D1571155

No Such Thing As A Good Blind Date

A Brandy Alexander Mystery

Shelly Fredman

Bloomington, IN  Milton Keynes, UK

authorHOUSE®

AuthorHouse™
1663 Liberty Drive, Suite 200
Bloomington, IN 47403
www.authorhouse.com
Phone: 1-800-839-8640

AuthorHouse™ UK Ltd.
500 Avebury Boulevard
Central Milton Keynes, MK9 2BE
www.authorhouse.co.uk
Phone: 08001974150

First published by AuthorHouse 9/28/2006

ISBN: 1-4259-5351-4 (sc)

Printed in the United States of America
Bloomington, Indiana

This book is printed on acid-free paper.

I would like to express my utmost gratitude to the following people:

Dudley Fetzer— Master of the one-liners. Thank you for being the yin to my yang, the cream in my coffee, the...well, you get the idea.

Corey Rose Fetzer—You are always right on target about what a scene needs and your (sometimes brutally honest) opinions are just what I need to do my best work.

Marty Schatz—I'm so grateful that you peruse the newspapers for quirky articles. Without you, I'd have no plotline!

Bruce Gram—Since I don't know a period from a comma, I'm sure glad you do. Thank you for all the time you spent going over the text. It was so very appreciated.

Caleb Fetzer—One heck of a brother-in-law. Thank you for giving me Toodie.

Susan Jaye—Thank you for getting out there and spreading the word. Your friendship means the world to me.

Renée Greidinger—My emotional rock and keeper of the memories—Thank you for always listening to me and for keeping me in a steady supply of chocolate TastyKake cupcakes.

Judith Kristen—(AKA my wonderful pal Judy) author extraordinaire and God's gift to teenagers—I don't know what I'd do without your support.

Franny Fredman—Simply the best mom anyone could hope for. I love you, kiddo.

And to: Bergundi Silva, Kris Zuercher and Michelle Warren —my new friends—thank you all for making me laugh, supporting my work and sharing your lives with me.

I'd also like to thank Marilu Coleman, Sharon Ayers, Kathleen Berryhill, Dawn Freeman and Angie Shearin for taking a chance on a new writer.

For my mom

Prologue

My name is Brandy Alexander and I am a recently re-instated native of South Philadelphia; more specifically, the proud new owner of the house I grew up in. Until five weeks ago I was the "puff piece reporter" for a local morning TV news show, out in Los Angeles. My job was to act perky and look like I was having the time of my life while reporting on "special events" around the L.A. area. There's really only so much enthusiasm a person can whip up for the Pacoima Chili Cook-off and the job fell a tad short of my dream of becoming the next Diane Sawyer, but it kept me off the streets and out of debt.

I'd left Philadelphia for the most clichéd of reasons—a broken heart. (I'm a firm believer in running away from one's problems. It's a great strategy, right up there with denial. Plus, it's the only exercise I get.) You'd think that my four year stay in the land of a million therapists would have taught me to confront my feelings head-on, but as my dad would say, I'm a tenacious little bugger. I stick with my game plan no matter how dysfunctional.

Then one day my best friend, Franny DiAngelo, called to say she was getting married, and there was a bridesmaid's dress down at Mama Mia's Bridal Shop with my name on it. She had launched a pre-emptive strike and there was no way

I could refuse her. So with much trepidation I packed up my emotional baggage and hopped a plane to Philly.

I didn't even realize how much I'd missed my hometown until I was back in the heart of it. My brother and my best friends in the world all still lived in the neighborhood. PrimoHoagies still made amazing hoagies, and the crazy guy in the top hat who sells Italian ice on Market Street still remembered that my favorite flavor is cherry.

My career in Los Angeles was stalled in the 6:00 a.m. "filler" slot of a third rate news station. My social life was non-existent, since I'd gone on a grand total of six dates in the entire time I'd lived out there. I missed the sights, the smells and the sounds of my neighborhood. I missed who I was and how I felt being surrounded by the people I love.

In the two weeks I'd been back in Philly, I had reconciled my differences with (if not my feelings for) my ex-boyfriend and could finally take a walk down memory lane without bursting into tears. In short, the time was ripe for a change. So when my parents announced they were selling our family home and moving to Florida, it seemed like the most natural thing in the world to buy the house from them. My boss at the TV station argued that it wasn't very mature of a twenty-eight year old to run back to the metaphoric womb, but nobody likes a know-it-all so I decided to ignore her advice. Had she pointed out that the metaphoric womb was over sixty years old, with really bad plumbing, she may have gotten my attention.

Chapter One

"Well, now here's your problem." Russell Hannigan, reigning expert on clogged pipes, waved a metallic snakelike object in the air. Speared on the tip sat a soggy oblong wad of cotton.

Eeww. I blushed in recognition.

"How many times do I gotta tell you women not to throw this crap down the toilet?"

"It's not mine. I think Mrs. Gentile was in here the other day." I was not above blaming my geriatric neighbor for anything embarrassing retrieved from the depths of my toilet bowl. "Um, do you mind just throwing that away?"

Russell gave a disgusted shake of his head and tossed the culprit in the trashcan. "Ya know these pipes are ancient. They're gonna give you a real headache if you don't replace them."

I sighed. "How much?"

"It's gonna cost ya."

Big surprise.

"Russell, you up there?"

"Yeah, Toodie, come on up."

Toodie? Toodie Ventura? I craned my neck over the railing as a lanky, red haired bundle of manic energy bounded up the stairs. Toodie was two years ahead of me in elementary school, the same class as my brother, Paul. By the time I'd graduated high school he was one year behind. Toodie reminded me of an Irish Setter puppy, all arms and legs and big dopey smiles. He laid one on me now and I couldn't help but smile back.

"Yo, Brandy. I heard you were back in town. Me too."

Toodie had just returned from an all expense paid vacation, courtesy of the Pennsylvania penal system. He'd been convicted of stalking his ex-girlfriend, Ilene, and burning cigarette holes in the crotches of all her panties as they hung on the line to dry in her back yard.

Toodie's grandmother was convinced it was all just a big misunderstanding, but the dead rats he'd left in Ilene's oven, along with the note that read: "Bon Appetit, you fucking bitch. Love, Toodie" cleared up any lingering doubts the judge may have had. Okay, so the "puppy" had a dark side.

Russell cleaned up his tools and headed downstairs. That left just me and Toodie, and I wasn't sure why he was here in the first place.

"I'm working for Russell now. He needed help with the overflow." Standing ankle-deep in toilet water, Toodie considered what he'd just said and cracked up.

I helped him mop up and we made our way downstairs. Russell was under the kitchen sink, banging away on the pipes.

"You've got a leak the size of Lake Erie. Ya don't do something about it, it's gonna ruin the drywall."

I did a quick mental calculation. Eighty-five bucks an hour plus materials came to more than an out-of-work new homeowner could afford.

"Can't do it, Russell. At least not until I get a job," which, at the rate things were going, could be *never*.

In the five weeks since I'd been back, I'd been on nine interviews at various news organizations, starting with the most prestigious and slowly working my way down, until yesterday, I found myself answering an ad for a new show called The Nosey Neighbor.

Basically, the job consists of a pair of binoculars and a cheap digital camera with which I'm supposed to spy on people in the neighborhood and catch them in embarrassing situations. Hilarity ensues. I told them I'd think about it and they told me not to wait too long, there's a real market out there for this kind of stuff. *And there are still people who think we couldn't possibly be descended from apes.*

Toodie hung back as Russell pulled away from the curb. I live in a predominantly Italian neighborhood on a narrow street filled with small, attached houses called row homes. My house is at the end of the block. The mezuzah on the doorjamb reflects my dad's half of my heritage, while the statue of the Virgin Mary peering out of a second story window represents my mother's.

Eighty-year-old Doris Gentile and I share a common wall. Mrs. Gentile hates me. It started with the decades-old feud she's carried on with my mother, over some holiday lawn ornaments. In Mrs. Gentile's world grudges are transferable and they pick up steam as time goes by.

At the sound of Russell's van, Mrs. Gentile poked her head outside "to see who was making all that ruckus." Like there was any doubt in her mind. She sniffed the early December air as if she smelled something distasteful on her shoe and glared down at me. Suddenly her eyes clamped onto Toodie and she furrowed her unibrow in recognition.

"Toodie Ventura, is that you?"

"Yes, ma'am."

"Shoo. Shoo!" she scowled, willing him gone with a flick of her wrist.

Toodie remained rooted in place.

"What's with her?" I asked.

"She's mad at me because I threw snowballs at her cat

when I was six."

"Oh."

Mrs. Gentile gave up and slammed her door.

I looked at my watch. I was late for an interview and didn't have time for small talk, but I didn't want to appear rude.

"Toodie, it was good to see ya—"

"So Brandy, I was thinking. You need some plumbing repairs and I need a place to stay until my granny gets back from her trip to the Bahamas…"

Oy, I could see where this was heading. "Toodie, why can't you just stay at her place while she's gone?"

"She says I can't stay there alone since I accidentally set her rug on fire with my wood burning set. But that's just because I was high at the time. I don't do that shit anymore," he added, but he didn't look me in the eye so I wasn't all that convinced.

"Gee, Toodie, I'd like to help you out and all, but I'm not looking for a roommate right now." Especially a pyromaniac girlfriend-stalker, no matter how tempting free plumbing is. I started backing away towards the house.

"Okay, so like if you change your mind, give me a call. You can reach me on my cell. It's 570-1250."

"Will do, Toodie." I made a big show of memorizing the number.

Back inside, I raced to get ready for my interview. I turned on the shower and jumped in, letting the warm water spray my five-foot-two-inch frame. Belting out the theme song from Friends, I slathered massive amounts of grape-fruit-scented shampoo on my shoulder-length brown hair and scrubbed hard.

It wasn't until I was ready to rinse that I discovered a noticeable decrease in water pressure. Uh oh. I cranked the faucet handles to the max, but the pressure just kept getting lower and lower until, finally, all that came out was a pathetic little dribble. And then it quit altogether.

The shampoo had stayed in my hair for too long and my head was starting to itch. I climbed out of the shower and wrapped my soap-encrusted body in a towel. After checking the water pressure on every conceivable faucet in the house, I threw on my dad's old raincoat and snuck around the outside of the house until I found Mrs. Gentile's garden hose. I bent over and turned it on full force. Freezing cold water hit the top of my head as I scrambled to rinse myself off before she discovered me pirating her supply. Turns out, Mrs. Gentile was the least of my worries.

"Hi, Brandy." I looked up, half naked and turning blue with cold.

"Oh, hi Henry." Henry is our mail carrier.

"Is this some sort of TV prank? I know you were famous for that kind of thing when you worked on that morning news show out in Los Angeles." Henry stepped closer to get a better look and I took a reflexive step back.

"No, Henry, this isn't a prank."

He didn't look like he believed me.

"Uh, this is a little awkward, so if you don't mind, I'm just going to hose off and get back in the house."

"Sure thing, doll."

Henry took out a bundle of envelopes from his mail sack and began stuffing them into my neighbor's mailbox. I waited a beat, and when I realized he was in no rush to leave I didn't bother getting the rest of the shampoo out of my hair. I straightened up and tightened the belt on my dad's raincoat. Then I dove back into the house and called Toodie.

"Honey, what in the world did you do to your hair?"

I was sitting in the window seat of Carla's beauty shop, studiously avoiding the mirrored wall in front of me.

"It's a long story." Actually, it's a short story, just eternally embarrassing.

Carla is the manager of the salon and my Uncle Frankie's longtime girlfriend. She's only thirty-seven, but she's more of a mother hen to me than a contemporary. She plunged her hands into the frozen bird's nest sitting atop my scalp.

"Smells like grapefruit."

"Good olfactory recognition. Can you help me? I've got an interview five minutes ago."

"I'm going to have to cut it," she said.

"No, Carla, *please!*" I begged, as if I'd just been told they were going to have to amputate a limb. "Anything but that."

Carla eyed me critically, her sixties style beehive encased in multi layers of hairspray. She was either hopelessly out of date or retro chic.

"You're not too good with change, are you?"

We compromised. She took me in the back, where Gladys (her ancient employee, who is rumored to be constipated, hence her unnaturally surly attitude towards the rest of human kind) spent fifteen minutes holding my head under water and dousing me with bottles of crème rinse. My head felt like it was coated in salad dressing and it didn't smell too good either.

"Just a little trim," Carla said, when I was back in the window seat again for all the neighborhood to see.

"Okay, but no more than an inch—and leave the bangs."

Carla sighed. "I should shave you bald and dye your scalp bright purple."

"But you're not going to, right?" I knew it was an empty threat, but it still made me nervous.

The door opened and in walked a young woman about my age—very pretty, with long, dark, tangle-free hair and flawless Latina features. Carla looked up and nodded hello. "Be right with you, honey." She glanced back down at me and tensed.

"Who is she?" I mouthed into the mirror.

"Bobby's wife," she mouthed back, apology written all over her face.

I never believed that turning "white as a sheet," was an actual physical possibility until it happened to me.

Robert Anthony DiCarlo and I had been friends since the day he swaggered into town, a sixteen-year-old kid with a chip on his shoulder the size of Detroit. I was fourteen and thought the sun rose and set on his magnificent Irish-Italian head.

Over the next two years I pined away for him as he treated himself to all that South Philadelphia had to offer in the way of pubescent female companionship. But on the night of my sixteenth birthday I claimed Bobby as my own. We sealed the deal behind the dumpster, in back of the South Street Boxing Gym, where Bobby used to hang out. In retrospect, it probably wasn't the most romantic place to consummate two years of unrequited love, but I knew that night that we'd be together forever, and anyway, I wasn't all that picky.

Bobby remained faithful to me for close to a decade, but we were young, and eventually, there was a parting of the ways. Wish I could say it was mutual—or that I even saw it coming. The breakup hurt, but the lies were devastating. I'd lost so much more than a lover. I'd lost my best friend.

A year and a half after I moved to Los Angeles I heard that Bobby had gotten married. It's not a happy union, but a two-year-old daughter keeps them together. After the up-bringing he'd had, Bobby would never abandon his kid.

Bobby and I got a chance to talk things out when I came back to town for Franny's wedding. I thought we'd reached a point where we could call each other friends again, but in the five weeks since I'd moved back I hadn't heard a word out of him.

I looked up and found the woman staring into the mirror

at me. I get really self-conscious when anyone inspects me too closely. I start feeling like I've got something hanging out of my nose or stuck in between my teeth, which I probably do.

I turned away and she began checking out the hair products that were for sale behind the cash register. I wondered if she knew who I was. As if she'd read my mind she suddenly appeared at my side.

"Excuse me," she said, looking directly at me.

Carla sprang into action. "Marie, this is Brandy. Brandy—Marie." No last names; keeping it anonymous, like an AA meeting.

"DiCarlo." Marie said pointedly. "Marie DiCarlo."

Okaaay. I *get* it.

"Bobby's wife," she added, just in case I didn't.

"Nice to meet you," I mumbled.

Marie heaved a begrudging sigh. "I'm sorry about my brother."

Due to an unfortunate misunderstanding, about a month ago her brother tried to kill me with a hatchet.

"Oh, that's all water under the bridge now," I said. "So how *is* your brother?" I smiled my most ingratiating smile. *See, we can all be friends.*

She didn't smile back. I honestly don't know what she was so bent out of shape about. I thought I was being really nice about the whole hatchet-wielding-brother incident. She turned to Carla.

"Put these on my tab, please, Carla."

"Sure thing, hon." Carla took the hair products out of her arms and went to get a bag.

Marie leaned into me. She was so close I could smell the Winterfresh gum on her breath. "I don't know what you've heard, but Bobby and I are very happy together."

"I'm glad for you."

"Are you?" She straightened up and walked out of the

salon, leaving her purchase at the counter.

"What was that all about?" Carla asked.

"Beats the hell out of me."

"She didn't threaten you or anything, did she?"

"No, why?"

Carla began combing my hair. It was so greasy the comb kept slipping out of her hand. She bent to pick it up, her spandex clad butt perched high in the air.

"Everyone knows that marriage is going south, sweet-ie. And you moving back to the neighborhood didn't help any."

"Carla, Bobby and I are over. I never even think of him that way anymore." I gave a surreptitious look heavenward to see if God was paying attention to my lie.

"Prove it."

"How can I prove it? That's ridiculous." A diversionary tactic I'd learned from my mother.

"I have someone I want you to meet."

I groaned, my intestines constricting into one gigantic knot. "Carla, I don't want to be fixed up. Don't I have enough to contend with right now? If you want to do me a real favor, get me a job."

"If you play your cards right, you could have both."

My eyes narrowed in suspicion. "What do you mean?"

"This guy I want you to meet—"

"How do you know him?"

"I don't—exactly. His mother comes into the shop. She says he's a real sweetheart, rich, successful and handsome too."

"Then why does he need his mother to get dates for him? Forget it, Carla. There is no such thing as a good blind date."

"He's some high power guy at The News Network."

Wow. I'd been trying to get an interview with them

since I got back to town.

"He sounds perfect. Can't wait to meet him."

Carla smiled triumphantly. Okay, I can be bought. So sue me.

Toodie's old Toyota pick-up was parked in front of my house when I got home. I pulled in behind him and got out of the car, careful not to scrape the door on the curb. I was driving my brother Paul's car—a mint condition, 1972 metallic blue Mercedes SL convertible—"a classic," he's quick to remind me. I knew I'd have to give it back to him one of these days, but I was reluctant to plunk down my practically non-existent savings on a new set of wheels.

Toodie leaped out of his truck, balancing a large carton on his shoulder. He galloped towards me, dragging an extension cord behind him.

"Hi, Roomie," he beamed.

I truly wished I shared his enthusiasm.

"Toodie," I said, grabbing my keys out of my pocketbook, "this is just temporary, remember? Until your granny gets back from the Bahamas." I pulled open the storm door and let him walk ahead of me into the living room. "When is she coming back, anyway?"

Toodie set his carton down and shrugged. "Dunno."

"She *is* coming back, though, *isn't she*?" Visions of my new "roomie" burning down my house with his woodworking set before I even made the first mortgage payment danced through my head.

"Oh yeah. She'll be back." He nodded his head vigorously, a gesture obviously meant to reassure. It didn't.

I showed Toodie to his room and laid out some clean towels for him.

"Just one thing, Toodie. This is a drug-free zone. Oh, and if you're planning on entertaining anyone, I'd rather they didn't spend the night."

Toodie's eyes grew wide. He sat down on the bed and patted the seat next to him. I reluctantly sat down too.

"Brandy, if this roommate thing is going to work, we've got to come clean with each other." His voice gentled. "Are you like 'hot' for me?"

Before I could ask him if he had completely lost his mind he continued. "Because I like you, Brandy. I really do. But I have to be honest. I don't think of you that way." He stared at me with baleful eyes. *Pity.* The man pitied me!

"Toodie, I can assure you that's not what I meant! And what do you mean, you don't think of me that way? What's wrong with me?" *Seriously, what's wrong with me? I felt insulted that a man with the IQ of a basset hound was spurning my affections. AS IF!*

"Nothing's wrong with you. You're great. But you and John Marchiano are a terrific couple, and I wouldn't want to, ya know, come between you two."

John Marchiano is my oldest and dearest friend, but he doesn't have a shred of sexual interest in me. John climbed out of the womb wearing Chanel and singing show tunes, a fact that has somehow eluded Toodie.

"Well, I'm glad we cleared the air on this, Toodie. I promise I won't make things awkward by coming on to you."

"Thanks," he said with the utmost sincerity.

I stood. "Come on, I'll make you some lunch."

Lunch consisted of peanut butter and jelly sandwiches and chocolate milk. We split a Family Size Hershey Bar for dessert. Chocolate and I have a spiritual connection. It fills me up, makes me happy and never lets me down. If it were legal to wed an inanimate object, I'd ask it to marry me.

After lunch Toodie dragged his toolbox in from his truck and buried himself under the kitchen sink. I sat at the dining room table, licking melted chocolate off the candy wrapper, the employment section of the newspaper spread before me. What is it that Franny is always saying about positive thinking? That you should start by envisioning the thing you want, make it real in your mind. "Okay," I thought. "I'll give it a try." I shut my eyes, the words formulating in my brain.

NOW HIRING: Investigative Reporter for nationally acclaimed news program. Little to no experience necessary. Great salary. Benefits. I opened my eyes. Toodie was staring at me.

"What are you doing?"

"I'm envisioning."

"Is it working?"

I scanned the employment section for my ad. "No."

The phone rang.

"I'll get it." Toodie reached for the receiver. "Alexander residence," he said in a ridiculously phony British accent. "This is the butler speaking."

I don't know why but I thought it was hilarious.

"Whom shall I say is calling?" He paused dramatically. "One moment please. It's your mother," he said, handing me the phone.

I made a face that any normal person would have interpreted as the "I-don't-want-to-talk-to-my-mother-now-tell-her-I'll-call-her-back-face." But Toodie is guileless and doesn't read social cues. I put the phone to my ear.

"Hi Mom."

"Since when do you have money to squander on a butler?"

"He's not a butler, Mom."

"Then why is he answering your phone?"

I suppressed the urge to scream and said instead, "How's Daddy?"

"Your father's fine. It's you I'm worried about."

So what else is new? "Why are you worried about me? I'm fine." Jobless, penniless, but fine.

"Brandy, don't you ever pick up the papers?"

"Of course I do. I'm browsing through the comics' section as we speak. Did you know that Cathy and Irving got married? What's it been, twenty years?"

"Don't get flip with me, Brandy Renee." Uh oh. She's pulling out the middle name. She must really be upset.

"I'm sorry, Mom. What's wrong?"

"Well," she said, mollified, "It seems that there has been a rash of break-ins in the neighborhood lately."

"How many is a rash?"

"Armed robberies," she said, choosing to ignore me. "In fact," she added, lowering her voice to the stage whisper she usually reserved for conversations about terminal diseases, "Mrs. Edelstein's neighbor was held up *at knifepoint in her own home*, two blocks down on Ritner. They took her jewelry and a bust of Beethoven. I just don't want to pick up the newspaper one day and see your name listed among the victims."

Oh why did I think it would be nice to get her that subscription to the Inquirer when she moved to Florida?

"Brandy, are you there?"

"I'm here, Mom. Listen, I don't want you to worry about me. I'm perfectly safe."

"Well, keep the doors locked—and call your brother." That's my mother's solution to everything.

She filled the next ten minutes detailing her trip to the podiatrist. I care, I really do, but I'm a little on the squeamish side. So when she started in with her toe fungus, I decided to wrap things up.

"I've got to run, Mom. The butler wants to use the phone."

Chapter Two

"Ya know the nose, ya know the man."—Janine DiAngelo, twin sister of Franny and the definitive expert on key male anatomy.

"I'd always heard it was the thumbs."

Janine took a swig of Rolling Rock ale and considered this. "No, Danny Margolis has huge thumbs." She shook her luxurious auburn haired head, lost in promises unkept. "He was a big disappointment."

Reflecting on my own meager experience in this department, I deferred to Janine's wealth of knowledge.

It was five p.m.—Happy Hour at the Pensacola Bar & Grill, an after-work hangout for the actual employed. Young urban professionals flocked here, presumably, after a hard day at the office, to unburden themselves of the pressures of the working world. Sitting among them at the bar, munching free snacks and nursing beers, Janine and I were Happy Hour frauds.

I glanced over at my cohort in unemployment. Janine looked like a goddess in her "weather be damned" short tight skirt, which accentuated her legs, and a form-fitting turtleneck, which accentuated other parts of her near perfect five foot nine inch body. I slumped beside her in my uniform jeans and sweatshirt, looking like the shortstop for a peewee softball team.

"So how's it going with Toodie?" she asked.

It had been a week since the big move, and I had to admit to being pleasantly surprised. He's sweet, in a loopy sort of way, and as a plumber he knows only too well what can befall a person who doesn't clean the hair out of the shower drain. Plus, he cooks. I reported all this to Janine.

"Brandy," she said, one eye on me and the other on a six foot two inch suit and Armani tie that was making its way over to the bar, "don't you think it's a little odd that in the all the time you've been back, the only socializing you've done is with a thirty year old jailbird who still lives with his granny?" Well, when you put it *that* way...

"I socialize. Yesterday I had a dental appointment, and just last week I took Rocky to the vet's to get spayed." Rocky is my twelve-week-old kitten, who, judging by the hordes of Tomcats sniffing around the house, has no trouble getting dates.

The Armani tie reached the bar and slid onto the stool next to Janine. His sandy-haired, equally well-dressed friend sidled up next to him, giving me the once-over. To his credit, he didn't try to slip me subway tokens or point me in the direction of the nearest homeless shelter.

"Hey," he said, reading the logo on my sweatshirt. "South Street Boxing Gym. Do you know Frankie Brentano? He's the manager there."

Janine flashed me the "thumbs up" sign and deliberately turned her back to me.

"Yeah, I know him," I said. "He's my uncle."

Uncle Frankie is my mother's significantly younger, formerly delinquent brother and one of my favorite people in the world. "How do you know him?"

Stan, it turns out, is an avid boxing fan. He is also an accounts exec at a nearby advertising firm, a Lacrosse player, divorced from his childhood sweetheart and a former spelling bee champion. I learned all this in the space of three minutes. I also learned that Stan likes to work with his hands. One arm leaned on the bar while the other snaked up my back, rubbing concentric circles along my spine and settling around the vicinity of my chest.

"Stan," I asked, smiling, "did we meet in a former life and it just slipped my mind?"

"I'm sure I would've remembered," Stan said, smooth as snake oil. And then, swear to God, he winked at me. I gave myself points for not throwing up.

"The reason I'm asking is, you've got your hand practically down my bra cup, and that's usually reserved for men I've known longer than six minutes." I disengaged myself from Stan and leaned across him to tap Janine on the shoulder. She tried her best to ignore me, lost in conversation with Eric Something or Other; another accounts exec, and judging by the placement of *his* hands, a "leg" man. I tried again.

"Yo, Janine. Isn't that Christine Yablonski over in the corner, by the plastic Fichus tree?" I waved a hearty hello in the general direction of the faux Fichus. A middle-aged woman with short, steel gray hair and a man's suit smiled and waved a tentative hello back.

"Who?" Janine asked, clearly not playing along.

I turned to Stan and Eric. "Old friend. Would you excuse us for a minute?" I shoved Janine off her stool and herded her out of the bar area.

"Brandy, what is wrong with you? Those guys are cute, rich and interested."

"Look, I don't mean to sound ungracious here, but unless Stan is an undercover gynecologist, he needs to keep his hands off my boobs."

Janine thought about this for a minute. "Maybe he's just a really affectionate kind of guy."

"And maybe he's just a *perv*. Janine, we just met!"

Janine looked downcast.

"Okay, what's going on here? Why are you pushing so hard for this?"

"Well," Janine said, "it's just that we've all been worried about you."

"Who all?"

"Everybody."

I felt a colossal headache coming on and with it, a minor epiphany. "Have you been talking to Carla?"

Janine refused eye contact. "Maybe."

Unhhh! "Carla thinks I moved back here to be near Bobby. Is that what you think too? Because that's ridiculous! Not to mention pathetic. *Do I look pathetic to you?*" My voice was starting to hit a range known only to dogs— and possibly whales.

Janine raised her arms in an "I surrender" gesture. "Okay. I believe you. You're not stuck on Bobby. But Eric and I are really hitting it off, so could you please be civil to Stan—at least until I can get Eric to ask for my phone number?"

"Fine," I grunted.

"Thank you."

We headed back to the bar, my new and improved sweet-as-pie attitude threatening to hurl me into a diabetic coma. The guys had ordered drinks for us while we were gone. Clear, dark amber liquid in tall glasses, with pink umbrellas peering over the top. I was smiling so hard my cheeks hurt. Janine kicked me under the bar.

"Too much?" I whispered. She rolled her eyes in response.

"What's this?" I asked, inspecting the glass.

"Long Island Iced Tea," Stan the Hand said.

"Oh, I love iced tea."

"Uh, Bran?" Janine started, as I picked up the drink and took a huge thirst-quenching gulp. The effects were immediate, the room spinning out of orbit being my first clue.

"This isn't iced tea, is it?"

"In name only," said Stan.

"What's in this thing, anyway? And by the way, it's delicious!" I grabbed hold of the straw and began slurping it down like there was no tomorrow.

"Vodka, gin, tequila..." He reached for my glass.

"Whoa, hold on there, cowboy."

Stan tried to pull the drink out of my hand but I was too quick for him. I downed the rest and set the glass back on the counter, grinning up at him. He had a certain *je ne sais quoi* that for some reason I hadn't noticed before. The arm was back around my shoulder and this time I let him keep it there.

"Hey, Stan," Janine said, eying his arm around me, "you didn't slip a little Ecstasy in there, did you?"

"No! What do you take me for, anyway?"

I tugged on Stan's sleeve, pointing to Janine's drink.

"Yoo hoo, can I have another one of those things?" I asked, leaning against him. He wasn't a bad looking guy. In fact, when I squinched my eyes closed real tight and tilted my head, he looked just like Bruce Willis in his old Moonlighting days. Before the pierced ears and shaved head.

"Ya know, you're kinda cute," I said. And then, *Oh God*, I winked at him.

Janine drove me home. I was a little fuzzy on the details but, apparently, Stan and Eric left shortly after I challenged the middle-aged woman wearing a man's suit to an arm wrestling contest.

"I guess I shouldn't drink on an empty stomach," I said, by way of apology to Janine.

Janine laughed. "It was fun. Ya know you could've beat that old lady, easy, if you hadn't fallen off the barstool."

I thought so too. "I'm sorry about Eric."

"Eh," she shrugged. "Did ya get a look at the nose on

that guy? Miniscule. And you know what they say? Ya know the nose..."

Janine pulled up in front of my house, turning on the interior car light while I searched for my keys. It was an unnecessary gesture, as the entire block was illuminated by the glow of Mrs. Gentile's latest holiday acquisition; a Disneyesque nativity scene, complete with revolving wise men and animatronic farm animals that neighed, baa-ed and bobbed their little robotic heads, welcoming baby Jesus into the neighborhood.

Toodie stood on a ladder on my side of the porch, stringing Christmas tree lights along the roof; a ragged display in green and red, with gaping holes where the burned out lights hadn't been replaced. I stood there watching him as Janine pulled away.

"Yo!" he yelled from the top of the ladder. "Pretty neat, huh?"

"Neat," I agreed. "Where'd ya get them?"

"Garage sale." Having run out of light strings, Toodie climbed down off the ladder, leaving half the roof in darkness. We looked skyward, admiring his handiwork. While it wasn't the extravaganza created by my neighbor, it had a kind of trailer park panache that appealed to me.

"Hey, what's this?" An ancient piece of machinery had taken up residence on my front lawn, its carcass held together by decades of rust. Upon closer inspection I saw that it was a Harley Davidson Shovelhead, circa 1973.

"My new set of wheels—once I get it up and running." Hope springs eternal.

"Garage sale?"

Toodie nodded.

"Maybe Paul can help you get it going." My brother is nuts about cars, bikes, anything with wheels, chrome and an engine that predates the disco era.

I helped Toodie maneuver the Harley into the basement, which was rife with the oddball stuff he's collected in the short time he's been staying with me. As I pushed the kick-stand down on the bike I tripped over a set of dilapidated, left-handed golf clubs.

"I'm thinking of taking up golf," he said.

"Toodie, these are left-handed clubs. You're not left-handed...and there's no head on the nine-iron."

"I know. That's how come they were so cheap."

We headed upstairs. Toodie's plumbing tools were sprawled all over the kitchen floor, the cabinet under the sink wide open. "You need a new garbage disposal," he said. "This one's leaking buckets."

I took this as an encouraging sign. At least the water was running again. Rocky lounged in a puddle on the floor, her gray and white fur matted into sorry little clumps. I'd always heard that cats had an aversion to water, but she thought this was great fun.

Something wonderful permeated the air. It was coming from the oven.

"I'm going out tonight," Toodie said, "but I made you a meatloaf. And there're some mashed potatoes in the fridge."

I have to admit I've eaten pretty well since Toodie's moved in. My dinners usually consist of cold cereal and half a box of Tastykakes or the occasional grilled cheese sandwich.

I opened the oven door and took out the meatloaf, digging in with my fingers. One nice thing about living with Toodie, I don't have to concern myself with social amenities.

"Oh, and some guy called while you were out. Randolph...Rudolph...?"

"Adolph?" I suggested helpfully.

"Barry," he beamed. "Barry Kaminski. Something

about dinner Saturday night. He wants you to call him."

After I ate all of the meatloaf and mashed potatoes, I called Barry back. He had a rich, mature baritone that reminded me of Ted Baxter on the Mary Tyler Moore Show, and his speech was very formal. You could tell this man worked for network news, not some crappy local station where the reporters are like stand-up comics, doing their personal "schtick" while reporting on a three car pile-up on I-95.

We agreed that he'd come here for dinner. I really wanted Barry to see that I'd gone to a lot of trouble to prepare a delicious meal for him, so that when I hit him up for a job he'd be hard pressed to turn me down. I made a mental note to call DiBruno Brothers to pre-order lasagna and stop by Perini's for dessert.

I cleaned up the dinner dishes and flopped on the couch, flipping through the stations until I reached Nick at Nite. Roseann was on. Oh goody. I've always found Dan very attractive. He's cute and solid and dependable. And he's always there for Roseann. Not like the men in my life. Not that I've had so many. Just one, to be specific. And then several weeks ago, there was the promise of one more—well, maybe promise is too strong a word— okay, a faint possibility, but that didn't pan out and I guess I've been in a bit of a funk about it. Maybe everyone's been right to worry about me. It's time I moved on. I decided to devote the evening to spiritual growth, but Full House was on next and I just love that little Michelle. I guess my path to enlightenment could wait another half an hour.

I woke up late and had to race to get ready for my appointment. Although I'd convinced myself that Barry was the president of ABC and was going to fall in love with me and make me co-anchor of Nightline, I thought it'd be wise to have a backup plan—just a little extra cash to tide me over while Barry and I worked out the details of my contract. Paul was looking for a waitress to fill in at his place. He owns a dance club downtown and one of his staff got nabbed on a DUI. Since it was her second offense she'll be out of commission for a while. Meeting with Paul was just a formality; it was either hire me or pay my mortgage.

I ran down to the basement to grab a pair of jeans out of the drier and banged my knee against a freezer that was plugged into the far wall. It was covered in Budweiser Beer decals and looked like it had seen better days.

I entered the kitchen to find Toodie lying prone on the floor, his head stuffed under the sink. "What's in the freezer, Toodie?"

He stuck his head out briefly and said, "Omaha steaks" before disappearing under the sink again. "I've got to get to work by noon, or Russell says he's gonna can my ass. But I just wanted to do a quick—uh oh."

Oh, that didn't sound good. I squatted down next to him to get a better view. It smelled like a sewage plant under there. I'm not a plumber but I don't think orange sludge oozing out of the disposal is a good sign.

"No worries. I've got it all under control."

I stopped at the car wash on the way to Paul's club. It had rained last weekend and I'd left the window open a crack to help de-fog the windshield. The problem was I forgot to close it again and the floor mats got soaked. They dried right up when I blasted the heat, but it left a foul odor reminiscent of old tennis shoes. I found some air fresheners on the counter by the cash register and I was trying to decide between Alpine Breeze and New Mown Grass when my cell phone rang.

"It's Franny."

"Fran! How's the honeymoon?" Eddie surprised Franny with a cruise, which was very sweet but maybe not the best choice for a woman three months pregnant and in the throes of morning sickness. I opted for Alpine Breeze and handed four bucks to the cashier.

"I don't think I'm cut out for marriage," she sighed.

"What's wrong?" I took my package and headed back to the car. Someone in a dark green Honda had pulled into the lot and had left their car idling alongside the building. I couldn't turn around so I put the car in reverse and backed out of the car wash.

"I've only been married for five weeks and he's already on my nerves."

"Franny, that's understandable. You're just getting used to sharing space with someone."

"No. He's just annoying. He keeps calling me Mrs. Bonaduce. He thinks it's cute. His *mother* is Mrs. Bonaduce." She paused. "Do you think I remind him of his mother?"

"You're on your *honeymoon*, Fran. I sincerely hope not."

"He wants me to change my last name."

"Well, you're just going to have to sit down with him and discuss it."

"We did discuss it." The discussion mostly boiled down to Eddie whining, *"But you promised,"* and Franny digging in with, "I lied. Get over it."

I pulled out onto Broad Street. Downtown rush hour traffic is an all day affair; it was bumper to bumper. Add to that the myriad of Philadelphians who feel it is their God-given right to double-park their vehicles wherever the spirit moves them, and the result is an urban nightmare. "Fran, I've got to go. We'll talk about this more when you get back."

The thing is I should be the last person giving relationship advice, considering the only men I've ever lived with are my dad and Toodie. Note to self: Work on Love Life.

I was stopped at a light on Market Street when I noticed

the green Honda again. It was two car lengths back in the next lane over. A gray ski cap and sunglasses obscured the face, but there was something feminine and familiar about the long dark hair cascading around the driver's shoulders. The light changed and the car in front of the Honda switched lanes, but the Honda made no attempt to fill the gap left by the other car. It slowed down and allowed another car to take its place.

I drove three more blocks and hung a left past the St. Regis Hotel. Two minutes later the Honda was in my line of sight again. "That's odd," I thought, and then the hairs on the back of my neck stood up in unison as I came to the sudden realization that I was being followed—by none other than Marie DiCarlo. Oh my God!

We stopped at another light and I tried to set my mirror to get a better look. Was she riding around tailing me with their two year old strapped into the back seat? Or did she get a babysitter for an unfettered afternoon of stalking her husband's ex-girlfriend? I thought about her crazy brother and wondered if this stalking business was a congenital trait, in which case she couldn't help herself.

Oh jeez, now she sees me looking at her in the rearview mirror. Be cool. Act like you're just trying to pop a pimple on your forehead. I reached for my forehead and felt a small angry bump. Dammit, a pimple.

The light turned green, but I'd gotten all involved in popping the pimple and didn't notice. The guy behind me leaned on his horn, indicating he thought I should tend to my cosmetic needs at perhaps another time. I threw the car into gear and took off across the intersection, leaving the car in back of me to wait for a woman pushing a baby stroller to cross the street. By the time I'd made it to the next block, the green Honda was nowhere in sight.

"Paul, what kind of car does Bobby's wife drive?" I was sitting in a wide, red leather booth at Paul's club, eating

Dunkin' Doughnuts and drinking freshly brewed coffee. My brother sat down across from me, moving the doughnuts out of my reach.

"Hey, where are you going with those?" I asked.

"You've had four."

"So who's counting?"

"I am."

"Jeez, Paul. Who died and made you Doughnut Police?"

"Knock yourself out," Paul said, pushing the box towards me.

I didn't want another one, but I forced it down, just to prove a point.

"So why do you want to know what kind of car Marie DiCarlo drives?"

"I think she was following me."

"R-r-really?" Paul said, revving up for a stutter-fest. My brother has a wicked stutter that emerges whenever he's upset. John says it always seems to happen whenever I'm around, but I'm sure that's just a coincidence.

"Paul, it's okay, really. Maybe it wasn't her. I'm *sure* Bobby's wife has better things to do than to follow me around."

The thing is, I *wasn't* sure. A while back, Marie had left him, taking their baby daughter with her. When I came back to Philly for Franny's wedding, Bobby had confided to me that his relationship with Marie was based on a one-night-stand that had turned into an elopement when she found out she was pregnant.

Marie was crazy in love with Bobby and was not averse to using their daughter to keep the marriage intact. She let him know in no uncertain terms that they were a package deal. To prove her point, she ran off with baby Sophia to give Bobby a taste of what would happen on a permanent basis should he ever decide to leave her. My moving back to town must have thrown her over the edge.

Paul spent the next hour showing me the ropes. It seemed simple enough. Take food and drink orders, don't spill hot coffee in anyone's lap and be polite to all the customers, even the ones I think are jerks. I practiced balancing a tray full of dishes for a while and then Paul had to get ready for the lunch crowd. He walked me out to the curb, gazing at his Mercedes with all the love of a reluctant papa sending his first-born off to college. "I'm never going to get my car back, am I?" he sighed.

"Don't give up hope, Paulie. Never give up hope." I drove off before he could figure out just what I meant by that.

I stopped at DiVinci's Pizza on the way home for a medium pepperoni "to go."

DiVinci's is your basic hole in the wall, patronized, according to John, by the culinary-impaired. But I love it. The pizza's excellent, the beer cold, and the cockroaches deferential. They never show their faces until you're at least halfway through your meal.

I parked on the street and entered by the side door. Immediately, I was assaulted by a blast of warm, garlic-scented air. I unbuttoned my jacket; an old pea coat that once belonged to my dad, and maneuvered my way through the college crowd to get to the bar.

Sanford, the owner, was working the register. "What can I get ya, hon?"

"Could I get a medium—make that a large pepperoni to go?" I figured Toodie could have the other half for dinner.

I was reading the daily specials when someone snuck up behind me, pressing me into the bar. "I hope you're not gonna eat that all by yourself. You're gonna get fat."

I turned around to see who I was going to have to smack, when two bear-like arms wrapped around me and lifted me into the air.

"Glad to hear ya moved back to town, kiddo. It hasn't been the same without you."

"Vince!" I yelled, happy as hell to see him. Vince Giancola and I have been friends since kindergarten. He's now an assistant D.A., which is hard to believe, considering he used to boost cars for a living.

"I hear you're shacking up with Toodie Ventura. Brandy, tell me it isn't true."

"Heartbroken?"

"You'd better believe it. Seriously, Brandy, the guy's a whack-o."

"True, but he's my whack-o."

Vince steered me over to his table, which was littered with the remains of his lunch.

"Look, I don't mean to scare you, but ya know, he doesn't have the best track record with women."

"Oh God, Vince. It's not like I'm sleeping with the guy. He's fixing my plumbing." Shit. That didn't come out right. "No, *literally*, he's fixing my plumbing in exchange for room and board. Besides, he's very sorry for what happened with his ex-girlfriend. He's harmless—*really!*"

Vince gave me a look.

"So," I said, getting comfortable in the scarred, wooden booth, "how are things at the D.A.'s office?"

Vince extracted his wallet and threw a twenty on the table. "Good. Busy. Crime is up, I'm working my tail off." He hesitated a brief moment before adding, "You just missed Bobby. He left about thirty seconds before you got here."

My heart rate climbed into the stroke-zone. "Oh." I tried to keep my face blank, but it was like trying to keep the world from turning.

"Sorry."

"Don't be. We're cool."

Sanford signaled to me that my pizza was ready. I stood

and Vince walked me back to the bar. I reached into my pocketbook for my wallet, but he beat me to it and handed Sanford a couple of bills.

"My treat."

I protested, but Vince stood his ground.

"Let me guess. My mother called your mother and told her I don't have a job and to look after me so that I don't starve to death."

"Something like that. You be careful, you hear?"

I reached up and kissed him square on the mouth. "You're a good friend, Vincent."

"Keep that up and next time it'll be a full course meal with cloth napkins and candles on the table."

"I'm going to hold you to it."

The ride home was mercifully uneventful. I positioned the pizza box on my lap, popped in a Green Day CD and munched down a slice of heaven. Before I knew it, Toodie's half of the pizza was gone. Poor Toodie, he would have really enjoyed it.

I spent the rest of the day perusing the Internet for work, on the off chance that a job with Barry didn't pan out. Rocky curled up beside me, inside the now empty pizza box. My kitten has a fascination with tomato sauce. She must have some Italian blood in her.

At nine p.m. I turned off my computer and flipped through the TV Guide in search of entertainment. I was feeling restless, but I couldn't put my finger on why. And then it dawned on me. Toodie hadn't come home. Could it be that I actually missed him? The house was strangely quiet.

Down time is dangerous for me. My mind starts to wander to places I have no business visiting. I started thinking about Bobby but I quickly shook those thoughts away, only to replace them with the man I'd met a little over a month ago; a man who captivated me completely and then disappeared from my life as quickly as he'd come. Thinking of him made me feel lonely and sorry for myself, two feelings I could definitely live without. Screw this. I decided to be productive and learn a new skill, so I stayed up until past midnight, eating Oreos and trying to teach myself how to French braid my hair. The hair thing didn't work out but the Oreos really hit the spot.

I fell asleep on the couch and woke up at around one a.m., the television light flashing in an otherwise darkened room. I went to turn it off and caught the tail end of a local news report about the recent disappearance of some young woman. Not exactly the bedtime story I needed. My mother's voice echoed in my brain, break-ins and armed robbers looming large in my mind until I was sure I heard someone trying to climb in through an upstairs window. Just as I began to work up a full-on panic attack, Rocky charged down the stairs, clenching a flying insect the size of Mothra between her teeth. Relieved, I rolled over on my side and fell back to sleep.

The ringing of the phone woke me up. I struggled awake and ran into the kitchen to grab the receiver before the answer machine picked up. It was Russell, looking for Toodie.

"The son of a bitch never showed up for work, yesterday afternoon. He knew I had a big job and I was counting on him to help me."

"Hang on a second, Russell." I took the stairs two at a time and knocked on Toodie's closed bedroom door. No answer. I peeked inside. It looked like a cyclone had struck in there. Clothes, bike parts and all sorts of worthless crap littered the carpet and bed. But worst of all was the ammonia-scented stench that permeated the rug. How long had Rocky been using this room as a litter box?

Just as I started to close the door again, I heard the same eerie noises that, last night, I'd attributed to an overactive imagination. They were coming from the closet. I picked up one of Toodie's size twelve work boots and cautiously opened the closet door. In a flash a furry, twenty-pound mass of energy leaped out at me, knocking me to the ground. "Son of a bitch," I yelled, echoing Russell's sentiments. *Toodie snuck a dog into the house and then just dumped it in my lap!*

I tried to grab the little yapper, but Rocky strolled by at that moment, stopping in the doorway to lick her crotch. The dog bolted out of reach and took off after her. Rocky freaked and puffed herself up to three times her normal size. She hissed and clawed at him and then flew down the stairs with the dog in hot pursuit. I stumbled after them, pausing briefly to pick up the phone extension. "Russell, I'll call you back."

I found Rocky cowering under the sofa. The dog was playfully swatting at her, wiggling his shaggy brown butt in the air as he tried to join her under the couch. He was actually very cute, with huge dark eyes and a water fountain tail. He was about as big as a cocker spaniel and seemed inordinately good-natured—somewhat like Toodie. *Toodie!*

"Okay, toughie, leave the kitten alone." I tugged on his belly and he immediately rolled over onto his back, gazing up at me with those big brown eyes.

"No. Don't look adorable. I refuse to be taken in by your cuteness. You peed in my guest room. I'm mad at you." It was hopeless. I was hooked.

I wondered if the little guy was hungry. As if he could read my mind, he followed me into the kitchen and jumped up onto a chair, seating himself at the table. I looked around for a suitable meal for him and settled on Rocky's cat crunchies. I poured a little into a plastic bowl and placed it in front of him. He sniffed at it for a minute and then took a swipe, knocking the bowl onto the floor. I wanted to be mad, but he gave me such a bewildered look I just cleaned up the kibble and made him a fried egg instead.

I sat down at the table next to him, watching him plant his face in the dish, egg yolk smeared all over his snout. Leaning back in the chair, I assessed my situation: jobless, penniless, mate-less, dining at the kitchen table with a stray mutt of undetermined origins. My mother would be so proud.

After I cleaned up his face I took him into backyard to pee. When I say yard, I'm exaggerating. It's really more of a four by four slab of concrete with weeds sticking out of the cracks in the cement. The dog wandered around in a circle, stopping once or twice to chase something that wasn't there. It was cold and I was running out of patience.

"Come on, *do* something already."

On cue he squatted and did his business. At least he tried to, but nothing came out. Finally, he gave up and waddled back into the house.

I tried calling Toodie's cell phone but all I got was his voice mail, so I left a brief message urging him to call me. In all probability, Toodie had gone on a bender and had forgotten where he lived. He was no doubt shacked up somewhere sleeping it off. At least, that's what I hope happened. Because, like it or not, I'd really grown to care about the guy; he was like the pet I'd never had as a child and I kinda felt responsible for him. If he didn't show up, how was I going to tell his grandma that I'd somehow misplaced him? I had enough trouble already. The dog was eating my shoe.

"Am I as boring as I think everyone else is?"

"If I say yes, will you still help me make dinner?" It was Saturday afternoon and John was seated at my kitchen table, arranging layers of fresh pasta into a large casserole dish. John is an expert photographer and an excellent cook all rolled into a five foot three inch, adorably egotistical package.

My blind date was due to arrive in three hours and fourteen minutes and dinner wasn't half ready. I would have gone ahead and ordered out, but Toodie had volunteered to make lasagna for me. Only I hadn't heard a word from him in two days. I'd called his cell phone numerous times and tried to leave messages for him, but after a while the voice-mail wouldn't accept any new calls, which meant he wasn't retrieving his incoming calls. I didn't want to be worried about him, but I was.

"Ya know," said John, "you could try being a little more diplomatic. I'm up to my elbows in wet noodles here. I don't do this for just anyone, ya know."

I rolled my eyes heavenward.

"I saw that."

Rocky sauntered into the kitchen and jumped up onto the counter, pausing to lick the marinara sauce off the ladle.

"Will you get her off of there? That's disgusting."

I reached over and set Rocky on the floor next to Toodie's dog. In the two days since he's been here, they've become thick as thieves. I don't know if I like it. They always seem to be plotting against me.

"How're ya doing, Spike?" I asked, rubbing the soft spot behind his ear.

"Spike?"

"I'm trying it out."

John shook his head. "Too butch. How about Leonardo?"

"Too gay."

"Shut-uh up! What's wrong with that?"

"I may want grandpuppies some day."

"You mean you're going to keep him?" John shoved the tray of lasagna into the oven and began tearing up lettuce for the salad. I reached over and grabbed a carrot out of the salad bowl.

"Wash your hands, for God's sake. Where were you

born? In a barn?"

I flashed him a huge smile. "Thanks, John. You know how much I miss my mom."

Just as I finished squeezing my size six butt into size five pants the doorbell rang. Fido (okay, I'd have to work on the name thing) started running around in circles barking his head off and chasing his tail while Rocky dove under the couch. I did a quick check in the mirror. No stains on my shirt, both shoes matched and although I don't use make-up, there was a healthy glow to my cheeks from turning my head upside down to blow dry my hair, which lay poker straight and to my shoulders. "Well, I'm good to go." I opened the door.

Barry Kaminski stood on my porch, impeccably dressed in a gray mohair overcoat and holding a bouquet of long stemmed roses. The man was drop-dead Cary Grant gorgeous. *And about as old! What was Carla thinking?* I tried not to let surprise register on my face as I led him inside.

"Thank you for the flowers. They're lovely." Seeing as the only vase I had was the empty jar of marina sauce I'd just tossed into the recycle bin, I laid the flowers on the end table next to the couch.

Earlier, I'd chilled a couple of Buds for our pre-dinner aperitif, but Barry didn't strike me as the beer swillin' type. Unfortunately, all I had left was a bottle of Gatorade and some instant coffee, both of which he graciously declined.

"I'm sorry about the mix up," he said when we were settled on the couch. "My mother forgets it's been forty-five years since my Bar Mitzvah. In her mind it was just last week."

"No problem, Barry. I'm from Los Angeles. May-December romances are a dime a dozen out there." *Oh my God. What just came out of my mouth?* "What I meant was I'm sure we have tons in common. For instance, Carla mentioned you're an executive with The News Network." *All right!* Nice segue into the whole "I need a job" discussion. I was practically high-fiving myself when I heard Barry sigh. "What's wrong?"

"You wouldn't believe how many Woodward and Bernstein wannabees there are out there. And it seems that every one of them wants a job at my network. So, what do *you* do for a living?"

The phone rang and I ran to the dining room to answer it.

"So what's he like?" Janine screamed into the phone. The drunken roar in the background told me she was calling from Fritzy's Sports Bar.

I cupped my hand around the mouthpiece. "He's old," I whispered.

"What?"

"He's old," I said again, only slightly louder.

"I can't hear you. Say it again," Janine bellowed.

"She said, 'He's *old*.'"

I whipped around to find Barry smiling back at me from the couch. He may be old but he has excellent hearing.

"I gotta go." I hung up the phone.

"Brandy," Barry said, rising up from the couch, "you're delightful. But I'm sure I'm not what you had in mind when you signed up for this evening. Maybe we should call it a night."

"No. Really. We're just getting to know each other. Um, I'm just going to go check on dinner."

Barry followed me into the kitchen where we found Rocky stretched length-wise on top of the lasagna, digging her claws into the freshly baked noodles. *Unhhh!* If Barry hadn't been standing right there, I would have just spread some more sauce on top and prayed he wasn't allergic to cat fur, but seeing as he'd just witnessed this culinary debacle, I was hard pressed to pretend it was still edible. My chances of looking like a competent, employable person were disintegrating along with the meal.

"Rocky!" I admonished, acting like this was the very first time she'd ever done such a thing. She didn't look one bit sorry that I was going to spend the rest of my working life fetching margaritas for Paul's lowlife customers. "Barry, I'm sorry."

"No, really, it's not a problem," he said, trying hard not to look nauseated. "Look, maybe this is a sign that the evening just wasn't meant to be." He reached for his coat and began walking towards the front door, taking my dreams for the future along with him.

"Don't be silly," I said, hauling him back in. "Just a minor setback."

Frantically, I wracked my brain for something else to serve him. There were some kosher hotdogs in the back of the freezer, but they just didn't seem festive enough. Then I remembered Toodie's steaks. "I've got some steaks in the freezer in the basement. We can defrost them in no time." I could tell he didn't want to, but he was too polite to turn me down.

"Here we go," I said, sidestepping Toodie's left-handed golf clubs and the broken bike. I tugged on the freezer door but it wouldn't open. Something seemed to be jamming it. I tried again. Nothing. Oh great. The stupid door won't budge.

"Ya know, Brandy, I'm not even hungry. Why don't we just forget dinner?"

"No, no. If you can just give me a hand here." I picked a golf club out of the bag and nudged it through the door handle. We each grabbed an end and pulled. Nada. "I think we've got it. Just one more, good tug and—"

"It's not doing a bit of good and—look out, the damn thing is tipping over!"

"Don't worry, I've got it."

Barry gave up and moved to the side while I continued to battle the door. I yanked as hard as I could and suddenly the freezer pitched forward practically on top of my head. The door flung open, spilling the contents onto the floor.

"Dinner!" I yelled, oblivious to what had tumbled out of the freezer.

Barry stared back at me in unabashed horror.

"What? Oh no, don't tell me you're a vegetarian. You should have *told* me you don't eat meat before I went to all the trouble of opening the door."

"You're insane," he gasped, all signs of civility gone. He began backing away from me, crab-crawling his way to the farthest corner of the room.

"Well, that's the thanks I get for trying to provide a nice meal for you, and—hey, what's that leg doing on the floor?" The words were out of my mouth before the thought fully registered. I looked around. *And an arm, and a torso, and—Oh my God!* The sound of my own screams echoed in my ear as the floor rose up to meet me.

Chapter Three

"Brandy. Honey, wake up." The voice belonged to Homicide Detective Robert Anthony DiCarlo of the Philadelphia Police Department. Bobby. What was he doing here? I struggled to open my eyes and found his smoky blue ones staring back at me. My head ached and it took me a few seconds to remember why.

"Bobby," I croaked, battling a tidal wave of nausea, "there are b-body parts in the f-freezer." Either the concussion was affecting my speech or I was morphing into Paul.

"I know, honey," he said, kneeling next to me. "We're taking care of it." He felt the back of my head. "Shit. You're bleeding. Just lie still until the paramedics can check you over." He tried to sound reassuring, but he couldn't mask the concern on his face.

I glanced around the basement, which had gotten noticeably more crowded since Barry and I had come down in search of dinner. Apparently, after I'd passed out, Barry called the police and while he was at it, a few of his closest friends from the newsroom. Reporters gathered outside the door while uniformed cops milled around collecting arms and legs, pieces of a jigsaw puzzle that used to be a person. The coroner came in and pronounced the victim dead. *Like it took a genius to figure that out.*

A sudden horrifying thought occurred to me. "Bobby, the-the body—it wasn't Toodie Ventura, was it?"

"Why would you think it was Toodie?"

"Because—" I stopped, too overwhelmed by pain and circumstance to explain.

"Far as I can tell, the victim was female."

"As far as you could tell?"

"It was—headless." My stomach pitched a fit at the mental image. Good thing I'd missed dinner.

Bobby stayed by my side while the paramedic checked the crack in my skull. I took this time to study him. He looked wonderful. Dammit. Dark wavy hair, slightly disheveled, five o'clock shadow on his near-perfect face and newly formed muscles traveling up and down his lean, six-foot-one-inch body. Uncle Frankie had told me Bobby was spending a lot of time at the gym lately; seems he's not too anxious to go home to the lovely Marie. I knew how she must feel. He's certainly spent the last six weeks avoiding me. I understood why, but it still hurt.

The paramedic finished checking me over. "You should go to the hospital, ma'am. You need stitches."

I looked beseechingly at Bobby. I'd spent some time at Jefferson last month when a psychopath decided to use me as a human punching bag. I didn't relish the thought of a return visit. Then again, I couldn't stay here. I squeezed my eyes shut, but the sight of those chopped up body parts was already implanted in my brain. I felt another wave of nausea coming on and I forced myself to sit up.

"Don't Barry and I have to give statements or something?" I looked around. Where was Barry, anyway?

"If you're wondering about your friend, he's upstairs talking to my partner. And by the way, isn't he a little old for you?"

"I don't think that's any of your concern." Or mine, for that matter. As soon as Barry saw what came tumbling out of the freezer, he'd looked at me like I was Hannibal Lechter's first cousin, once removed. I don't think we'll be swapping spit any time soon.

"You're absolutely right. None of my business." Bobby stood up, all traces of personal involvement gone. "We'll need your statement, but Officer Terrel can do that."

"Bobby—"

"A head injury's nothing to mess with, Brandy. Let them take you to the hospital." He turned and walked upstairs.

Officer Terrel accompanied me in the ambulance. I answered her questions to the best of my ability, but it was hard, seeing as I kept drifting off to sleep every three minutes.

No, of course I didn't know there was a dismembered body stashed away in my basement. Would I have spent so much time trying to open the damn freezer in front of my date if I had something to hide?... No, I don't live alone; I've got a temporary roommate...Toodie—Mitchell Ventura...I don't know where he is. He hasn't been home in a few days... Yes, that's right, Toodie brought the freezer home a few days ago...said they were Omaha steaks...Did I think what? Oh my God! I had been so afraid that something bad had happened to Toodie, it never occurred to me that Toodie...and I've been living under the same roof as him!

It was all too much. I began to hyperventilate, sucking in short gulps of air like the proverbial guppy out of water. The attendant made Officer Terrel stop talking while he stuck an oxygen mask over my nose. "Better?"

I nodded. I was glad Bobby wasn't there to see me acting like such a wimp. When I was a kid I had the reputation of being fearless. I wouldn't want to shatter anyone's illusion.

I guess Bobby had called my uncle, because Frankie was waiting for me at the hospital when the ambulance pulled in.

I was comforted beyond words to see him.

"Yo, Midget Brat."

"Yo, Uncle Frankie." He gave my hand a reassuring squeeze.

"So, I guess you heard about my date tonight."

"Carla mentioned something about a fix-up." He smiled. "This may fall under the category of 'Worst Blind Date Ever.'"

"I don't know. The night's still young."

They wanted to keep me overnight. Seems I could slip into a coma—and that would be bad, why? It seemed a great alternative to the images floating around in my head.

"But who will take care of Rocky and the dog?"

"Since when do you have a dog?"

"Long story." I couldn't ask anyone to stay at the house, at least not until the place was fumigated, or exorcised or whatever it is people do after the victim of a grisly murder turns up in pieces in their basement.

It was decided that Frankie would take them back to his place and then pick me up in the morning if I was fit to be released. Then he'd drive me over to the police station so that I could make an official statement. In the mean time, Frankie would field the inevitable questions from Paul and the rest of the gang. I had some questions of my own, like where the hell was Toodie and what exactly was his involvement in all this.

I had plenty of time to think about it, because the nurses woke me up every hour to make sure I hadn't "slipped over to the other side." But try as I might, I just kept coming up empty.

In the morning I was pronounced "good as new" by a very perky resident, living, for the past six months, on No Doze and was told that I could resume normal activities. I think she'd gotten my chart mixed up with the woman down the hall who'd just had breast augmentation surgery, but it was still nice to be given a clean bill of health.

Uncle Frankie picked me up in his silver F150 and drove me to the police station. He played it cool but I could tell he was worried about me. "Are you sure you're up for this? You could go home, rest awhile." Funny thing, the house sort of lost its appeal when body parts started flying.

"I'm fine." The back of my head felt like it was on fire, so I popped a handful of Hershey's Kisses, because everyone knows that caffeine is good for getting rid of headaches.

"I think your dog is constipated," Uncle Frankie said. "You should get him some Pepto Bismol. He sure is cute. What's his name?"

I thought about this. "Homer," I told him, thinking about The Simpsons.

Uncle Frankie shook his head. "Doesn't strike me as a Homer."

I decided to give it some more thought.

Frankie dropped me off in front of the station and went to park. I knew my way around the building from when Bobby first joined the force and we were still a "happy couple." Seemed like a million years ago. A young, female cop greeted me and led me down the hall into an empty cubicle. The sign on the desk read Detective Robert DiCarlo. My heart did a little skipping around thing, which I attributed to nerves but may actually have been lust. Okay, sometimes I get really inappropriate urges at inconvenient times.

Bobby walked in with a Styrofoam cup filled with coffee, which he handed to me. There was an easy familiarity that was somehow very reassuring.

"Thanks."

He walked around the desk and sat down. He was wearing faded jeans and a gray t-shirt, with a long sleeve button down shirt on top of that. He was so bad-boy beautiful he looked like a Gap commercial. "So, how're ya doing?"

"Well, aside from the boulder growing on the back of

my head, I'm doing okay."

Bobby picked up some index cards and started shuffling them around, a prelude to getting down to business. So much for pleasantries. He put down the cards and looked at me. He was clearly uncomfortable. Well, tough. I wasn't loving this either.

"Brandy, I'm sorry I haven't been around much since you moved back—"

"Oh, hey," I cut him off. "I heard about your wife and baby coming back. I'm glad for you Bobby. I know how much you missed your little girl."

He nodded, relieved not to have to spell it out for me. "Listen, in case you were worried, your statement matches up with Barry's and you haven't been implicated in any way in this murder." *Should I have been worried? I hate missing an opportunity to needlessly fret over something.* "And since it's been determined that the actual murder didn't take place there, we've 'cleared' the premises so you're free to use the basement again."

Actually, I was thinking of having it surgically removed from the rest of the house.

"Bobby, do the police know who she is—I mean was?"

He shook his head. "There are no prints on file and without the head it makes things a little difficult. Why didn't you tell me you and Toodie Ventura were living together?" The question came out of the blue and there was more than a hint of accusation in his tone.

"Why are you saying it like I'm his common law wife? He needed a place to stay, I needed some plumbing work done. Period."

"So, you're not—"

"God no!" Jeez, how desperate for a man did he think I was?

"Okay. Sorry. I'm just relieved you're okay, is all.

We've got an APB out on the guy. In the mean time I want you to change your locks."

"Are you saying you think Toodie killed this woman?"

"Well, given his history and the fact that he brought the freezer into your home, it's not out of the realm of possibility."

"But that doesn't make any sense. I mean, why would he kill her and then leave her body in a freezer in my basement?"

"Gee, I don't know. Why would Toodie buy a set of headless golf clubs? Because he's *crazy*, that's why!"

"It was only the nine iron."

There's a little vein that sticks out on the side of Bobby's forehead when he's trying to control his temper. It was sticking out now.

"Look, I've gotten to know Toodie over the past couple of weeks. I know he's been in trouble before, but I can't believe he'd do something like this."

"Maybe you don't know him as well as you think."

"What's that supposed to mean?"

"If Toodie's innocent, why did he disappear?"

"I don't know," I admitted. And it really bothered me.

Bobby leaned across the desk until he was mere inches from my face. His voice was hard. "Stay out of this, Brandy. Let the police handle it." He slid a card over to me. It had his work number on it. "If he tries to contact you, give me a call."

I stood up. "Am I free to go?" I tried to keep the pissiness out of my voice, but it was hard. I'm not exactly known for following orders.

"Free as a bird." He relaxed back into his chair again, expelling a breath of utter frustration.

"See you around, Bobby."

"Change your locks!"

"Alright, who wants another brownie?" It was eight-thirty at night and the "Alexander Ghost Expeller Pajama Party" was officially under way. Janine made up the menu—chocolate, to appease the spirit of the woman who had "passed" and tequila shooters, "because alcohol is a disinfectant, right? So we're just purifying our surroundings." When I'd come home from the police station, I'd spent a hundred and fifty dollars on a cleaning crew to do the same thing, but Janine's way was a lot more fun.

Carla tossed back a shot and burped. She was wearing a powder blue sheer mini nightgown with a gauzy matching robe.

"Aren't you cold?" I was bundled into red and white striped fleece pj bottoms that made me look like a giant candy cane.

Carla shrugged. "I'm very warm blooded."

I looked around the living room at my friends, grateful for their companionship.

Paul, Frankie and John had been here earlier, but they left when we put on Steel Magnolias, Carla's favorite movie. I would have preferred to watch Anchorman. I really could've used the laugh. But after three tequila shooters even Steel Magnolias was funny.

When Frankie and I got back from the police station, we had to circle the area four times before we could find parking on my block. Hordes of cars trickled down the narrow street, stopping in front of my house to take pictures. The power of morbid curiosity is astounding.

I'd called a locksmith—not because Bobby told me to. It just seemed like a good idea. I still couldn't accept that Toodie had anything to do with this woman's murder. He really is too much of an innocent. But there was no denying he was involved somehow, and until I figured out how, I thought it best to err on the side of caution.

My mother called. She'd seen the footage of me on the

evening news. I'd rather have been reporting it, but hey, I made national headlines. She advised me to get a new room-mate and to call Paul.

Franny called too. She said she was sick of the boat, sick of Eddie and she was coming home on the first flight out. I knew she was doing this for me and the tears sprang up so suddenly they threatened to choke me. I fought them back, allowing Franny her charade.

"So, how are you dealing, Bran?"

"I'm fine."

"You're fine?"

"Really, Fran, it wasn't that bad. It was just the arms and legs. It's not like I found the head."

"Oh," Franny said. "It was just the arms and legs. No head. That's good, because *that* would have been gross. Why do you always do this Brandy?"

"Do what?" I asked, knowing perfectly well what she meant.

"Pretend that everything's no big deal. That you can handle it all on your own."

If you can call anesthetizing myself with booze and a six-brownie sugar high handling it. I sighed. "Is this the part where you tell me I need to see a therapist to help me through my ordeal?"

"No, this is the part where I tell you I love you and I'll see you tomorrow."

"...and then he punched a hole in the wall." Carla was giving Janine a facial. She'd smeared some slimy green gook all over her cheeks and forehead, leaving a thin strip where her mouth is. The mouth was working in what Janine thought was a quiet whisper, but in actuality was loud enough to wake the dead. God forbid, as my mother would say.

"Who?" I asked. I'd just returned from the kitchen,

where I'd found Rocky and Bullwinkle curled up together near the stove. The dog's belly was beginning to look a little bloated. I made a mental note to pick up some Pepto Bismol, like Uncle Frankie suggested.

Janine looked up, her face a mask of green guilt. "Nobody."

I gave her my most searing look, which was all the more scary with chocolate crumbs falling out of my mouth.

"Okay, you're only going to hear about it from somebody else, so I might as well tell you. It was Bobby."

Turns out, right after I left the police station, Bobby got another visitor. Marie. According to Janine's friend, Cathy, who works in Records, Marie stormed into his office yelling a whole bunch of stuff in Spanish. It took a few minutes for Cathy to track down someone to interpret for her what Marie was saying, but by that time Marie had switched to English. "What was she so mad about?"

Janine shrugged. "Your name came up a few times."

Oh boy.

"She seems to think you and Bobby are carrying on some kind of illicit affair."

"But that's crazy. We barely speak to each other. What does she think? That I planted the body in my basement just so Bobby would have a reason to come around?"

"Um, now that you mention it, yeah. She told him she wanted him to quit the case. And that's when he punched a hole in the wall."

Wow. This called for another brownie.

We got to bed at around three. Every light in the house had been turned on, plus the radio and the downstairs TV. We were all huddled together in my queen-sized bed, Janine in the middle, flanked by Carla and me on either side. Carla slept sitting up, her beehive pressed against the headboard. "It's a small sacrifice for this work of art," she told me, when

I asked her about it.

Inside of two minutes, they were both asleep. Janine began to snore, lightly at first, and then with a steady rise in volume. I wanted to stick my head under the pillow, but Rocky was lying on top of it and she swiped at me when I tried to nudge her off.

After fifteen minutes of this I gave up and made my way downstairs. The dog followed me, wide-awake and ready to play. Typical male. He snuggled up against me as I stretched out on the couch.

Just as I began to drift off to sleep, I heard my cell phone go off. Oh great. Some pervert insomniac calling to tell me he wants to see me naked and covered in Jell-o. I let my voicemail pick up and tried to go back to sleep. A minute later, curiosity got the better of me. I pressed *86 and "retrieve".

"Brandy. I'm in trouble." The voice was just a whisper, but I knew it all the same. I clutched the phone to my ear, waiting to hear the rest of the message, but that was it. Toodie. Master of the understatement. *"I'm in trouble."* *No duh!* My heart started beating in triple time. Should I call the police? Wake up Janine and Carla? Call The News Network and offer them an exclusive in exchange for a job? He sounded so scared and he hung up so abruptly. Toodie, what the hell is going on?

I woke up with the cell phone welded to my hand. After I'd calmed down, last night, I punched in "received calls" and Toodie's number came up. Okay, so it wasn't a dream. I tried to call him back, but he didn't pick up. I knew I should be making a beeline to the police station to report this latest turn of events, but something held me back. It was the desperation in his voice. This was not the voice of a vicious killer. This was the voice of a little boy in *big* trouble. I kept hoping he would call me back. But then what? Ask him if he'd done it? That just seemed rude.

I was spared having to talk to Janine and Carla about this because they were already gone. They'd left a message on the coffee table.

"You were sleeping so soundly we didn't want to wake you. Fed Rocky and 'What's his name'. Call us." I could tell Carla had written the note because it was signed with a bunch of hearts and x's and o's at the bottom.

Paul needed me for the lunch shift, so I hopped in the shower and then threw on a clean pair of jeans and a black pullover sweater. I figured that way if I spilled anything on me, it wouldn't show too badly. I grabbed my bag, stuffed a TastyKake in there for nutrition and headed out the door.

My cell phone rang just as I pulled into the parking lot of Paul's club.

"Hey, it's Bobby."

I smiled at the sound of his voice, before I remembered that we had a strictly professional relationship these days. He probably had a lead on the freezer or something.

"What's up?" I maneuvered, one-handed into the spot marked "Reserved for Owner." Well, it *is* Paul's car.

"I uh, just wanted to see how you were feeling this morning."

"Oh. Fine. I'm fine. So, do you have any leads on the dead woman?"

"You know I can't talk about the specifics of an on-going investigation."

"You got nothin', right?"

Bobby laughed and the sound went straight to the pit of my stomach. "I got nothin'."

I pictured him leaning back in his chair at work, his long blue jean clad legs stuck out in front of him. I thought about the hole in his office wall and wondered if he had gotten it fixed. I thought about Marie and what she would think if she knew he had called me. It never once occurred to me to tell him I'd heard from Toodie.

"I've got to go, Bobby," I said, guilt rearing its ugly head. I knew from past experience that he frowned on me withholding evidence in a murder investigation.

I started across the parking lot, the cell phone cradled against my ear. I could hear him breathing softly on the other end.

"Okay, well, take care. And change your locks." I hung up without telling him that I already did.

Paul was waiting for me behind the bar. I took a moment to study him as he happily swabbed down the mahogany. My brother is one of the sweetest guys ever. He's handsome and smart and infinitely kind. But he has no common sense when it comes to women. He always ends up with pound puppies, women who need to be rescued. The last girl he was serious about lived in Camden, in a doublewide trailer she shared with her alcoholic ex-husband and her six children. She was twenty-four. I guess bad relationship karma runs in the family.

"Yo," Paul smiled, looking up. "The lunch crowd will be here any minute and it's going to be jammed today. Grab a pad and start taking drink orders over at table four."

"Right," I said, wondering which one was table four. My cell phone went off again, probably Bobby, wondering if I'd changed my locks in the last three minutes. I held up my index finger to Paul. "One sec," I mouthed. "Hello?" I said into the phone.

"Brandy, it's Toodie." Oh, crap.

Chapter Four

"Paul, give me a minute."

"Is someone there with you?" Toodie asked. The fear in his voice was palpable.

"Yeah. Hold on. Don't hang up." I covered the mouthpiece. "Possible job interview."

Paul gave me two thumbs up and headed off to table four. I bolted for the Ladies' Room and locked the door.

"Are you still there?" My hands were shaking but I kept my voice steady.

"Yeah. Where are you?"

"At Paul's club. Where the hell are *you?*"

Toodie hesitated. "I'm not at liberty to say."

"You've gotta be kidding me. Toodie, you left a freezer full of human remains in my basement, I think that warrants an explanation."

"Oh, you know about that—"

"Not to mention the dog!"

"Oh, shit. I forgot about the dog. Is he okay?"

I took a deep, cleansing breath. "He's fine, except he's a little constipated. Listen, I hate to ask, but—"

"I didn't do it, Brandy, I swear to God. I thought there were steaks in that freezer. I didn't know until I looked in there."

It was my turn to hesitate. "Do you know who she was?" In my mind I'd been referring to this woman by disjointed body parts. It was less painful than thinking of her as someone's loved one.

"I didn't even know it was a 'she'. When I saw what was in there, it freaked me out so much I just slammed the door and bolted."

"Well, where did the freezer come from in the first place?"

"It belongs to a guy I know named Glen."

"So if it belongs to Glen, why'd you open it?"

"I got hungry."

A small, hysterical giggle escaped my lips. I believed him. "Listen, Toodie, there's an APB out on you. You've got to turn yourself in. You've just made things worse for yourself by running away."

"You don't believe me."

"I *do*. Look, you can talk to Vince Giancola. He's the Assistant D.A. I'll go with you."

"I don't think so. He's the one who prosecuted me over that little incident with Ilene."

"Oh." I could see where that might pose a problem.

"Ya gotta help me."

What did he want me to do, drive the getaway car as he hightailed it out of town? I had a million questions, but they would have to wait. Someone was rattling the bathroom door, trying to get in.

"Be out in a second," I yelled. "Look, I've got to go. Give me a number where I can reach you. You haven't answered any of my messages."

"I'll call you."

"When?"

"Tonight. So, like, don't tell anybody I called, okay? At least not until you hear me out."

"Alright, but if you don't call me tonight, I'm calling

the police."

"Fair enough. Thanks, Roomie. I knew I could count on you."

Dammit. Why does he have to be so…so…pathetically endearing? I must be nuts.

Waiting tables is harder than it looks. There are so many things to remember; who ordered what, which customer is allergic to onions (especially important) and where the Epi-Pen is kept in case you forget. The customer is always right (even when they're not) and if you want a good tip, don't suggest to overweight people that they substitute salad for the fries, even if you're doing it for their own good.

Paul approached me midway through the shift. "I was thinking, maybe you're more suited for hostessing. Ya know, the "meet and greet" type."

"No, no, I'm really getting the hang of this. Oh, and could you tell the people at table three that French Onion soup doesn't stain. For some reason they don't believe me."

Paul gave me a long look. "How about you be the hostess and I raise your salary to compensate for lost tips."

"That's alright, Paul. I haven't made any tips anyway."

I managed to get through the rest of the shift without incident but with newfound respect for people in the service industry. Paul caught me just as I was leaving for home.

"Are you going to be alright tonight? Because I can come by after the club closes if you want."

"I'll be fine, honest. Paul, you don't have to baby sit me."

He slung his arm around my shoulder and walked me to the door. "But you're my baby sister. Plus mom would kill me if I didn't watch out for you."

"I'm the worst waitress in the history of customer service and you haven't fired me. Nepotism notwithstanding,

I think you've gone above and beyond the call of duty." I kissed him on the cheek and told him I'd be back tomorrow. I'm not sure, but I think he blessed himself as I walked out the door.

I stopped at the Acme on the way home. Since Toodie left I was back to eating Cheerios for dinner. It had started to rain, a slow, steady drizzle that picked up speed as I exited the car. By the time I made it inside the store, my hair was hanging in limp, sodden strands and my jacket, the ancient, woolen pea coat, was soaked through to my skin. I smelled like a Border Collie.

I was perusing the frozen food aisle to see what was new in the world of Macaroni and Cheese, when I heard a small child's voice about three feet in front of me.

"Doggie," she giggled. I looked up, wondering who would bring a dog into a supermarket. A two year old with the face of a Botticelli painting smiled innocently up at me. She was pointing a tiny finger in my direction.

"Sophia, come here, sweetheart."

The voice stopped me cold. Bobby and I locked eyes as he scooped his beautiful daughter into his arms. His cart was filled to the brim with diapers, household essentials and fresh produce. It was the cart of a married man, a daddy. "Hey," he said.

"Hey." I love being caught off guard. It really sharpens my conversational wit.

"This is my little girl, Sophia. Can you say hi to Brandy, honey?"

A droplet of water from my bangs began making its way down my cheek. At that precise moment Marie DiCarlo rounded the bend from aisle twelve in search of her husband and daughter. Even with her face contorted in anger, she looked radiant. Bobby nodded to her. "Marie, this is an old friend, Brandy. Brandy, my wife, Marie."

"Um, we've met."

"What a touching scene," Marie said, linking arms with Bobby. "But if you need consolation, I suggest you go somewhere else to find it."

"What?" Oh, she thought I'd been crying. I swiped away the raindrop. "No, I was caught in the rain."

Bobby's face tensed under the fluorescent lighting. "Brandy, you don't owe her an explanation."

"But she could use a bath," Marie smirked. "She stinks." All right, enough was enough. That bitch was goin' down.

"For your information, Marie, it's the coat. And ya know I've had enough of your snide remarks. I've done absolutely nothing to warrant this attitude. If you're insecure about your marriage, deal with it with *him*, and leave me the hell out of it!"

There was a moment of dead silence, followed by an ear splitting wail.

"Now you've upset the baby. Come here, mija." Marie lifted Sophia out of Bobby's arms and stalked off, showering me with a field of death rays as she went.

"Ah, look—" Bobby started.

"Just go," I said, not bothering to look at him. I picked a frozen Mac n'Cheese out of the display case and threw it in my cart. "Your wife is waiting."

It was ten p.m. and still no word from Toodie. I waited all through The Gilmore Girls and two Will and Grace reruns. If it weren't for the Hershey bars I'd consumed on the way out of the store, I would have been asleep by now. I scanned the newspaper in my obligatory job search and did the crossword puzzle, making up words just so I could fill it all in. I was just crawling into bed at midnight, when the phone rang.

"Are you alone?"

"Yeah, now spill it."

According to Toodie, Glen was a friend of a friend from

prison. He'd called Toodie the other night and told him he had a freezer full of very expensive steaks, and if he helped him move them he'd cut Toodie in on the action. Long on enterprise and short on ethics, Toodie figured this was a harmless way to make a little extra cash. He drove out to meet Glen, and when he got there, the door was unlocked but Glen wasn't home. He went around back and there was the freezer in a shed.

"Glen didn't tell me where he wanted the freezer moved to. Only that it was really important to get it out of there ASAP. I tried to call him but he wasn't picking up his cell. So I figured as long as I was there, I'd pull the dolly out of the truck and take the freezer back to your house. I didn't think there'd be any harm in that."

Wow. Hindsight is a truly worthless thing.

"Did you ever get a hold of Glen?"

"No, I called him a bunch of times, but he never answered his phone."

I thought about this for a minute. "Toodie, is it possible that Glen never intended to meet you there? That maybe he wanted you to move the freezer on your own?"

"But why? He wanted a cut of the steaks too."

I sighed. "Toodie, they weren't steaks, remember?"

"Oh yeah."

"Toodie, where are you?"

"I can't tell ya. Look, I want to, I really do, but it's too risky. Glen must know by now that I know what was in the freezer. And he knows I can nail him. This guy is really bad news, Brandy. I mean, psycho meth-freak kinda bad."

"Then come out of hiding. Talk to the police. Bobby Di-Carlo's on the case. You know he'd give you a fair shake."

I could feel Toodie mulling this over in his brain. It was burning up the cell waves.

"Not yet. I was sort of hoping you could do a little investigating for me. Like, check out Glen's house, maybe gather some clues. I know you're really great at that sort of thing."

Once, I did it once, and it almost got me killed in the process.

"I don't know, Toodie. You said this guy is psycho."

"Yeah, well, I don't mean for you to knock down his door or anything. Just kinda scope it out. If you can find anything at all to prove what I've been telling you, then maybe I can go to the police."

It actually sounded reasonable to me. "Okay. I'll do it. But if I come up empty, I'm going to have to tell the cops." Before we hung up, I asked him about the dog.

"I found him wandering around about a half a block from Glen's house. He looked all sad and pathetic. I had to help him."

Sort of like me and Toodie.

I woke up feeling vaguely depressed. I hate to admit it but the situation with Bobby was really getting to me. The old Bobby would never turn his back on a friend. Then again, the old Bobby didn't have a wife who threatened to disappear with his kid so that he'd never see her again. And after meeting Marie DiCarlo I had no doubt she could make that happen.

In a way, I feel sorry for Marie. She's in love with a man who doesn't love her back, and she's fighting to keep her marriage together. I really couldn't fault her for that. Maybe if I had fought for Bobby four years ago, things would be different now. There's that damn hindsight again. Anyway, the point is, she thinks I'm the problem, but I'm not.

The address Toodie gave me was a seedy looking 1940's duplex just off of Frankford Avenue. I was parked next to Jolly Jack's bar, which, judging by the people staggering out of there, was a neighborhood hangout for the criminally insane. Glen's apartment was a few doors down on the right; a wood and brick abomination that looked like it was in the throes of hurricane season. A filthy storm door hung precariously by one hinge. There was a trashcan, filled to overflowing, next to it. Garbage spilled out onto the street, causing the gutter to become clogged with the overflow.

I was afraid to get out of the car, so I reached under the seat and pulled out a pair of mini binoculars that Paul had left after a Flyers' game. I put them up to my eyes and zeroed in on the front window. The drapes were open and I had a clear view of the activities.

A ruddy-faced woman in her sixties was sponging down the windowsill. Beyond her, I spied two beefy men in overalls, hauling huge bags of trash through the house. From what Toodie had told me, Glen didn't seem like the Spring Cleaning type, so I gathered up my courage and unlocked the car door.

I approached the apartment and gave a tentative knock. The front door opened, allowing me to see into the living room. If Glen lived there, he certainly couldn't be accused of being a pack rat. The place was almost completely bare. "Yeah?" The woman with the ruddy face stepped out from behind the door.

"Hi," I said brightly. "I'm looking for Glen."

The woman narrowed her eyes so close together she looked like a Cyclops. "Stand in line. Does he owe you money?" she added as an afterthought.

"No, um, can I come in for a minute?"

She moved her ample body off to the side and allowed me to pass through. Clearly, Glen no longer resided there. A quick glance around the room told me I was lucky not to have crossed paths with him. A large, crudely drawn swastika was etched into the door jamb, leading into the bedroom. There was a hole in the ceiling that could only have been left by a high-powered rifle. Lucky for his neighbor, it was a side-by-side duplex and not the stackable kind. The walls had been washed down, but the outline of some cartoon-like, anatomically impossible pornography remained. A bucket of lemon-scented ammonia sat in a corner. The apartment was unbearably hot.

"Broken thermostat," the landlady shrugged. "You know you look too clean to be a friend of Glen's," she added. What do you want with him?"

"Oh, I—"

She interrupted me before I could think of a good lie. "Hey, you're not one of those yuppie drug addicts are you? I've read about your kind in the paper."

I assured her I was not, although at this point I would have killed for a Xanex.

The roar of an engine had me running to the door, but I was too late. The truck carrying Glen's belongings had disappeared around the corner, and with it, my chance to rifle through his personal effects.

"Where are they going with that stuff?" I asked.

The woman shrugged. "City dump. It was all worthless crap anyway. Just clothes, an old mattress."

"I'm sorry, I didn't catch your name." During my tenure in Hollywood, I learned a few tricks about personalizing conversations. It tended to make people trust you.

"Didi."

"Do you mind if I take a quick look around, Didi?"

"Be my guest. Help yourself to anything that's left over. That sonovabitch owes me two months rent. Snuck out in the middle of the night and left me with a stinking mess."

I was tempted to ask her if the mess included a woman's head, but she was the chatty sort, and I figured if that were the case she would have mentioned it.

I poked around some, but the cleaning crew was disappointingly thorough. There was no smoking gun, bloody knife or confession note left behind to point to Glen as the killer.

I wandered into the kitchen. An old landline phone was tacked up to the wall and next to it, a bunch of numbers had been scribbled down. Ginos' Pizza, Dale's Pharmacy and a 900 number that, if my memory for late night cable TV commercials served me correctly, belonged to PhoneDatePlaymate. I took down the pharmacy number and walked into the bedroom.

It was empty, except for a small waste paper basket that had somehow eluded the cleaning crew. I picked it up and examined the mostly revolting contents. There was not much to go on; an old lottery ticket, a broken hairbrush with a small tangle of hair stuck to it, some used Kleenex and an old TV Guide with a picture of Reba McEntire on the cover and her front teeth blackened out.

I pocketed the lottery ticket and rooted through my pocketbook until I found a baggie. It was half filled with Cheez-its. I ate the Cheez-its and then placed the hairbrush in the baggie, in case the police needed it for DNA evidence somewhere down the line. Even as I went through the motions, I knew it was all a fruitless effort, but I'd promised Toodie I'd try to help. At least I established there really was a Glen.

"One more thing, if you don't mind," I said to Didi. "Did Glen have a girlfriend?"

"Are you a cop? Because I don't want no trouble."

"No, I'm not with the police. I'm just looking for someone and I thought Glen might know where she is."

Didi was a lot more cooperative when she thought I had any actual authority over her. She picked up a broom and pointed it at my chest. "I've got work to do and you've been here long enough."

I agreed, but I wasn't quite ready to go. I bent my head and made loud sniffing noises.

"You crying?"

I nodded vigorously. "It's just that the woman I'm look-

Shelly Fredman

ing for is my sister. She's missing and someone told me she may have hooked up with this low-life, and—and—"

"That's alright, honey." She leaned the broom against the wall and gave me an awkward pat on the back, which I'm sure was meant to comfort, but actually really hurt. "I wish I could tell you more. I don't live on the property. Maybe the guy next door can tell you something."

He wasn't home but Didi took my phone number and promised to have him call me if he had any more information.

Okay. I'd kept my promise to Toodie and checked out Glen. The logical thing to do now would be to tell the cops what I know. There was just one problem. While I was thinking of my little detour to Glen's as a minor delay in disseminating information, they might interpret it as withholding evidence and obstruction of justice.

If I had called them as soon as Toodie contacted me, they could have sent officers over to Glen's to check out his place. He may even have still been there. But now any evidence of a crime being committed was washed away by Didi or hauled to the city dump. I could just hear my mother's voice if she ever got wind of this: *"I'm very disappointed in you, Brandy Renee."* Well, mom, I'm very disappointed in me too. I really screwed up.

Maybe if I could somehow locate Glen, I'd be able to go to the police with something substantial. Toodie had given me a fairly detailed description of the guy—about 5'9", one hundred and thirty-five pounds, with a shaved head and a tattoo of a naked woman on his right forearm. I mean how hard could it be to find a methadrine-lovin,' tattooed skinhead psychopath in the city of brotherly love? There's one on every street corner. The trick was finding the right one.

I took a quick cruise around the neighborhood before I headed home. I don't know what I expected to find. Maybe Glen lurking in a dumpster but life is rarely so accommodating.

I'd made some fliers about a lost dog and stuck them up haphazardly along Frankford Avenue. The thing is, I really liked the little guy and I wasn't too anxious to find its rightful owner. But as John pointed out, what if it belongs to a lonely old lady, or some kid who cries himself to sleep every night wondering if his dog will ever come home. I'd lived in L.A. too long not to worry at least a little about Karma.

It was Open Mic night at Paul's club and the place was packed. Someone started a rumor (okay, it was me) that Keanu Reeves' band was playing there, and all the locals flocked to the place to see a bonafide celebrity. *I* even got a little excited before I remembered I was the one who'd started the rumor.

"Bran," Paul said, rubbing his goatee in a gesture of frustration, "I know you're just trying to help me out here, but do me a favor and be a little less helpful."

"Ya know," I said, ignoring him, "I have some really good ideas for the club, Paul. For instance, Karaoke is very popular in L.A., and maybe we could put in an oyster bar and strobe lights over the dance floor and—"

"Bran, you're still looking for a real job, right?"

"Oh, Paulie, if you're worried that I'm going to leave you in the lurch, you can stop right now. You know I wouldn't do that to you."

"You could, though. Honest. But in the mean time, do you think you could deliver these drinks to table six?"

"Yeah, sure. But just think about those strobe lights, okay?"

I got home a little after two a.m. and fell into bed exhausted, too tired even to worry about Toodie.

A light snow had fallen during the night, blanketing the street with a pure white powder. I looked out my bedroom window and there was Mrs. Gentile, outside in her housecoat, sweeping the snow from her steps. Nature wasn't going to have one up on her, not if she could help it.

I turned from the window and a moment later was struck by a loud grunting sound, followed by some creative Italian cursing. I looked out again and there she was, butt on the pavement, calling for help. I was tempted to ignore her, but I couldn't just leave her there with her scrawny legs flailing about in the cold, winter air. I yanked open my window and called down to her. "Are you okay, Mrs. Gentile?"

"Do I look okay?"

She didn't, but I had high hopes.

"Come down here and help me up."

I sighed and silently prayed she hadn't broken anything, so that I'd have to cart her off to the emergency room.

Thankfully, she was just a little banged up, nothing life threatening. I helped her into her house and eased her down into a chair. Wow, she'd been our neighbor for over twenty-five years and I'd never stepped foot inside her home. It smelled like cat pee, although to my knowledge she doesn't have a cat.

"Can I get you anything before I go?" I was trying to be gracious but it was hard, seeing as the last time we conversed she informed me that I was going to "burn in hell" for sins both real and imagined.

"A little broth would be nice. There's some on the stove."

I followed the cat pee smell into the kitchen. Mystery solved.

After delivering Mrs. Gentile her broth, I propped her legs up on the ottoman and made a half-hearted offer for her to call me, should she need anything. I then made a hasty retreat to my house. Two minutes later the phone rang. Oh crap. I must not have wiped my feet when I walked on her rug and now she wants me to shampoo her carpet.

"Hello?"

"Hi," said a pleasant sounding male voice. "I'm calling about the lost dog. I think it's mine."

My heart sank. "Oh, well, do you mind describing him for me?"

"No, sure. He's light brown, mixed breed, shaggy—"

"I'm sorry, but anyone would know that. I wrote it on the flier. Could you tell me something special about him? Something only the owner would know?"

The voice on the other end hesitated a beat. "His favorite color is green."

I didn't want to laugh, but it was funny. "I'm sorry. I just want to make sure I give him back to his rightful owner."

"Sounds like he's won you over."

"He has," I admitted. "What's his name, anyway?"

"Fluffy."

"Fluffy?"

"My niece named him. Personally, I would've gone with something more macho, like Brutus...or Buttercup."

I laughed again.

"I'm Keith, by the way."

"I'm Brandy."

"Brandy. That's an unusual name and yet it seems like I just heard it recently." There was a slight pause while Keith tried to remember that he saw me on the evening news, courtesy of Barry Kaminski's "on the scene" reporting. "Hey," he said, the light dawning, "you wouldn't by any chance be the woman who found the dead body in her basement, would you?"

If he'd had a hopeful note in his voice I would have slammed the phone down in his ear, but he sounded properly sympathetic so I confessed.

"As luck would have it, I am. So, how'd you lose your dog?" I asked, signaling an end to that part of the conversation.

Turns out, Keith is a lawyer who has a client near the 2200 block of Frankford Avenue. He took Fluffy with him to drop some papers off at the client's house, and the woman's young son accidentally let the dog out the front gate.

"I've been really worried about him. He's got some stomach problems."

"Yeah, I noticed. He's been constipated for a few days. I was going to run him over to the vet's."

"He's on special medication and it's important that I get him back on his regimen as soon as possible. I was wondering when I could pick him up."

I wasn't too anxious to have a stranger show up at my door—not after everything that's happened.

"Why don't we meet somewhere?"

"Great idea. Listen," he said, "you've been so nice, taking care of Fluffy for me. How about we meet at La Boheme at Penn's Landing? My office is half a block from there. I can drop the dog off and then take you to lunch."

"Oh, that's really not necessary."

"No, I'd really like to."

I did a quick inventory. Keith's a lawyer with a good sense of humor, who's nice to his niece and loves his dog. I thought about the peanut butter and jelly sandwich that awaited me and made a snap decision. "Sure," I said. "Sounds great."

By our bits of conversation I surmised that Keith was in his mid thirties, never been married—could be gay, but when I ran it by John he said it was unlikely.

"La Boheme is a definite 'date' restaurant. If he just wanted to thank you he'd take you to Sal's on Broad Street. He's trying to impress you, Sunshine."

Now that I thought back on it, Keith could have been flirting with me. "But I don't even know this guy, John," I pointed out. "What if he turns out to be a weirdo?"

"Well, I could eat lunch there too in case you need some

back up. I'm trained in the martial arts, you know. I've been taking Tai Chi."

"Isn't Tai Chi those syncopated stretching exercises that old people do in the park?"

"It's very muscle strengthening." He sounded offended so I didn't argue the point.

"I think I'll be okay, John, but thanks for offering."

Before I left to meet Keith I tried calling Toodie's cell phone again. No answer. Dammit, Toodie, pick up the phone. Not that I had anything to report. There hadn't been anything about the murder in the paper or on the news in the last couple of days, and since Bobby and I didn't seem to be on speaking terms, I was at a loss for information.

I pulled Fluffy out from under the bed, where he was happily chewing on a tube of toothpaste and I wiped the gel from his mouth. He looked like he'd contracted rabies, but his breath was minty fresh.

The wind had picked up down by the wharf, causing the temperature to drop about fifteen degrees. I rooted around in the downstairs closet and found a ratty old afghan that my mother had crocheted back in college. It was orange and brown, with a bright yellow sunburst zigzagging across the center. It looked like a prop from the musical "Hair." I wrapped Fluffy up in it and set off to meet Keith.

He was standing on the sidewalk, wearing a black Burberry overcoat and gray slacks. At least I hoped it was him. Age-wise we looked to be in the same decade, which was a real plus, after Barry. As I got closer, I noticed he was very cute, in a collegiate, WASPY sort of way, with a boyish charm, which I'm sure, served him well with women jurors.

"Brandy?" Keith smiled, extending his hand in greeting. Okay, when he got a look at me, he didn't run away screaming. So far so good. Fluffy was in my arms, stuffed inside the afghan. He poked his furry head out and sniffed the air. "Well, there you are," Keith said, making no move to take him. "How about we walk over to my office so I can leave him with my receptionist. He hasn't uh, gone to the bathroom lately, has he?" I shook my head.

"No, sorry."

Keith's office was in one of the new buildings on Dock Street that were built to look old and picturesque; an ivy covered red brick structure overlooking the water. It had to cost a fortune to rent space there. We took the elevator up three flights and walked down a plush hallway until we reached the last door, on which was painted "Keith Harrison Attorney at Law" in gold block letters. A young woman was seated at the front desk. She seemed to be the only one who worked there.

"Hi, Mr. Harrison," she said, looking up as we entered. Keith flashed her a toothy smile and she blushed the color of rutabaga.

"Do me a favor, Ali, put the dog in my office and close the door. I'll be back after lunch."

"Oh, how adorable," Ali gushed, taking Fluffy out of my arms. I felt like she'd ripped a piece of my heart out along with the dog.

"Ready to go?"

If I marry Keith, I'll be able to keep Fluffy.

"What? Oh, yeah."

I spotted her as we walked from the bar to our table. She was wearing a fur coat. Can you believe that bitch? I tried to duck behind Keith, but he was having a bathroom emergency—too many Pelligrinos—and made a beeline for the little boys' room, leaving me to contend with my high school nemesis and all-around pain in the ass, Mindy Rebowitz. "Bran-dee," she screeched. "What are you doing here?"

"Uh, eating?" I ventured. *Sorry, God. I know I gave up sarcasm for Lent, but she just begs for it.*

Mindy glanced down at Keith's empty seat. "All by yourself? Poor Brandy. Why don't you join Terrence and me? I'm sure he wouldn't mind." Terrence is Mindy's hapless better half.

"Actually, I'm not alone. My date will be back any minute now. But thanks for asking," I added politely. "Oh, and please don't feel like you have to keep me company. I'm sure Terrence is missing you already."

Mindy's bottle blond head bobbed in agreement, but she angled herself into the empty chair, anyway. The waiter came by and plunked down a basket of assorted breads. I reached for the panini, but Mindy got there first and began chowing down. Through a mouthful of my lunch she caught me up on the antics of her children, a three-year-old "genius" and a six month old with "star quality."

After the bread was gone she looked around the room. "Are you sure you don't want to join us?" I was almost tempted to, just so's I could eat all of *her* bread. But I knew what she was implying.

"Mindy, I really do have a date. He's in the bathroom."

"For fifteen minutes? You'd better check. He might have fallen in." She laughed so hard at that she almost tipped over. God I hated her. She was right, of course. *The fucking jerk ditched me!*

I was so furious I didn't notice the commotion in the back of the restaurant. The din got louder and I shouted to be heard.

"Look, Mindy, just go on back to Terrence, okay? I'm not some charity case. Men are dying to go out with me! Oh, here he comes now."

Only he wasn't walking. He wasn't even vertical...or conscious. A gurney carrying Keith Harrison's seemingly lifeless body whisked by our table on its way to the ambulance. His face was a bruised and swollen mass of lumpy flesh.

I caught one of the paramedics going out the door. "Oh my God, what happened? Is he going to be okay?"

"We'll do our best. He was pretty badly beaten."

"Where are you taking him?"

"Jefferson."

I was so shook up, I actually turned to Mindy for comfort, only to discover she was already halfway across the room, on her cell phone, spreading the news of my latest dating debacle. Just then a thought occurred to me. I didn't want Keith to die. Of course not! But if he did, I wondered if I could keep the dog.

Chapter Five

I sought out the remaining cop on site and introduced myself as Keith's lunch companion. From what they could piece together, after Keith had gone to the bathroom, he went out to the parking lot to retrieve something from the car and was ambushed on the way back in. A busboy taking out the trash spotted Keith crawling on all fours back into the restaurant. He collapsed just inside the kitchen.

"Was this a random mugging, ya think?"

"Could be. It's been known to happen. This is a pretty touristy neighborhood. Drug addict comes along, spots an easy prey—"

"But the attack was so—so vicious. Don't muggers usually just take the money and run?"

"Maybe the guy wasn't carrying as much cash as he would have liked and it pissed him off. Hard to say."

I was half way home when I remembered about the dog. Ali wouldn't know what happened to her boss. She'd wait all afternoon, maybe try to call him, but he wouldn't be able to answer his phone. Five o'clock would roll around and Ali would pack up her things and leave, without a backwards glance to the poor little would-be orphan trapped in Keith's office. How could Ali be so insensitive? I had to go back and rescue him.

Fluffy was sitting on Ali's lap, eating raisins out of her hand when I walked into the office suite. "Oh, hi," she said. "Where's Keith? I mean Mr. Harrison?" And she went all rutabaga again.

As briefly as possible, and in the least alarming way I could find, I told her about the mugging. Ali's shoulders began to heave up and down as fat teardrops rolled down her face and plopped onto Fluffy's head. Gently, I removed the dog from her grip. "I'm sure he's going to be fine," I said. "Don't you worry, Keith's a survivor!" How the hell would I know that? I just met the guy. But it sounded good and seemed to reassure Ali.

"Look, as long as Keith is going to be laid up for a little while, I thought I'd come back for Fluffy. He's used to being at my house and I'm sure Keith will feel better knowing he's being well cared for."

"Oh," said Ali, thinking. It seemed like a strenuous task for her. "Why don't you just leave her here and I'll have Mrs. Harrison pick him up and take him back to their house?"

Mrs. Harrison? Keith didn't strike me as the kind of guy who'd live with his mother, which meant…I sighed.

"Give me the address, Ali. I'll take the dog to her. I'm sure Mrs. Harrison has enough to contend with already." *Her maggot of a husband heading the list.*

Jeez, I hoped the police had already called Keith's wife because I really didn't want to be the one to break the news to her. Well, at least she was getting her dog back.

The address Ali gave me turned out to be a magnificent brownstone in Society Hill. There were no available parking spaces so I double-parked and left the engine running. Gathering Fluffy in my arms I marched up to the door and rang the bell.

A woman who appeared to be in her late thirties answered the door, holding a lit cigarette in one hand and a cordless phone in the other. I quickly scanned her face. She didn't look to be crying. Maybe she hadn't heard the news yet. Oh great.

"Mrs. Harrison?"

"Yes?" she said, expectantly, looking down at her beloved pet.

"I found your dog."

She gave me a peculiar look and spoke into the phone. "Nancy, I'll call you back." Mrs. Harrison disconnected and turned to me. "That's not my dog."

"What? But your husband identified it. He said he saw my lost dog poster and he called me. Maybe it looks like your dog?"

Mrs. Harrison chuckled without mirth. "Honey, we don't have a dog. I'm allergic. My husband is a lying bag of shit."

"But why—"

She cut me off, a weary smile playing about her mouth. "My guess is he was riding around town and saw you posting the signs. He probably thought you were cute and figured he'd use the dog angle to get to you."

"But why would anyone go to all that trouble? I'm not exactly Pamela Anderson."

"My husband can't keep his dick in his pants," she said, matter of factly. "He sees a pretty face—" She shrugged and drew on her cigarette. "It's all about the challenge."

Son of a bitch.

"I'm sure he didn't mention the fact that he's married. Don't feel bad," she added. "You're not the only one who's been duped by Keith. And you won't be the last."

Actually, there was a good possibility that I would be.

"Um, Mrs. Harrison—"

"Connie."

"Connie, I don't know if you're aware of this, but I've— I've got some bad news about Keith." Turns out she'd already heard.

"He'll be fine," she said, echoing the words I'd told Ali. "His face will look like raw hamburger for awhile and he'll have to get his perfect teeth fixed—that should put a little crimp in Romeo's style." This time we both laughed.

I wanted to ask her a million more questions, like, did Keith have any enemies—I still wasn't convinced a beating that thorough was the work of a mugger—and why an attractive, intelligent woman like herself would stay with a creep like Keith. But I spied the parking enforcement guy working his way down the street, so I thanked Connie for setting me straight and ran back to the car, the dog firmly secured in my arms.

There were three messages on my machine when I got home. I put Fluffy down on the floor and he scampered off to find something inappropriate to eat while I pressed the play back button.

"Hi sweetie, it's your dad."

Oh my God. My dad never calls me. Something must have happened to my mother.

"Nothing's wrong," he assured me. "I just wanted you to know that Paul told me you were having some financial difficulty—now don't get all upset with your brother, I'm glad he told us. Anyway, your mother and I just wanted you to know that if you need something to tide you over, just say the word."

In the background, my mom's version of whispering came through loud and clear.

"Tell her not to let her pride get in the way. You know she always wants to do everything herself."

There was a muffled response from my dad before he spoke into the phone again.

"Okay, doll. We love you. Talk to ya—bye honey."

I got a little teary eyed as I heard him hang up the phone.

Message number two was from Uncle Frankie. "Carla wants to know do you want to come for dinner tonight. I've got to warn you, she's cooking."

Sure, why not. My lunch today consisted of a smashed up TastyKake and four tic tacs. I'm sure Carla and Frankie had already heard what happened at La Boheme this afternoon and this was their way of taking care of me.

I was caught totally by surprise by call number three. It was Barry Kaminski.

Barry's message was brief and to the point. He said he had something to discuss with me and could I meet him at his office tomorrow morning. Maybe he'd heard of my amazing exploits on The Early Edition News in L.A. How I'd taken a relatively obscure show to major prominence with my in-depth reporting on the best fast food restaurants in the San Fernando Valley or the piece I did on dog parks, and he wanted to snap me up before some other network grabbed me. I knew in my heart it probably wasn't anything like that, but it never hurts to think positive.

"So the wife says her husband saw you out on the street and he had to have you! Way to go, Midget Brat!" Uncle Frankie flashed me two thumbs up.

"Stop teasing her. She's had a traumatic day." Carla punched him lightly on his arm and began clearing the table as the rest of us trooped into the living room. We all offered to help, but Carla said it was easier if we just let her do it herself.

Nobody argued. We were all stuffed; we being me, Franny, Janine, John and my uncle. After Carla burned the pork roast, Uncle Frankie had sent out for PrimoHoagies. I had a "Pal Joey" and the other half of John's "Soprano." John's watching his weight. I flopped onto the couch and undid the top button on my jeans.

"Ya know, " I said, "as much as I'd like to think men

go wild just by the sight of me, the wife was off base on her theory. The thing is, Keith knew that Fluffy is having stomach problems. How would he know that unless he'd had prior contact with the dog?"

We didn't have time to discuss it because just then Carla emerged from the kitchen carrying a blueberry cheesecake. "Dessert," she called.

Everyone groaned. Everyone except me, that is. I dug right in.

"So how come Eddie didn't come tonight?" Franny eyed me as I scraped the last bit of cheesecake off my plate and into my mouth.

"He went to the Flyers' game with Bobby."

"I'm surprised Marie let him off the leash." *Oh Jeez, that wasn't supposed to be said out loud.*

"Good one," Janine snorted, but Franny cast me a sympathetic glance.

"I'm *fine,*" I told her. "I just feel bad for him, is all."

"Ya know, this reminds me of something," Carla said.

"What does?"

"This whole 'I can't be friends with you because my wife won't let me' thing." She scrunched up her eyes in concentration.

"Friends," I sighed. "When Emily told Ross the only way she'd come back to him is if he broke off all contact with Rachel."

"That's it!" Carla exclaimed, which was followed by an awkward silence.

"So, who wants more cheesecake?"

I dropped Franny off at her house. She didn't get out of the car right away and I could tell she wanted to say something.

"What's up, Fran?"

"Okay, so like, you may not be the best person to talk to

about this, but I'm really worried about Bobby."

"Worried? Why?"

"Eddie says he's miserable at home. Oh, Bobby hasn't come right out and admitted it—you know it's not his style to confide in people—but Eddie ran into Vince Giancola yesterday and Vince said Bobby's getting into fights at work, taking stupid chances. That's why Eddie insisted Bobby go with him to the game tonight. He wanted to get him alone, see if he'd open up. Personally, I think he should just dump her ass. He's married to a lunatic."

I parked and turned off the engine. "Fran, swear you won't tell anyone, but Marie's been following me."

"Get out!"

"Well, it's either her or her evil twin." I told her about seeing Marie in the green Honda, and how she'd shown up at the police station, not ten minutes after I left Bobby's office.

"You need to tell Bobby."

There were a lot of things I needed to tell Bobby, but I don't always do what I'm supposed to.

I walked into the house and tripped over Rocky and Fluffy, who were busy mangling an empty Cheerios box. Funny, it hadn't been empty when I left it on the kitchen counter this afternoon. I vacuumed up the crumbs and plunked down on the couch. Fluffy jumped up and snuggled in beside me.

"You never struck me as a 'Fluffy'," I told him, scratching behind his ears. "We're going to have to work on a new name."

He wagged his water fountain tail in agreement.

"So, what do you think about this whole Bobby situation? Rocky thinks it's not my problem he got himself into this mess, and it's up to him to get himself out. But you strike me as the more compassionate type."

Fluffy rolled over on his back and offered his belly for me to rub.

"You're right. I do tend to want to take care of everyone. And as much as I'd like to fix everything, there are some things people have to do for themselves. You're a very good listener. I'm glad we had this little chat."

It was almost midnight so I headed upstairs and got into bed, but the nightlight in the bathroom was burned out, so I had to get up and look under the sink for a replacement bulb. I had just snuggled under the covers again when my cell phone went off.

"Hello?"

"Yo."

"Toodie?" He sounded exhausted.

"Were you able to find Glen?"

I told him what happened when I went over to Glen's house.

"I should have told the police. If they had this information, they could have gone over to Glen's that night and maybe found evidence to clear you." There was dead silence on the other end of the line. "Toodie, ya still there?"

"Yeah. Look, thanks for all your help, Brandy. I know you tried your best." I heard a soft click and then nothing.

"Toodie? Toodie!" Unhhh!

I dreamed that Marie DiCarlo had turned into her brother and was chasing me around town with a hatchet. I tried to get away, but somehow got caught up in the Mummer's Parade. The next thing I know I'm strutting down Broad Street with a forty pound headdress balanced on my neck and my head tucked under my arm. I'm sure it would have made a terrific scene from a Fellini film, but it didn't do much for a good night's sleep.

Eight a.m. I dragged myself out of bed and took a quick shower. The water pressure still wasn't great, but if I lathered minimally I'd be okay. I was supposed to meet Barry at nine. I wore my most mature outfit—a tweed suit with sensible pumps—and stuck a copy of my resume in my pocketbook. Then I fed Rocky and took Fluffy outside to do his business. He squatted, per usual, and lo and behold, something came out. Not much, but it was a start. Must've been the raisins.

I got to Barry's office with two minutes to spare. It was way up on the twenty-ninth floor, where all the executive suites are. I missed the hustle and bustle of the newsroom. While my old job was mostly pre-taped segments, on rare occasion I'd get to sit in for someone suffering the "holiday flu"—a phenomenon that usually hits on Christmas or Thanksgiving morning.

Barry was back to his charming self, having apparently gotten over the shock of thinking I was the neighborhood cannibal. He offered me a drink and said it was good to see me again. *Yeah, because we had so much fun the first time around.*

After meandering through the requisite pleasantries, he cut to the chase. "I've been doing some research on you. Why didn't you tell me you were an investigative reporter in Los Angeles?"

"I never like to mix business with pleasure." *YES!*

He leaned back in his chair. "In that case—"

"Oh, but I can make an exception. I mean the date was a disaster, so it's not like a conflict of interest or anything..." I let my voice trail off before I uttered another asinine thought.

Barry drummed on the top of his desk with his fingers. I'm not sure, but it sounded like the theme to The Andy Griffith Show. He stopped drumming and focused in on me.

"I need information, Brandy. And you seem to holding all the cards."

"What do you mean?"

"We've been investigating this murder and my reporters have been coming up empty. They've gotten nothing from their sources at the police station." The light dawned.

"And since you've been investigating me, you know that I have a history with the primary investigator on this case."

"That, and you lived with the prime suspect. I just thought if you had any inside information, you might consider passing it along— to your colleagues."

"I don't have any colleagues, Barry. I'm unemployed."

"You get me something substantial and I'll see to it you're a working reporter before the next full moon."

It was tempting. Boy, it was tempting. I rose out of my chair. "Barry, I know this is your job, and normally I'd kill for an opportunity like this. But I'm not in the habit of using my friends to further my career."

Barry rose too. "While I admire your principles, it often takes a cutthroat attitude to get the story." *What? He didn't think I could be cutthroat? I could be cutthroat...if I felt like it.* "I appreciate you coming in." He offered his hand and I shook it.

"Look, if I hear of anything that could be helpful to you without jeopardizing the police investigation or personal confidences, I'll pass it along." After all, his mother got her hair done at Carla's. We're practically family.

I swung by Jolly Jack's on the way home. I know, I should've taken the cat and dog's advice and steered clear of the whole mess, but Toodie sounded so sad. I had to try to help him. I pulled into the parking lot and sat there, gazing over the dashboard at broken Miller Light bottles, cigarette butts and what looked like a couple of used condoms. Well, they may be litterbugs but at least they weren't propagating their species.

I parked in the spot closest to the building and locked the

car. It had begun to drizzle, so I reached into the back seat and grabbed my umbrella. There were some drunks hanging around outside, wrestling over a half empty bottle of Jim Beam. I sidestepped them and opened the door.

The stench of stale cigarettes and beer hit me the minute I entered the room. As my eyes adjusted to the dim lighting, I picked my way carefully over to the bar. I found an empty stool next to a man wearing a Phillies' cap and what appeared to be a dead beaver wrapped around his ears. Upon closer inspection, I realized they were woolen socks.

"Hi," I said, brightly, shaking the excess water off my umbrella. I felt a little overdressed in my tweed suit and pumps, but who would notice in this crowd.

The guy with the socks on his ears turned to no one in particular and said, "Look, it's Mary Poppins."

Someone laughed. *Oh, like you're all fashion mavens. What was I doing here?*

I ordered a coke and scanned the room, trying to search out the least Neanderthal-looking one of the bunch. It was a tough choice. I settled on the bartender. "Excuse me, I was wondering if you could help me. I'm looking for a guy named Glen. He lives down the street—"

"Don't know him."

"But I haven't even described him yet."

"Still don't know him."

Oh, I see how this game is played. I plunked down a twenty on the bar. "*Now* do you know him?"

He picked the bill up and pocketed it. "No, but thanks for the tip." Crap.

"Does anyone know a guy named Glen? About 5'9", shaved head, one hundred thirty-five pounds...anyone?" I called out lamely. Either the bar was filled with deaf mutes or they were acting that way exclusively for my benefit. *Oh fine.* I hopped off the bar stool and headed for the door.

"Sounds like you're looking for Glen Davis."

Shelly Fredman

I turned to see who had spoken. It was a woman about my age, wearing a hooded sweatshirt with the words, "Boys are stupid. Throw rocks at them" on the front.

"Mean spirited little bastard. He gave me this." She turned her cheek to the light. A four-inch scar ran the length of it. Wow.

"Any idea where I might find him?" I gulped.

"You sure you want to?" *No, not sure at all.*

"It's kind of important."

She cast an eye around the room. No one seemed particularly interested in our conversation, but her caution made me real jittery.

"Look," I said, digging into my bag for a pen and scratch paper, "if you think of anything, would you mind giving me a call?" I quickly scribbled my name and number on the paper.

She took the paper and stuck it in the pocket of her sweatshirt. "You might try his brother. He works at Dino's MasterCarb. Turk Davis."

"Thanks."

"Don't thank me, honey. I didn't do you any favors."

Okay! I have a lead on Glen and there's parking right in front of my house. Life is good. I hopped out of the car and ran up the steps. It was 3:30 p.m., and I had just enough time to shower and change before heading over to Paul's for the evening shift.

As soon as I walked through the door I knew something was wrong. The foyer smelled like cheap tobacco. I did a quick scan of the living room. Where was the dog? He usually greeted me the minute I came home. I took a few steps inside and found him cowering under the couch. On the floor I found the bottom half of a gingerbread man tree ornament I'd made in the third grade. The rest, I assume was his mid morning snack. No wonder this dog is constipated.

I bent down to pet him, but he whimpered and receded further under the couch. I was about to crawl on all fours to coax him out of his hiding place, when I caught a shadow of movement out of the corner of my eye. *Oh shit. Company.*

Panic surged through me, making me dizzy with fear. *Okay, maybe if I act like nothing's wrong and just slowly make my way to the front door*—Instantly, a hard body slammed into me, knocking me to my knees. Blindly, I reached out and caught the guy by his ankles. He smashed into the end table, knocking over a lamp. I scrambled to my feet but he was quicker. He shoved me sideways, sending me spiraling onto the couch.

The dog went nuts, barking and snapping. He latched onto the guy's pant leg and chomped down. The intruder howled in pain and made a grab for him, but I launched myself off the couch and lunged for the guy. With a violent twist he shook me off him and jammed out the door. My first instincts were to bolt out of the house and chase the bastard down. I decided to go with my second instincts instead and locked the door behind him.

I slumped down onto the floor as the adrenaline slowly seeped out of me. The dog came over and began licking my face, offering his brand of canine comfort. I buried my face in his soft fur and then wobbled to the kitchen and dialed the police.

Officer Mike Mahoe was the first to arrive on the scene. Mike is a big, beautiful, golden-skinned transplanted Hawaiian. We met here last month, after Marie's brother tried to kill me.

"If you're looking to set some kind of neighborhood record for 'most bizarre happenings in a single family residence', so far, you're winning." I know he was just trying to put me at ease, but I wasn't quite ready to laugh about the situation.

Mike set to work gathering evidence while I gave his partner a description of the man who broke into my house. "He's a white guy, medium height, with a stocky build and wearing a drab olive green army jacket. He's got a shaved head and a round face with a wide, flat nose."

The officer wrote it all down. Then he asked me if anything was taken.

"I don't know. At least it didn't look like he had anything in his hands when he left. I think he must've just broken in when I walked in."

Bobby's partner, Detective Lindley came up to the door.

"Nobody's dead," I said. "How come you're here?"

"Heard the call and thought maybe Ventura decided to put in an appearance."

I shook my head. "Wasn't him. I saw the creep."

"Can you make a positive I.D. on the guy?"

"I don't know. I only caught a glimpse of him. Everything happened so fast."

Mike came back into the living room, followed by his partner. "Looks like your visitor broke a window in the back of the house. The method of entry matches a couple of other break-ins in the neighborhood."

Mike offered to stay with me until the repair guy came to fix the window. I told him what I really needed was someone to run interference for my mother's inevitable phone call. And with cops cars parked outside my house twice in one week, it was going to be a doozy of a phone call.

"He likes you," said Franny, when I replayed all this for her an hour later.

"No he doesn't. He was just being nice."

"Nice is offering to make you a cup of tea. The guy practically suggested he move in with you."

Note to Self: Don't tell Franny *anything!*

"Fran, you're making way too big a deal out of this."

"Okay, fine...but I'm telling ya, he likes you."

I called Paul and told him I wouldn't be able to come in to work tonight. He could barely contain the relief in his voice, but he made all the obligatory noises about how he'd try to muddle through without me.

I managed to make it to the police station and back without incident. After sifting though about four thousand mug shots, I narrowed it down to a handful that may have been the guy, but I just couldn't be sure.

"I'm sorry I can't be more specific," I said to Mike, who seemed to take a real interest in the case.

"That's okay. You've given us something to go on. Man, you've had a rough couple of days, huh?"

"I've had better ones," I admitted. I waited a beat. "Mike, I know you're not supposed to talk about it, but do you have any suspects in the—ya know, lady in the freezer case?"

"You mean besides Mitchell Ventura?"

"Does *everybody* on the force think he did it?"

"Look, Homicide's not my department, but he'd be on the top of my list. The guy did time for stalking. That's a serious offence. And he was in possession of the freezer. Plus, he has priors for drugs. A person under the influence of certain drugs can commit really horrendous acts of violence."

"Toodie smokes pot, Mike. I'm not advocating it, but I just don't think he got lit and went on a weed-induced killing frenzy."

Mike shrugged affably. "Like I said, it's not my department."

I cried all the way home. Tears of frustration over everything that'd gone down over the past few days poured out of me, rendering me a soggy mess. My house was broken into, I had no job, my blind date got mugged and my plumber was on the run from the fuzz. Toodie was depending on me to help him. The police seemed sold on the idea that he was guilty of murder, and my stupidity in not telling the cops about his phone call may have cost him his chance to clear himself. If I could only find Glen...but then what? Go up to him and say, "Hey buddy, you're comin' with me," in my best tough guy voice? I'm sure that would work.

John says I have a "control issue." I have to be in it at all times. But I was in way over my head here. I needed help and I knew where to find it. Only the prospect of making this next phone call was scarier than anything that had happened so far. I took a deep breath and dialed.

Chapter Six

He picked up on the third ring. Instantly, I broke out into a sweat and tried to hang up, but the sound of his voice, soft and husky and erotic as all get-out kept me rooted to the phone. "Brandy Alexander," he said, and I could hear the smile in his voice. Damn that caller I.D.

"Um, hi Nick." Smooth, Alexander, really smooth.

Nicholas Santiago belonged on the cover of People Magazine under the banner of "Sexiest Man Alive." It wasn't so much the way he looked, although he was more than qualified in that department, with long, wavy hair, compelling, almond shaped eyes, sensuous mouth, high cheekbones and a lithe, yet muscular body. No, the man was so much more than the sum of good genes. There was the easy confidence, the quiet air of authority, the calm, almost hypnotic cadence of his speech and the knowledge that he was capable of killing you in an instant should the occasion warrant it.

I met Nick last month, through the course of an investigation. He helped me out of a jam, which is to say he saved my life, and then he disappeared, but he'd left an indelible impression on me. Enigmatic and dangerous, Nick was the first man I've had feelings for since Bobby and the last man I *should* be feeling this way about. Boy, isn't that always the case?

I pictured him now, sitting behind the desk in the office of the martial arts studio he owns, a three days' stubble on that beautiful face. I heard music playing in the background, Django Reinhardt and Stephane Grappelli.

"So, uh, I hope I'm not calling at a bad time."

"Actually, it's perfect timing. I've been out of town for a while. I just got in about thirty minutes ago, and I stopped by the studio to check on things. So, I hear you've been having some adventures without me." Again, the smile in his voice.

"How did you know?"

"Word gets around." I'll bet it does. Nick's associates range from United States senators and presidents of third world nations, to street thugs named Lefty. There's not much he doesn't know.

"Listen, I really hate to impose on you—especially since you were almost killed because of me the last time out—"

"What do you need, angel?" My insides flipped at the familiar term of endearment.

"And I know I said I'd repay you for all you did for me, but then you went out of town, and—"

"Brandy." His voice had gone soft as a whisper. "Tell me what you need."

The heat in my belly grew, and now that feeling spread to other, more intimate parts of my body. Did that man have any idea what kind of effect he had on me? My guess is he did.

"Um, I need to run something by you. Do you think we could meet?" I didn't want to talk about it over the phone, in case it was bugged—and maybe in the back of my mind I was just a little bit excited about the prospect of seeing Nick again. But that was just a bonus. I swear.

"Do you remember where I live?" he asked.

Like I remember my own name. "I think so."

"Good. How about you come over tonight, around seven. I'll make us some dinner and you can tell me all about it." *Dinner with Nick? Alone? At his place? Oh boy!*

Nick lives in Center City, on the top floor of an elegant, old world style apartment building overlooking Rittenhouse Square. At ten 'til seven I pulled into the loading zone, remembering to scoot all the way forward, in order to leave room for Marie. She was following me again. I punched in Nick's number as the green Honda slipped off into the night.

"Hey. Where are you?"

"I'm parked in the loading zone."

"Come on up."

"But I'll get towed."

"It's okay. The owner won't mind."

Before I got there, Marie and I stopped off at a chocolatier's and picked up a two-pound box of truffles, because my mother says you should never show up at someone's house empty handed. I shifted the chocolates into my other hand and stopped for a moment to check myself out in the beveled mirror, adjacent to the elevator. I was wearing a low cut white silk blouse and a push-up bra (okay, it could have been worse; at least it wasn't padded) and some black bikini underwear, in case I got "lucky", which I didn't even know what that meant, since these days, lucky has taken on a whole new meaning for me, i.e. not getting myself killed.

The elevator stopped on the fourth floor, opening onto a dimly lit hallway. I felt myself get all sweaty again and just prayed I didn't break out in hives like I did when I was four and went to see Santa for the first time.

The door to Nick's apartment was slightly ajar, allowing the most amazing aroma to waft into the hallway. I gave a tentative knock.

"Come on in."

He was in the kitchen, standing over a large pot of something garlicky and wonderful. He put down the spoon he was holding and crossed the room to greet me. He was wearing a tight black t-shirt and faded blue jeans. His hair, shiny and thick, grazed the base of his neck. As he came nearer he smiled and it took my breath away. And then he closed the gap and I was swept up in a hug, as he placed a kiss on either side of my cheek, his lips warm and soft on my skin. "I've missed you, Brandy Alexander."

"I-I've missed you too," I croaked, reeling from the contact.

It took me a full minute to realize we weren't alone. Nick turned toward the living room. "Hey, Raoul, you remember Brandy, don't you?"

I spun around, and seated on Nick's beige leather couch sat Raoul Sanchez, his gang-scarred tattooed head bobbing up and down in recognition. The last time I saw Raoul he tried to knife me, and I ran over his hand with my car.

I was happy to note the cast was off and he had almost full range of motion back. Raoul grinned and stood, gold teeth gleaming in the lamplight. Nick walked him to the door, where they spent a few minutes quietly conversing in Spanish. I took this time to look around. I love Nick's apartment, with its high-beamed ceilings, simple but elegant furniture, and, most especially, the beautiful baby grand piano that sits in the corner by the window.

They chatted a moment longer and then the front door opened and Raoul stepped out.

"Nice to see you again," I called out, weakly.

"Any friend of Santiago's," he replied, nodding to me. And he was gone.

"Raoul works for me now," Nick said, by way of explanation.

"Oh." I didn't think I wanted to know exactly how a guy with a murder conviction on his rap sheet earned his paycheck, and besides, I knew Nick wouldn't tell me anyway.

"I hope you like Cajun," he said, returning to the kitchen.

We ate at the bar. Nick pulled up two stools and poured us each a glass of red wine. He'd prepared Shrimp Creole. It was spicy and delicious, but it made me really thirsty, which was fine because it gave me an excuse to keep drinking. Being with Nick made me nervous on so many levels and the wine really took the edge off.

We ate in comfortable silence and then he refilled my glass and we moved onto the couch. The box of truffles lay between us. "Take one," he said. "You know you're dying to."

"No I'm not." I took two and then shoved the box out of reach.

"Now," he said, settling back into the cushions, "tell me everything."

The story poured out of me, at times becoming so jumbled and disjointed I had to stop and catch my breath. In the daily living of this nightmare, I'd acted on pure impulse, never stopping to think about what a toll it was taking on me. But when I gave voice to it, I realized how dangerously close I was to an emotional breakdown. That's why it's never good to talk about your feelings. It turns you into a wimp.

"So. Your date was beat up—was that before or after you were burglarized... oh, *after* the body parts, *before* the burglary. And the guy who broke in—what did he look like?" I told him. "Did he hurt you?" Nick's face remained impassive, and yet there was something fractionally different about him. I'd seen him react that way about someone once before. The man is dead now.

"No. He didn't hurt me."

"And you trust this guy, Toodie, absolutely?"

"Absolutely." Nick picked up his glass of wine and took a sip. "What does your cop friend think about all this?" I picked up my glass as well and tossed back the remains before I answered.

"I wouldn't know. We're not exactly speaking. Did I mention his wife is stalking me? But I digress."

Nick didn't know of Glen Davis, off-hand, but he said he'd run a check and help me find him. Keith Harrison, however, had a familiar ring to it. "I seem to recall something about an attorney by that name—the guy was brought up on charges of co-mingling of funds or something—anyway, they couldn't prove anything and the case, ultimately, was dismissed." Why did this not surprise me?

I didn't want to leave the comfort and security of Nick's place, but I had to get home for the dog's midnight feeding, before he ate something crucial, like the television set. Nick walked me down to my car, which, miraculously, was right where I'd left it, no Marie in sight, no bald burglars jumping out from behind the bushes. Just the way life's *supposed* to be.

We stood on the curb while I opened my bag and fumbled around for my keys. It had grown seriously colder, but my chattering teeth were more a function of nerves than the weather. Nick took my bag and extracted my car key. He inserted it into the lock and opened the door and handed me back the key.

"Thanks. Listen, dinner was great, and um, I hope you know how much I appreciate you helping me out—but, hey, don't worry, once I cultivate my own gang members and street derelicts I won't keep hitting up your sources."

Nick's mouth turned upwards into a grin. "No rush. You going to be okay?"

I nodded. I bent down to slide into the driver's seat; when, abruptly, he pulled me back up. His voice was gentle but serious.

"Listen angel, from what you've told me, Davis is not a nice guy. I know you want to help your friend, but you're not going to be much use to him dead." I remembered the four-inch scar on that woman's face and nodded again. "Be careful." He stepped back from the curb and watched me as I shifted out of neutral and drove away.

"He kissed you on both cheeks? Was it a brotherly kiss, or something more romantic?" It was nine a.m. and Franny was in hot pursuit of the details of my evening with Nick.

"Neither. It was—European," I said, remembering a conversation we'd had months ago in which Nick revealed that his mother was part French.

"Did he kiss you goodnight?"

"No." And I have to say, I was really disappointed.

"Hang on a second." Franny cupped her hand over the receiver. *"Hello,* can't you see I'm trying to have a conversation here? They're in your top right hand drawer. Sheesh," she muttered, turning her attention back to me. "Men are so inept."

"What? Eddie couldn't find his socks?"

"Not Eddie—my boss."

"You talk to your boss like that? How do you get away with it?"

"They're afraid of me. And now that I'm pregnant they just chalk it up to mood swings. So when are you going to see him again?"

"It's not like we're dating, Fran. He's helping me out with—" *uh oh.* Too late I remembered I hadn't told her about Toodie.

Franny lowered her voice to a whisper. "Helping you out with what? And this better be good. I can always tell when you're lying." It's true. She could.

"Franny, I swear, I'll tell ya, but not now, okay? I need to get ready to go to work." *With a little pit stop at Mastercarb.*

"Oh, right. Who goes clubbing at nine in the morning?"

"Paul's got a group flying in from New Zealand. It's the

middle of the night, their time."

"You're up to something. I can feel it. That's alright. You can tell me all about it on Saturday."

"What's on Saturday?"

"You're not the only one who can be mysterious, ya know. You'll find out on Saturday."

Before I left, I put out a little bowl of raisins for the dog. He really likes them, and it seemed to help with his elimination problem. There was still nothing to write home about in that department, but at least *something* was coming out. I didn't know how long I was going to be gone, so I called John and asked him to stop in and let "Herman" out, mid afternoon. (I'd fallen asleep watching "The Munsters" last night and the name got stuck in my mind.)

I looked up the address for Mastercarb, on Passyunk Avenue, about a twenty-minute ride from my house in morning traffic. The closer I got the more I started thinking this was a really stupid idea. I mean what if Turk Davis turned out to be as dangerous as his brother? Nick offered to help me. Why couldn't I just wait to see what he turned up? Because I have the patience of a flea. That's why.

Now that I mentioned Nick to myself, I couldn't stop thinking about him. Not that he spends an inordinate amount of time thinking about me. I'm not his type. I've *seen* his type. Okay, not *seen* her exactly, but she's easy to imagine. Tall, voluptuous, long-limbed, exotic. A natural blonde. Probably owns her own business. Oh crap. I missed my turn. I did a quick "U"ie in the middle of the intersection and stepped on it before the guy in back of me completed his middle finger salute.

I parked on the street and fed the meter. I didn't have a clue what I was going to say to this guy. *"Hi. Did your brother by any chance whack some girl and stuff her in a freezer, and if so, do you know where I can find him in order to obtain a full confession? And could you check my oil?"*

He was around back, in the garage. The kid at the front desk called for him over the intercom and told me to have a seat in their reception area. I spent a few minutes staring up at a poster of a semi-naked woman on a motorcycle who was, apparently, too poor to buy clothes, because she just blew all her money on a new twelve thousand dollar bike, and then a guy appeared and the kid directed him over to me.

With a pleasant face, a soft, round body, and dark, furry tufts sticking out from the open collar of his shirt, Turk Davis looked like Winnie the Pooh in coveralls. Not exactly a dead ringer for his brother. "Hi, I'm Turk. Did you want to talk to me?"

I stood up and extended my hand.

"Hi, Turk. I'm Brandy. I was hoping you could help me. I'm trying to locate your brother, Glen."

Instantly, Turk's congenial face clouded over. "What's he done now?"

"Oh, no. It's nothing like that. He's—a friend of a friend and I was told to look him up when I came to town—"

He cut me off with a shake of his head. "Look, you seem like a nice girl. Do yourself a favor and stay away from my brother."

"I really need to find him."

"Then you came to the wrong person. The family wants nothin' to do with Glen. He's a freakin' nut. And if you had any brains in your head you'd steer clear of him too."

I guess he thought the conversation was over, because he turned and headed back towards the garage. I caught up with him and yanked hard on his arm.

"Yo! Let go!"

"Look, I'm not screwing around here, Turk My friend is in trouble, and Glen's the only one who can clear his name. Now I need you to help me out here." I whipped out a paper with my name and number scrawled on it and handed it to him. "You hear of his whereabouts, I need you to tell me, see? I could make things rough for you, see?"

I almost threw in a "you dirty rat" but that might have been pushing it.

Turk laughed. He *laughed*. "You watched White Heat with Jimmy Cagney last night, didn't you?"

"Okay," I admitted. "But I'm desperate, Turk."

"Christ," he muttered, "If Glen's your friend's only hope, he's in a shitload of trouble." But he promised to call me if he came up with anything.

It was only noon and I didn't have to be at Paul's until two, so I stopped off at DiVinci's for some lunch. The place was packed with kids from the college, so I looked around for a friendly face to share a booth with. What I found instead was Bobby. There were two empty Coronas parked in front of him and a third one on the way, along with a gigantic pepperoni pizza. As far as I could tell, he was dining alone.

I recognized the waitress, Lindsay Sargenti, one of fourteen Sargenti children and a junior at U of P. Lindsay cleared the empties and set the pizza down on the table.

"Careful, it's hot."

"Thanks, Linz."

"You sure you want this beer, Bobby? Aren't you on duty or something?"

I wasn't eavesdropping. I'm sure of it. I was just studying Lindsay for pointers on how to better serve my customers at Paul's. I drew the hood up on my jacket and moved a little closer.

Bobby grabbed Lindsay's hand and held it, a thoroughly seductive grin on his face. "I'm not on duty, Linz. But thanks for caring." He lowered his head and placed a tender kiss on the back of her hand. Lindsay gazed back at him, a sly smile on her pretty face.

"Get bent, DiCarlo. Hey, there's Brandy. Hi, Bran." She started waving like mad with her free hand. I tried to pretend I didn't see her and moved away from the table, but she kept on yelling for me until I couldn't ignore her any longer.

"Oh, hi, Lindsay. I didn't see you there." I gave a quick nod to Bobby. "How's Monica? Did she deliver yet?" Lindsay's older sister Monica and I went to school together. She's on, like, her eighth kid.

"Yesterday. Another boy. Are you eating here? Because there's a wait—unless you guys want to share a table."

"I, uh..." Bobby's legs were stretched out under the table, resting on the seat opposite him. He moved his feet, allowing me access to the booth. I eyed his pizza. It was dripping with grease and calling my name. "You gonna eat that whole thing yourself?"

"I was planning on it. Want some?" He offered me up a slice.

I sat down and dug in. Bobby had a slice too and along with it another beer. He wasn't drunk, but he wasn't feeling any pain either. He had an air of resignation I'd never seen in him before and it scared me.

"Why are you sitting here alone, drinking and stuffing your face with pepperoni in the middle of the day?"

He pushed his plate away and belched. "She doesn't want me hanging out at Eddie's because Franny's your friend. I can't go to the gym because Frankie's your uncle. The only thing I'm allowed to do is sit here and get fat. So that's what I'm doin'. You got a problem with that?"

"Yes, I have a problem with that!" I gave his leg a swift kick under the table.

"Ow!"

"For Christ's sake, Bobby, have you checked your pants lately, because you seem to be missing both your balls." I might have said that last part a little too loud because the people in the next both over laughed. Bobby shot me a look that would have annihilated a weaker person. I lowered my voice and added, "Well, I'm sorry, but it's true."

"You're all about the compassion, aren't ya?" He stood up and threw some bills on the table.

"Oh, sure. Run away. That's really going to solve it."

Bobby stood there a minute, glaring at me. I didn't know what else to do, so I kept on eating.

"Ah, shit," he said, finally, slumping back into the booth. "I hate when you're right."

"I am?"

He nodded. "What am I going to do?"

I was pretty sure this last question was rhetorical, since he said it mostly into his beer.

I slid out from the booth, grabbing another slice of pizza along the way. "Bobby, all I know is if I dropped off the face of the earth, Marie would find someone else to fixate on. It's never going to be any different until you take charge of your life again. Thanks for lunch."

Paul thought it would be fun if I tried my hand at valet parking. "You get to drive really hot cars and there's not a lot of customer interaction."

"You're just upset because of that guy at the bar," I said. "Look, *someone* had to tell him girls don't go for cheap tippers."

Paul rubbed his goatee so hard it was in danger of falling off. "Ya know, c-come to think of it, I overstaffed for today. I'm g-gonna p-pay you anyway. It's club policy."

As I pulled out of the parking lot my cell phone rang. It was John. "Hey John. I was just going to call you. Turns out I don't have to work, so I can let the dog out myself."

"Actually, I'm at your house now…are you coming home soon?"

I pulled out into traffic and hung a left onto Market Street. "I'm on my way. You sound weird. Is there something wrong?"

"No...not wrong, exactly." Fuck.

"Has anyone died in my house or general living vicinity?"

"Shut-uh-up. No one's died. Just get your buns home, okay?"

"Eewww. What *is* that?" John and I sat hunched together on my back patio, staring down at a big gooey mess. I guess the raisins finally kicked in, because whatever had clogged up the dog had suddenly unclogged, along with the entire contents of his bowels. The culprit measured an inch and a half long, wrapped in a colorful bit of paper and held together with a rubber band. I ran back inside the house and returned a moment later with a pair of tweezers and some paper toweling.

"This is so gross," I announced, poking around with the tweezers. I grabbed the mini package and laid it down on the towel.

"Now what?" John asked.

"Now somebody has to clean it off." I waited a beat, but John didn't volunteer. I didn't really think he would. "Fine. I'll do it. No big deal. It's only digested food."

"You keep telling yourself that, Sunshine," he said and went back into the house.

I followed him in and stuck the paper towel in the kitchen sink. There was a pair of disposable gloves under the sink. I pulled them on and sprayed some Windex on the mini package. Then I wiped it thoroughly with fresh paper towels. It didn't smell anymore so I decided it was safe to touch. Finally, the mystery behind the poor little guy's stomach problems would be solved. I tore off the paper.

"What is it?"

"I have no idea."

John came over and took a look. "Hmm. It looks like a thumb drive."

Shelly Fredman

"A what?" I washed my hands and reached into the cabinet for a TastyKake. I was all out, so I went to plan B and took a frozen Milky Way out of the freezer.

"A thumb drive. It's a computer device for storing information. Kind of a new age floppy. It plugs into your computer's USB port."

"That came out of him? It's a miracle. Hey, can we see what's on it?"

"I've got to go," John said. "I've got a date."

"With who?" I dug into the back of the freezer and retrieved another Milky Way.

"Friend of Richard's. I haven't met him yet." Richard is a performance artist. His idea of a good time is sticking pins through his cheek and peeing on the audience.

"A blind date? I don't know, John. Mine haven't worked out all that well."

"Maybe Richard knows someone for you too."

"Yeah, maybe."

After John left I took out my laptop and booted it up. There was a ton of junk mail and a letter from my friend Michelle, from L.A. She told me how the new reporter they hired to replace me on the Early Edition News (a former Olympic shot putter) was doing a piece on Go Carts, only once she climbed into the cart she got wedged between the seat and the steering wheel and they had to use the "Jaws of Life" to pry her loose. I felt bad for her, but it was comforting to know there's a job out there that's more humiliating than having none at all.

The thumb drive was still sitting on the kitchen table. Where did it come from and how did the dog end up swallowing it? I was dying to know what was on the disk, but it seemed impolite to just open some stranger's files. *Unless... it wasn't a stranger's. Maybe the disk belonged to Keith.* When I looked back on his interactions with the dog, Keith's only real interest was in its bowel movements. Now

I understood why he'd kept asking me if the dog had gone to the bathroom. He had to get the dog back before it pooped out the disk! There was only one way to test this theory. I had to open the files.

Seeing as all I really know how to do on the computer is surf the Internet and cut and paste, I spent about fifteen minutes poking around, trying to figure out how to access the information. Finally I gave up and called John.

"Hi. It's me. I need to know how to plug the thumb drive in."

"Can I help you with this later?"

"But I really need to do it now."

"I'm on a date," he hissed.

"Yeah, I know. It's really rude to keep him waiting, so if you'll just tell me how to plug this thing in, you can hang up and get back to your date."

"Or, I can just hang up."

Oh fine. I left messages for Franny and Janine to call me, and then I made myself a tuna melt, which I shared with Rocky because the dog ate her cat crunchies.

I sat in front of the television, eating my tuna melt and watching Dr. Phil. The topic was obsessive-compulsive personalities. I changed the channel, because I just couldn't relate. My thoughts turned to the scene in the restaurant, when Keith was wheeled out on the gurney. Maybe it *was* an irate mugger who had inflicted all that damage, but my gut instincts told me otherwise. Could it be possible that someone else was after the disk too and thought Keith had it on him?

I picked up the phone and punched in the police station; the number was burned into my brain by now. I asked to speak to Mike Mahoe. Luckily, he was there.

"Hi Mike, it's Brandy Alexander."

"Hey. How're ya doing?"

"I'm fine, thanks. Listen, I was wondering if the police

have had any luck finding the mugger who beat up that guy at La Boheme."

"How'd you hear about that?"

I figured I might as well tell him, because he'd find out about it anyway.

"I was sort of his date."

Mike stifled a laugh.

"It's not funny."

"I know. I'm sorry."

"Then stop laughing."

Mike took a deep, calming breath and exhaled slowly. "Okay. It's just that I've never run across anyone with your track record for ending up in the wrong place at the wrong time." The man had a point.

"It's an art form. So have they arrested anyone?"

"I just started my shift, but I'll check it out and get back to you."

"Thanks, Mike. I really appreciate it. By the way, have they gotten any leads on the guy who broke into my house?" I hoped I sounded more casual than I felt. The truth is, I've been really creeped out about staying alone since the whole thing happened.

"There was another break-in yesterday afternoon, a few miles from your place. The guy made off with some jewelry and a wad of cash. I guess you were lucky."

"I guess so."

I was feeling restless and bored and all my friends were busy. John was on a date—he'd made it abundantly clear he was incommunicado. Fran was eating dinner at her in-laws', Paul was at the club—I thought about heading over there but I figured he deserved the night off from me—and Frankie and Carla were at the Flyers' game.

I took out a pad of paper and a pen and stretched out on the couch. At the top of the page I wrote "THINGS TO DO." Underneath that I put: #1—Make more friends. I couldn't think of anything else for my "TO DO " list, so I decided to watch a movie.

John had bought me the "Rocky" DVD for a house-warming gift. I made a bowl of microwave popcorn, melted the last frozen Milky Way on top of it and settled back onto the couch. The dog was snuggled next to me, none the worse for wear from his enormous dump. I was actually happy to be alone now, because I always cry at the end of this movie. It's highly embarrassing, but there you go.

"Adrienne! Adrienne!" The water works were in full swing as Rocky's beloved battled her way through the crowd to get to her man. Just as Adrienne fell into Rocky's waiting arms, the dog bolted upright and hopped off the couch. He ran around in circles and squatted directly in front of the TV, his water fountain tail thumping a mile a minute.

"Here boy." I tried calling him back to the couch, but he only had eyes for Rocky. I tried again. "Yo, Adrienne." He whipped his shaggy head around to me, and I swear he was smiling. *I think we have a winner.* I'd have to change the spelling to the male equivalent, but at least now I could quit calling him "the dog".

It was only 10:30 p.m.; too early to go to bed, so I decided to get into my jammies and read. I was closing the bedroom blinds when I happened to look out onto the street and noticed an unfamiliar, dark colored sedan parked across from my house. It had been there hours earlier when I had taken out the trash. There was someone in it and he seemed to be looking directly into my bedroom. Panic overtook me. I grabbed the phone and dialed 911.

Five minutes later a patrol car cruised to a stop in front of the sedan. The officer got out and went around to the window side of the car. The guy in the sedan rolled down his window. I couldn't see real well, but it looked like he was showing the cop his I.D. Then he rolled up the window and the cop walked across the street and rang my bell. I flew down the stairs, Adrian at my heels.

"It's okay," he said. "He's a cop."

"A cop? What's he doing here?"

He shrugged. "Somebody thought you needed looking after."

I picked up the phone and punched in a number. "I don't need a baby sitter, DiCarlo. Get rid of him."

"Just doin' my job, sweetheart. Ventura was spotted in the area. Makes perfect sense that he might try to contact you. Maybe even kill you."

"Bobby! That's just plain mean. What is your problem?" I could feel that vein in his temple throbbing right through the phone.

"My problem?" His voice dropped to a deadly calm. "You're in a restaurant and your date gets beaten within an inch of his life, and *then* you walk in on a burglary in progress and nearly get yourself killed, and where do I hear about all this? Down at the station, because you never bothered to tell me yourself. That's bullshit."

"Oh, sorry. I left a message with Marie. Thought she'd pass it on." My sarcasm was met with a stony silence. "Sorry," I said again, so close to tears I could taste it. "Look, Bobby, I didn't mean it. I don't want it to be this way between us."

"Neither do I." The frustration in his voice was palpable.

"It's just that you're mad at me for something that's not my fault."

"I know. Jesus, Brandy, I've known you since you were fourteen years old. How am I supposed to stop caring about what happens to you?"

"Listen, I know you're concerned about me. Frankly, I'm concerned about me too. And it's not that I don't appreciate it, because I do. But I think Marie needs some time to adjust to the idea of me being around. So—maybe we ought to give her that time."

"What are you saying?"

"I think you should ask to be taken off the case."

"Is that what you want?"

"That's what I want."

Chapter Seven

"Why are your eyes so puffy?"

"They're not puffy."

"Yeah, they are."

"Will you quit staring at me and keep your eyes on the road?"

It was Saturday morning and I was riding shotgun in Franny's new Chevy mini van, a gift from Eddie to the "mother to be." We were on our way to pick up Janine for an undisclosed adventure. Fran's been a little weird lately.

"I shoulda gotten the T-Bird," she said. "It's more my style." *Oh yeah, baby drool and crushed up Cheerios really say T-Bird to me.* "So," she continued, "do you want to tell me what's wrong, or do I have to beat it out of you?"

"I don't even know where to begin."

"Let's start with why you've been crying."

By the time we reached Janine's, Franny knew *everything* and she wasn't thrilled.

"How the hell am I supposed to keep my mouth shut when your life could be in danger? I can understand not wanting to involve Bobby. I can even understand not wanting to go to the cops. There *is* that little matter of you withholding evidence, but for Christ's sake, Brandy, stop sticking your nose where it doesn't belong. If Toodie's innocent, the police will sort it out. Now," she ended, briskly, "what can I do to help?"

Janine was standing on the corner waiting for us, wearing a black mini skirt and fishnet stockings. It was twenty-six degrees out. Franny pulled up beside her and Janine climbed into the back seat. "So, where're we going?"

"You'll see," said Fran. "And you're going to love it!"

"I gotta tell you, Fran, so far, I'm not lovin' it."

"No?"

"Not so much."

"Me neither," Janine chimed in.

We were parked in front of Philadelphia Eddie's, the premiere tattoo parlor on the east coast. For some reason, fathomable only to pregnant women whose hormones have gone kablooy, Franny thought we should all get tattoos—each one reflecting our inner selves.

"Which one says you're a crazy pregnant lady who's so afraid of change she has to get a tattoo in order to reaffirm she's still young and desirable, even though she's married with a baby on the way?" Janine asked.

"I think the dagger."

Franny glared at the two of us. "Screw both of you. You have no idea what it's like to put your life on hold because suddenly you're responsible for another human being."

"I'm sorry, Fran," I said.

"Me too," added Janine. "But it's not like anything's really going to change. This is the twenty-first century. You don't have to alter your lifestyle just because you're pregnant."

I was about to jump in with my own reassurances, when a husky, bald headed guy wearing a drab olive green army jacket exited the hoagie shop across the street. He was chomping on a twelve-inch sandwich. "Holy cow! That's him!" I scrambled to unbuckle my seat belt and flung open the car door.

"Who?" Janine shouted from the back seat.

"Th-the burglar! The guy who broke into my house." As I propelled myself out of the car, my foot caught in the seat belt and I fell flat on my face on the curb."

"Are you all right?" Franny asked, leaning over to get a better look.

"I'm fine," I yelled. Blood was streaming out of my nose and dripping all over my jacket. "Janine, quick. He's getting away. Franny, call the police!" I began sprinting across the street, cutting a diagonal path against the oncoming traffic. Janine, in fishnets and heels whipped open her door and followed me into the street.

"Why do I have to be the one to call the police?" Franny shouted from the car. "Why can't I give chase and one of you sit here and call the cops?"

"What are you nuts?" Janine called over her shoulder. "You're pregnant."

"Nothing's gonna change, huh?" Franny sulked.

"Franny, not now." I was breathing so hard I almost heaved. "Just-call-the-cops!"

By the time we caught up with him, my burglar was four blocks down on a deserted side street. My face was a bloody mess, my lungs were burning so bad I thought they'd spontaneously combust and clutched in my hand was the only weapon I could find on such short notice—a Bic pen.

"Hey, you. Asshole." He stopped and turned around to see what kind of an idiot would call him that without a semi automatic to back them up. I was wondering the same thing. Janine stood next to me, waving her hands in the air like a Kung Fu Fighter. We circled him, stalling for time until our backup arrived. I must say, he looked a little confused and it suddenly occurred to me that he didn't know who the hell I was. How could a person invade your home, scare you half to death and then not even have the decency to recognize you on the street?

"Helloo, you broke into my house. Ring any bells?"

The light dawned and he threw his sandwich onto the ground, pastrami flying everywhere. He spun on his heel and dove straight at me, knocking me onto my butt. *Oh God, he's going to kill me. Where are the friggin' police?* On cue, the wail of sirens echoed in the street. Janine stood rooted to the spot as he leaped to his feet and bolted down the alley. Boy, for a husky guy, he sure could move. Crossing over to the Italian Market he disappeared into the throng of mid day shoppers.

By the time the police arrived on the scene, there was no scene. It wasn't their fault; Franny had told them we were traveling east on Arch instead of west. I hope she has at least a few brain cells left by the time this baby is born. After the inevitable lecture about the foolishness of our actions, the cops took our statement and told us they'd be in touch.

Janine called Fran on the cell and asked her to come get us. I limped over to the curb and sat down, inspecting the jagged holes I'd ripped in the knees of my jeans when I fell out of the car. Dried blood had formed a crust on the tip of my nose and on my exposed kneecaps. My butt hurt, my face hurt and my pride didn't feel too good either. Janine came over and sat down next to me, looking as fresh as a runway model. "Here," she said, handing me a Wetnap. I began wiping the crud off my face, trying to envision how I'd look tomorrow when the bruising set in.

Franny rounded the corner and I crawled back into the car. She looked disgruntled.

"So," I said, trying to fend off the mood swing, "ready to get your tattoo?"

"I'm sort of out of the mood."

"Oh, Franny, don't be mad," Janine told her. "It wasn't nearly as fun as it looked. And I promise you, as soon as this kid is born, we'll have a real kick-ass adventure."

Franny perked up. "With guns and everything, Neenie?"

"Okay, Fran, now you're being just plain weird."

"Oh, Hey," Franny said, having suddenly shifted back to her rational self, "I got a picture of the guy, coming out of the hoagie shop."

"You're kidding. How?"

She took her right hand off the steering wheel and dug around in her purse until she found her phone. "Here, take a look."

Holy cow. There he was, plain as day.

"Franny, you're brilliant!"

"I know."

Fran double-parked while I ran into the hoagie shop holding tight to her phone.

It was crowded but I squeezed my way to the front and flashed the picture around the deli case. There were two men working the counter. "Excuse me, but do either of you recognize this guy?"

The older of the two held my wrist steady as he examined the photo. "Yeah, hon. he's a regular here. Goes by the name of Bulldog."

I thanked him, bought three kosher pickles for the ride home and got back in the car.

When I got home I called the cops and Nick to tell them both about Bulldog. It was a race to see who would come up with his identity first. My money was on Nick. An hour later the phone rang.

"His name is Ivan Sandmeyer. He works as a bouncer at The Diamond Casino in Jersey." Nick. The man is superhuman.

"Wow, that was fast. I wouldn't want you to give away any trade secrets, but how'd you manage to come up with it so quickly?"

"Easy stuff, angel. You walk around with a street tag

like Bulldog, people are bound to remember."

"He's a long way from home."

"Guess there's more money in breaking and entering, although it did strike me as odd that he'd come all the way up here to make the hit. Especially if he's working the neighborhood on a regular basis."

It struck me as odd too.

"So have you heard from your friend lately?"

"No, and it really worries me. I heard he's been spotted in the area." I was overcome by a sudden sadness. Toodie didn't deserve to feel this alone and scared. "Any word on Glen Davis?"

"Not yet. Hopefully something will turn up soon. Hey, on an up note, Raoul has forgiven you for the mishap with his hand. In fact, he wondered if you'd go out with him."

"Are you serious?" Frantically, I wracked my brains for plausible excuses to turn him down. *It's against my religion...I'm a vegan and I make it a policy not to date carnivores... I'm really a man...*

"Don't worry, angel. I took care of it for you." *Whew.* "I told him you were my woman." *Oh my God!* This man is so unabashedly sexy he could recite names out of the phone book and make it sound like the Kama Sutra. Hearing him call me his "woman" nearly sent me into orgasmic overdrive.

"You told him I was your woman?"

"Oh, I'm sorry. Did you *want* to go out with him? I could call him back, say we broke up—"

"No, no. That's okay. I—uh—appreciate you uh, covering for me."

"Any time, darlin'. Speaking of which, I may be going out of town again at the end of the week. Can I trust you not to get into mischief while I'm away?"

"Define mischief."

Nick laughed softly. "Maybe I'd better wait on this trip.

Something tells me hanging around could prove a lot more interesting."

I felt inordinately relieved that Nick wasn't going away. It's not that I didn't believe the press on him. Bobby had him investigated, and although he could never pin anything directly on him, it was obvious that Nicholas Santiago made things happen. Sometimes very bad things. Oh, it was usually for a good cause, and only to people who weren't so nice to begin with, but Bobby says no matter how you justify it, it's still breaking the law. Only, I didn't see what was so wrong with that.

Then there were his mysterious enterprises, his alliances with shady characters, his dubious relations with renegade foreign countries, his women. And if all that weren't enough to have me running in the other direction, there was his powerful, almost drug-like ability to seduce me with a look, a word, a whisper. Nick told me once that I should never mistake him for a nice guy, because I would only end up disappointed. But all I know is I trust him completely. And in the end, that's all I really need to know.

My body ached all over from the events of the day, so I went upstairs to run a bath. It took half an hour for the tub to fill up, but the water was hot and I climbed in and soaked my scab-encrusted wounds. Two minutes later the doorbell rang. *My life sucks!* I thought about ignoring it, but what if it was a neighbor, coming to tell me my house was on fire and I had to leave right away or get burned to a crisp. Okay, I'd probably know by now if the house were on fire. But it could be important.

"Hang on a minute," I yelled from the tub. I climbed out and threw on some sweats and a flannel shirt. My hair was matted from the tub and had copious amounts of dried blood stuck to the strands around my face. I looked like I felt and I felt like caca.

Mike Mahoe stood outside on the porch, his face lit up

by the electrical circus emanating from Mrs. Gentile's lawn. It looked like the Aurora Borealis out there. I opened the door and let him in. He eyed me up and down and shook his head.

"They told me at the station you were at it again, but I didn't believe it."

"Is that all you came to tell me, because I've had a really busy day." I turned and went into the kitchen to make myself a sandwich. Under the circumstances, I didn't feel the need to offer one to Mike.

"Alright, I'm sorry for giving you a hard time. I've got some news about that Harrison guy."

"Yeah, what?"

Mike helped himself to some Hershey's kisses that were sitting on the counter. He's new and didn't know the rules about me and my candy, so when he turned around I just moved the bowl out of sight.

"I paid a visit to him at the hospital today. He's still in pretty bad shape so they're going to keep him a few more days. But here's the interesting thing. Harrison says whoever did it snuck up from behind him and tried to grab his wallet out of his back pocket, but when he fought back, the guy beat him senseless and then got scared off by a noise and took off. He says he never even saw his attacker's face."

"I guess it could've happened that way."

"Nuh uh. According to an eyewitness who happened to be passing by, Harrison was out by his car when some guy in a hooded jacket came up to him and started talking to him. He couldn't see the guy's face. Couldn't even guess what color he was. But right before he hit him, he heard the guy say something like, 'This is for Conley.' And then Harrison went down and the guy kept on beatin' on him. But he never once tried grabbing for his wallet."

"Did anyone question Keith about the discrepancy in the two reports?"

Shelly Fredman

"All he says is the witness was too far away to know what was going on and it happened just the way he said it did."

Mike couldn't stay. He was on a dinner break and had to get back to the station. I made him a peanut butter and honey sandwich for the road.

"Thanks for coming by, Mike. I appreciate you letting me know."

"Sure thing."

I walked him to the door and opened it.

"Hey, I know this is none of my business, but—" He hesitated and I could tell he was really uncomfortable.

"It's okay. What?"

"Well, is there anything going on between you and Bobby DiCarlo, because I'd like to get to know you better, but I don't want to step on anyone's toes."

I closed my eyes and counted to ten. And then I counted another ten for good measure. When I opened my eyes Mike was staring at me.

"I don't know who or what gave you the impression that there's something going on between DiCarlo and me, but I can assure you there isn't. He's a married man, to start with, and—come to think of it—we can end it right there."

Mike gave me a very sheepish look, which, on a six foot three-inch Hawaiian was actually kind of endearing.

"Sorry. It's just that he's so protective of you, I thought—"

"We go back a long way, Mike. Old habits die hard."

Mike left and I tried to get back into the tub, but the water had gone stone cold by now. I put on Nick At Nite and tried to relax, but my mind kept drifting back to something Mike had mentioned. What was it the guy said to Keith just before he beat him up? "This one's for Conley." Who the hell is Conley?

In the middle of the night I bolted upright in bed. The

guy didn't say Conley. He said *Connie!* Keith's wife must have paid someone to beat the living crap out of her philandering husband. She certainly had good reason to, and she didn't seem overly surprised or concerned about the news. Now it all made sense. He didn't want to rat out his own wife—maybe it was too embarrassing to admit she'd put a hit on him—so he made up that story about being mugged. I'm right. I know it. This realization got me all hyped up and I couldn't fall back to sleep, so I went downstairs, flipped on the computer and Googled Keith Harrison.

There were a couple of items here and there, nothing noteworthy, and then I typed in Connie Harrison and hit the jackpot. It seems that Connie is the daughter of Real Estate mogul Tyler Benson, a big deal developer on the east coast. She married Keith four years ago in a lavish ceremony on the ultra upscale Main Line, where she grew up. Although the Harrisons live quite comfortably, it is definitely a step down from her former surroundings.

I wondered if Connie confided in her dad about Keith's indiscretions and maybe Mr. Benson decided to avenge his little girl's honor by having her husband rubbed out. He certainly has the means to do it. Not to mention the motivation. On impulse, I clicked on "print" and made a copy of a picture of Keith. Then I made a note to call Mike in the morning and pass along my theory.

Sunday morning brought on an inexplicable urge to go to church. Maybe it was the constant threats on my personal safety that prompted me to make sure I was all square with God, should anything happen to me.

I decided to walk to Saint Dom's, which is just around the corner from my house. It had snowed last night and a thin sheet of ice clung to the sidewalk. I went back inside and pulled on my shitkickers—the only waterproof shoes I own, and grabbed a handful of Special K out of the box for breakfast. (I'm watching my weight.) I also snagged the last

Oreo, because one can't live on diet food alone.

When I got back outside, Mrs. Gentile was there, sweeping the snow off her side of the porch onto mine. I decided to do the Christian thing and turn the other cheek.

"Good morning, Mrs. Gentile. How are you today?"

She scrunched up her unibrow—you could really see the brain waves working—and finally settled on a reply. "I've got rats."

"Oh, I'm sorry to hear that."

"I never had rats until you moved back to the neighborhood."

I cast my eyes skyward. *Is this some kind of a test to see if I'm heaven-worthy?*

"Maybe it's all that pukey smelling soup you leave laying around on the stove." *Guess I'm going to Hell.*

"You watch your mouth, Miss Freshie." *Miss Freshie? She's old and bitter. Be more tolerant.*

"I'm sorry. I could come by later, set a few traps for you," I offered.

"We'll see," she said and went back to sweeping the snow onto my side of the porch. Unhhh!

I got to church late and slipped into one of the back pews. It was hot and damp in there, and I didn't mean to, but I fell asleep. I woke up just as they passed around the collection plate. I began fumbling around in my pocketbook for some money, but being out of work has put a real crimp in my wallet, and all I could come up with was one sorry looking torn up dollar bill. I gave an apologetic smile and quickly added it to the plate.

As we were exiting, I noticed a tall, slender woman with long dark hair, holding the hand of a gorgeous, dark haired two-year old. She was talking to the priest, who was finding her absolutely captivating. Shit. Marie. I tried to sneak past her, but she was blocking the doorway with her height and her beauty and her—her—I don't know what all, but she looked great and I didn't especially want to see her. I turned around just a tad too late. She gave me a look one usually reserves for serial rapists and went back to working her charms on Father Vincenzio. After that I felt pretty depressed, so I stopped off at a Starbucks for a peppermint mocha and some chocolate grahams and charged it to my Visa card.

When I got home I saw that the answer machine was blinking.

"Brandy, it's your mother. Daddy and I thought it would be wonderful if you could come down to Florida for Christmas. We would love to have Paul come too, of course, but he has a real job and can't get away. We'll send you the ticket. We love you honey. Bye bye."

There was a lot of noise on the other end as my mother struggled to place the phone back in its cradle, and I could hear my dad talking to her on the other end of the line.

"Lorraine, why'd you bring up the job? You know she feels bad enough."

"Don't be ridiculous, Lou. Oh, I can't hang this damn thing up." Click.

I called my brother. "Paul, am I being helpful to you at work? Be honest."

"Why do you ask?"

"Never mind." I hung up. I probably didn't really want to know.

Next, I called John. I was anxious to find out what was on the drive and thought he could come over and help me with it. He picked up after four rings. "So, how did your blind date turn out?"

"I'm still on it." Oh, guess it turned out okay.

"I'll call you later."

"Much later."

The last call was to Mike Mahoe. I left a message for him to call me.

The minute I put the phone back on its hook, it rang.

It was Franny and she seemed to be her old, read: "before pregnancy" self again.

"You want to meet me for lunch? My treat."

"Fran, you don't have to treat me like some charity case. I'll get a real job eventually."

Franny paused, thinking. "Have you been talking to your mom? You always get so touchy after a conversation with her."

"No," I lied. I hate being so predictable.

"Okay, so I'll pick you up at noon. We'll go to Henry's Bar and Grill. I feel like having steak."

I was wrong. Franny wasn't her old self. She was actually buoyant.

"What put you in such a good mood, Fran?"

"Hang on a sec." There was the sound of a door closing and then Franny got back on the line. "When we got back yesterday afternoon, I traded in the mini van for a T-Bird."

Way to go, Franny!

"So what did Eddie say?"

"He doesn't exactly know yet."

I had some errands to run, so we agreed to meet at the restaurant. It had been days since I'd last heard from Toodie and I couldn't help but feel I was letting him down. I thought I'd swing by Glen's old neighborhood and try to catch his neighbor at home. Maybe he could shed some light on Glen's whereabouts. While I was up in that neck of the woods, I would also take down the missing dog flyers. As far as I was concerned, anyone who really wanted his dog back would have called the number by now. Besides, what kind of conscientious dog owner would allow their dog to swallow a thumb drive? He could've choked to death! Before I left the house, I retrieved a foot long electrical cord that was hanging out of Adrian's mouth, replaced it with a couple of doggie biscuits and told him I'd be back soon.

By the time I reached Glen's neighborhood the sky had

turned a threatening gun metal gray. I really didn't want to be there, but I'd run out of leads. New tenants had already moved into Glen's old apartment. The screen door had been fixed and there was an old hibachi sitting right outside on the step. Someone was cooking a hotdog.

I slid out of the car and knocked on the neighbor's door. A minute later a guy in a white wife beater undershirt came out and stood on the steps.

"Yeah?" He gave me a curious but friendly smile.

I introduced myself and said I was looking for Glen.

"Oh yeah, Didi said you might be coming around. I'm Tom. Sorry about your sister."

It took me a minute to recall the lie. That's why I should always tell the truth. Life is so confusing otherwise.

"Thanks," I told him. "So, any idea where he may have gone?"

Tom shook his head. "Not a clue. When that guy left I thought to myself, 'good riddance to bad rubbish.' He is bad news any way you look at it."

I thought for a minute. "Tom, did you ever notice anyone coming in or leaving the apartment, besides Glen?" Maybe I could find a lead in the company Glen kept.

"People would come and go all hours of the day and night. I think he was selling 'ice' out of the house. Sorriest bunch of losers you ever did see. I tried to mind my own business, ya know what I mean?"

I knew what he meant. "Did you maybe ever notice anyone in particular? Somebody who might have come over on a more regular basis?"

"Now that you mention it, I did see this guy here, a couple of times. I wouldn't be able to pick him out of a lineup, but the reason I remembered him was he seemed a cut above the usual creep that hung around. I never paid much attention to him. I'm sorry. I know you really want to find your sister. Wish I could've been more help."

Me too, Tom. I thanked him for his time and asked him to give me a call if he remembered anything else.

I still had an hour before I had to meet Franny, so I cruised the area on the crazy hope that I'd spot Davis standing on a street corner, shooting up or walking his dog or something. When I hit Jolly Jack's I spied the woman I'd spoken to a few days ago, coming out of the bar. "Hey," I yelled out the window.

She seemed confused for a second and then she looked away and started walking in the opposite direction. I double- parked and hopped out of the car.

"Excuse me," I said, catching up to her. "Remember me? We met the other day and you gave me a lead on Glen Davis."

She cast a furtive glance around, her head bent to block the wind. "I don't know anything about the guy." She walked on a few feet and I trailed her, close behind. "Hey, stop following me. I told you I don't know anything."

Wow. She was so helpful the other day. Something must have happened in the mean time to change her attitude. And then it struck me.

"Have you seen Glen? Is that it?"

"Leave me alone." She broke into a trot and I had to run to catch up with her.

"That's it, isn't it? You saw Glen and he threatened you, didn't he?"

She turned to face me and I got a good view of the scar that ran down her cheek. An involuntary shiver rippled through my body. "Look, I don't want to get you in trouble. I just need to know if he's still in the area."

Her head moved a fraction of an inch, indicating I was right.

"Please. Just leave me alone," she said, and took off full speed down the street.

I thought about following her, but what good would it

do? She was clearly scared out of her mind. Glen was still in the area and word must've gotten back to him that she had spoken to me—which meant he knew someone was looking for him. The question is, did he know that someone is me?

Henry's Bar & Grill is a white collar-casual restaurant located in Center City that specializes in seafood and steaks. Franny was already seated at the table when I arrived.

"Hey," I said. "Am I late?"

"No, you're right on time. I got here early."

I sat down and picked up a menu. I was starving. "So did you tell Eddie about the T-Bird?"

"Sorta. I wrote him a note."

"Oh." It didn't seem like the best approach, but like I said, I'm not an expert on relationships.

While we were waiting for our meals to arrive I filled Franny in on the latest developments.

"It came right out of his butt?"

"Yeah. Weird, huh?"

"Weird," she agreed.

"I've been waiting for John to help me boot this thing up, but he's been a little busy."

"I could help you," said Fran. "But let's get back to the Mike thing."

"Franny, there is no 'Mike' thing. He's a really sweet guy, but...I don't know, the chemistry just isn't there. Ya know?"

"Gee," Franny said, "I wonder why not. Could it be he's too normal for you? He's not mad at the world, he doesn't have a secret life, he's not an outlaw. Sheesh! What a loser." She rolled her eyes at me.

"Okay, DiAngelo, I get your point. Can we drop it now?"

The server arrived and placed a 20-ounce steak in front of her. Franny cast him a critical eye. "That's the biggest one you've got? *What?* I'm eating for two now."

I picked up my burger and took a bite.

"Ya know what your problem is?" Fran said, pointing a steak fry in my direction.

"My best friend is a pain in the ass?"

"Your problem is you fall for the bad boys. Look, I love Bobby like a brother, but the guy is messed up." I opened my mouth to protest, but she shut me up fast. "And don't try to deny you still love him. It's me you're talking to. Then there's the ultra mysterious Nick, who, according to Carla is on a first name basis with mafia kingpins and third world devil worshippers."

"Franny, I'm not involved with Nick!"

"No, but you'd like to be." *Who wouldn't? The man is a walking pheromone.*

"Did I tell you that Monica Sargenti gained sixty-five pounds during her last pregnancy?" Okay, so it was mean, but at least it got her off the subject of my nonexistent love life.

Chapter Eight

At ten-thirty the phone rang.

"Hello?"

"I'm coming over."

Fifteen minutes later my doorbell rang. I spent the interim fourteen minutes and fifty-nine seconds in a deep and abiding panic. I knew that voice. That was not a happy voice. That was the voice of trouble hitting the fan. I just wasn't sure why.

I thought briefly about not answering, but curiosity got the better of me, and I unlatched the deadbolt and pushed open the storm door. Bobby didn't wait to be invited in. He walked though to the living room like he owned the place and sat down heavily on the couch. He was wearing his leather cop jacket and a ski cap that said Phillies on it, which he pulled off and stuffed in his pocket. Now I could see lines of exhaustion around his eyes and the grim set of his mouth. Something told me this wasn't a social call.

"Ya know where I was earlier this evening?"

I shook my head no.

"Picking a dead girl out of a dumpster."

"Bobby," I said, taking a seat on the other end of the couch, "I'm so sorry. It must have been awful."

He nodded. "She was about your age."

I wanted to reach out; to pull him towards me and hold him until the image of what he'd left behind was wiped from his memory. Instead, I offered him a TastyKake.

He gave a mournful little snort. "I didn't come here to be fed."

"Why did you come here, Bobby?" I asked as gently as possible. "I thought we agreed to put our friendship on hold for a while."

He stood up and rubbed the palms of his hands against his thighs, a gesture meant to calm himself down. After a moment he pulled a slip of paper out of his pocket and tossed it on the coffee table. "This was found in the dead girl's jacket pocket. Look familiar?"

I stared at the paper, afraid to open it. Anyway, I already knew what it was.

"Brandy," he said, and there was quiet rage in his voice, "what was your name and phone number doing in this woman's possession? How the hell did you know her?"

The irony is, I didn't know her. But I was the reason she was dead.

I sat in silence, holding my head in my hands, drowning in a sea of guilt.

"Answer me, Brandy. How did you know her?"

"I just met her the other day. I—I was looking for someone and she told me where I might be able to find him, and now—"oh shit—the tears started falling before I could do anything to stop them.

Bobby sighed and sat down on the couch again. He waited for me while I wiped my face on my shirtsleeve and took a couple of deep breaths. When he was sure the waterworks were over he tried again.

"You okay?"

I nodded.

"Now start at the beginning and don't leave anything out."

I told him everything—well, almost everything.

"You're holding something back. Who told you that the refrigerator was this Davis creep's?"

I hesitated.

"Tell me."

"I can't tell you. I'm protecting my source."

"And I'm trying to keep your ass out of jail. A young woman was murdered tonight and she had your name and phone number in your pocket. I pulled evidence for you. Do you have any idea what they could do to me if I get caught?" Bobby's face loomed mere inches from mine. "Now you tell me who this fucking source is or I'm going to rip your fucking head off."

"Oh, like that's really going to get me to open up."

Bobby slapped his hand against his head so hard I'd thought he'd knock himself out.

"It was Toodie, wasn't it?"

My non-response spoke volumes.

"Do you know where he is?"

"No. I swear it. He called me the night I discovered the body, but he wouldn't tell me where he was. He told me when he moved the freezer for Glen he had no idea what was in there. He thought they were steaks. And he asked me to try to find Glen. Toodie's scared, Bobby. He figures if we can find Glen, then maybe the cops will believe him."

Bobby got up again and began pacing the room, wearing little holes in my carpet. "Do you have any idea what kind of danger you put yourself in? Not to mention the legal trouble. Look, I know you thought you were helping Toodie, but if you had come to me sooner—"

"Don't you think I know all that? But by the time I thought it all through it was too late. I didn't want to involve you because I knew you'd try to help me, and I didn't want to put you in the middle."

"Well, I'm in it now." Neither of us said anything for a

few minutes. When he spoke again, it was with his cop voice. "Okay, here's what you're going to do. You're going to go down to the police station and make a statement that Toodie contacted you and told you about Glen. Then you're going to stay put and pray that they don't look too closely on the timing of events. And if you're very lucky, we'll be able to keep your butt out of jail. But I'm warning you, Alexander, from here on in, you stay the fuck out of this investigation."

"You're warning me?"

"Don't start."

"Don't tell me what to do."

Bobby pulled open his jacket and reached in, and for a brief panicky moment I thought he was going to whip out his .38 and shoot me. Instead, he pulled out a couple of Polaroids. "Maybe these will change your mind."

It was the girl from Jolly Jack's. Only she was lying in a pool of her own blood. Her neck was an open gash and stuff was oozing out of her. Bile rose up in my throat and I shoved Bobby's hand away.

"Look at them." He grabbed me by the wrist as I turned away and I struggled against him, knocking the Polaroids onto the rug. He swept them up in his hand again, forcing me to look. "Don't you understand, you idiot, this could've been you."

I yanked my arm hard and he lost his balance and fell, taking me with him. Bobby rolled and landed on top of me, heaving with anger and sadness, loss and frustration. All the fight drained out of me and I just gave in to the feel of his body pressed solidly against me. He laid his cheek against mine; the roughness of his unshaven face sending ripples of heat though my entire body. Finally, he raised his head and our eyes locked. Neither of us took a breath. And then the moment was gone. He rose up on his elbows and pushed himself off the floor. I didn't hear him leave.

I fell asleep on the rug, exhausted from an hour-long crying jag. He was right, of course. Bobby was trying to protect me and I was acting like a brat. It could have been me, lying in that dumpster. It was only by the grace of God that it wasn't. If there is any justice in the world the cops will find that bastard Davis. I only wish it hadn't cost someone else her life to make me see the light.

The ringing of the house phone woke me up. It was John.

"You sound terrible. Who died?"

I crawled to a sitting position and flopped down on the couch.

"No one you know."

"What?"

"Nothing. What time is it?"

"Six-thirty."

"In the morning? You couldn't wait until, say, nine?"

"I'm depressed."

Rocky sauntered into the living room, looking for something to eat. She followed me into the kitchen and I filled her bowl with cat crunchies.

"Why are you depressed?" I asked John. "I thought your blind date went well. It was certainly long enough," I added.

"It *was* going well…until his wife called."

"He's married?" Adrian padded into the kitchen and I let him out the door to pee.

John sighed. "Go figure. I really liked him, Bran."

"I'm sorry." I wasn't in the best frame of mind to be giving a pep talk, but I gave it a shot. "Ya know what my Bubbie Adele used to say? She'd say, 'every pot has a lid.'"

"No disrespect to Bubbie Adele, but what the hell does that mean?"

"I'm not sure," I said, letting Adrian back into the house. "I think it means there's someone out there who's just right for you." Or, as in my bubbie's case, lots of someones. Bubbie Adele was married five times.

After work I took the thumb drive over to John's so that we could take a look at it on his computer. John's a bit of a tech-head. He lost me after the first mumblings about a USB port, the gist of it being he had one and I didn't and we needed it to view the drive.

On the way over to John's apartment, my cell phone rang. It was Mike returning my call. I ran through my theory about Connie Harrison and her father. "Anything's possible," Mike conceded. "But it would be difficult to prove, seeing as the victim's version of events paint it as a standard mugging."

"Yeah, but it *is* possible, right?" I argued. "Mike, the guy is obviously lying. Harrison was almost beaten to death and yet nothing was taken. His wife admitted he cheats on her constantly. The witness overheard something about 'Conley,' which could easily have been 'Connie.' She's rich enough, or at least her father is, to hire someone to scare her husband into fidelity. The person who did this could have killed him, but he didn't. I think this was a warning."

Mike said he'd run it by his superiors and see what they had to say, but not to hold my breath.

There was no parking the entire length of John's block. I ended up around the corner on a side street, which didn't thrill me, but I parked right under a street lamp and ran like crazy until I reached John's door.

"Hey, Sunshine. Sorry about the parking. My neighbor is having a party."

"No problem."

"So let's see this mysterious thumb drive."

I spent the next few minutes hanging around while John booted up his computer, but he has a new flat screen television and pretty soon I was ensconced on his couch, watching Blossom—The E! True Hollywood Story.

There was a sudden explosion of laughter from John's

bedroom and then, "Come here, you've got to see this."

I took one look at the screen and sank back onto the bed. "Oh, you've got to be kidding. Porn? My dog swallowed a skin flick?" Unless Keith was starring in the damn thing, I just couldn't understand what all the fuss was about. *Ooh! Maybe he is starring in the damn thing!* John and I watched until it got really embarrassing and then he pulled the plug on it.

"Mystery solved," John said.

"I guess."

He gave me back the thumb drive. "Okay, I know that look," he said. "What's up?"

"Well, there are just too many unanswered questions, John. For instance, why did Keith pretend the dog was his, when his wife said they didn't even own a dog? And does the drive belong to Keith? And if so, why would he go to all that trouble just to retrieve porn? I mean he could easily get another copy...and how the heck did the dog end up swallowing the drive in the first place? And another thing, who is Adrian's real owner?"

"You named the dog Adrian?"

"Yeah, you know—Adrian! Adrian!"

John rolled his eyes. "You are seriously weird."

"I'm also starving. You need to feed me."

It was after eleven when I left John's apartment. He'd made pasta primavera, which, after I picked out the cauliflower, was delicious. In my opinion, cauliflower is the devil's work. It smells awful, tastes worse and looks like an albino brain. There is absolutely nothing redeeming about it.

The street was deserted so I stepped up my pace until I reached the car. I had my keys in my hand, sticking out from between my fingers like some funky brass knuckles, the way my mom taught me. I knew I was safe; this was one of the better neighborhoods, but I wasn't taking any chances. I felt anxious and scared but I didn't know why. And it didn't help that the street lamp I'd parked under had been blown out. Damn kids and their BB guns.

My phone rang and I jumped a mile. "Hello?" I said, fumbling with the keys in the lock. I opened the car and slammed the door behind me.

"It's Bobby." His voice was hard and professional. "You got lucky," he started, before I could tell him I was sorry about last night. If I was going to admit I was wrong, I wanted to get it over with.

Bobby continued in that same professional drone. "One of the regulars from Jolly Jack's called the station and said he'd seen Davis arguing with the victim the same day she was killed. When she tried to walk away from him, he grabbed her by the hair. He also stated that Davis is notorious for his abuse against women. There's an APB out on him, so there's no need to mention your involvement."

Tears sprang to my eyes and I quickly wiped them away. "What was her name?" I asked quietly.

His voice softened. "Andi. Her name was Andi."

"You were right, Bobby," I said, swallowing hard. "I made some really dumb mistakes, but I've stopped looking for Glen. And as for Toodie, I haven't heard from him in days. I don't know where he is, I swear, but if he does call I'll urge him to turn himself in." That was all I could think of to make amends, short of reciting a couple of Hail Mary's and offering to do his laundry. But Marie would probably take issue with that.

"Brandy, I just want you to be safe."

"I know you do. And I know I just said I'd butt out, but do you think this new info on Glen will help Toodie?"

"Beats me. They could have been in on this thing together. I'm still on the case, by the way. We're short-handed down at the station, and the chief says unless Toodie is my long-lost brother, I'm stuck working it."

"I understand." I just hope Marie will be equally understanding.

Ten seconds after we hung up, the phone rang. "What'd you forget to tell me, DiCarlo?"

"Guess again." The voice was male, unfamiliar and hair-raising creepy.

"Who is this?" I turned my head automatically to check the locks and started the engine.

"You were supposed to guess, bitch." My heart rate tripled as I struggled to keep down dinner. I didn't need to guess. I knew.

"Glen."

"You're quite the little detective, aren't ya? Ya know it's really unfortunate what happened to your new girlfriend. But guess what? You're next."

Before I could take a breath something slammed hard into the back of Paul's car and I flew forward, hitting my head on the steering wheel. *Oh my God, he's right behind me.* Reeling from the impact, I floored the engine and peeled out of the spot, too scared to see if he was following. I drove like a maniac; my only thought being to create as much distance as possible between us. With my free hand I tried to punch in 911 on my cell, but I dropped the phone under the seat and no way would I stop and look for it.

He kept pace with me for about ten blocks, his black Chevy Malibu shadowing my every move. How did he know where to find me? *And why couldn't I shake the son of a bitch?* I cut a sharp left and barreled headlong down a one-way street. Glen's headlights loomed in my rearview mirror for a brief moment and then—out of the blue—he was gone.

For some reason, his sudden disappearance panicked me even more. I knew I should go to the police, but there was no comfort in that thought. After all that's happened in the last several days, the cops think I'm some kind of whack-o and I could hardly blame them. I pulled over and kept the car idling while I searched for my cell phone. Then I punched in

Bobby's direct line at the station. He didn't pick up.

The adrenaline had worn off, leaving me drenched in sweat and shaking uncontrollably. I couldn't go home. He could be waiting for me. Paul's club was still open, but how could I put my own brother in danger? My life was no longer in my control and I hated feeling so helpless. I needed a safe haven. I needed Nick.

I swung the car around and headed in the opposite direction.

When I got to his apartment building, I picked up my phone and punched in his number. He answered on the first ring. Caller I.D. told him it was me.

"Hey, angel." His voice was low and relaxed. "What's up?"

"I'm parked out front. Can I come up?"

Nick was waiting for me at the door when I got there. It took every ounce of strength I had not to throw myself into his arms and cry myself silly. He was wearing a pale blue crew neck sweater, which brought out the rich chocolate brown of his eyes, and charcoal gray slacks. His face was newly shaved, accentuating his high cheekbones and angular jaw. For a moment I forgot all about the homicidal maniac who was out to get me, as I stood transfixed by Nick's extraordinary presence.

"Come on in," he said. "You sounded upset over the phone."

I was about to launch into the entire terrifying ordeal, when I saw her. She was sitting on Nick's beige leather couch, looking stunning in a simple, form fitting black dress and Jimmy Choo high heel pumps that cost more than I made in a week as a news reporter in L.A. Her hair was spun silk; a sharp contrast to my own disheveled mess. She was holding a wine goblet in her beautifully manicured hand. A small furrow in her brow creased an otherwise perfect, heart-shaped face.

She remained seated as Nick ushered me into the room and I felt a flush of embarrassment sweep over me. *Nick was on a date.*

"Brandy, this is Alana," he said, apparently completely unaware of the awkwardness I was feeling. "Alana, this is my friend, Brandy."

I felt like I'd been sucker punched. Just so that the Goddess Alana didn't get any wrong ideas, Nick let her know in a hurry I was just a "friend." At that moment I hated him, I hated her and I actually contemplated the possibility of going out with Raoul.

I grunted hello to Alana and she nodded vaguely in my direction.

"Can I get you some wine?" Nick asked.

"Um, no thanks. I can't stay. I was in the neighborhood and, uh, I thought I'd stop by to get that Shrimp Creole recipe. You know how it is when the old cooking bug bites you." *Oh my God. Somebody stop me.*

Alana eyed me coolly. "Yes, I often get the urge for crustacean at midnight."

Nick laughed and I wanted to punch her. And him too while I was at it. I fought the urge and headed towards the front door.

"I've got to go. Sorry to burst in like this."

Nick murmured something to Alana and then his arm was around my waist, guiding me back into the living room.

"You're obviously upset," he whispered, his mouth pressed to my ear. "You're not going anywhere until I find out why. Give me a minute."

I wanted to storm out of there on principle, but that only worked if he knew why I was mad, and I'd rather die than have him know how jealous I felt. Plus, the alternative was to sit home and wait for Glen to make an appearance. I wandered over to the baby grand and gazed out the window, too frightened and exhausted to argue.

Shelly Fredman

They spoke in hushed tones on the other side of the room, and then Alana walked over to the couch and picked up her coat, and held it out to Nick. He draped it around her shoulders and flashed her an apologetic smile. When they got to the foyer, she stopped and turned to face him. "I had planned on making you very happy tonight, Nicholas. Call me." She placed a lingering kiss on his mouth and walked out the door.

My stomach did a one-eighty at the sight of her lips plastered to his. *What was I doing here? I never should have just shown up at his place. He doesn't care about me. I'm just some hapless idiot he feels sorry for.*

"Nick, wait," I yelled, racing towards the foyer. "This is ridiculous. You were in the middle of—whatever—with Alana. I should be the one to leave." I yanked open the door and headed down the hall. "Maybe I can still catch her."

He grabbed me around the middle, hoisting me off the ground. My mind just snapped and I kicked out my legs, screaming for him to let me go.

"Are you aware that you're acting just a tad on the nutty side?" he asked mildly.

I did know. I just didn't know how to stop. Nick turned and dropped me gently onto the couch and sat down beside me.

"I'm sorry," I said, awash in abject misery. "I should have called first. It's just that I was so scared."

"What scared you, angel?" Just then he noticed the knot on my forehead. He reached over and brushed his thumb lightly over it and I flinched. Nick's voice took on a hard edge. "Who did this to you?"

So I told him.

"You're sure it was Glen?" It was a legitimate question. I seem to have pissed off a lot of people lately—through no fault of my own, of course.

"I'm positive. He killed that girl, Andi, he probably killed

134

the woman in the freezer—although I haven't figured out a motive for that one yet—and now he wants to kill me too."

I made my voice as flat as possible, but the involuntary trembling in my legs gave me away. Nick poured me a shot of single malt and waited while I tossed it back.

"Thanks. Christ, I don't believe this is happening just when I'd given up looking for the jerk."

"You'd already gotten the ball rolling and now the police have taken notice. In his mind you're responsible for all the bad press."

Just my luck, I'm taking all the heat of an investigative reporter, without any of the perks—like a paycheck.

"So—Davis was right on your tail and then suddenly he just vanished?"

I nodded.

"He's toying with you, angel. If he had wanted to finish you off tonight, you'd be dead."

"But why play around like that?"

"Think about it," Nick said. "It's actually pretty brilliant. He's screwing with your brain, making you look unstable. If you go to the cops with some story about him harassing you, there's no proof."

"But wait. What about the cell phone? His number would come up on my phone."

"Maybe. But I'm willing to bet he's using a stolen phone. My guess is he'll keep this up for a while until you're good and rattled, and then move in for the kill."

Wow, what a sad commentary on my life, that, compared to an ice freak, *I* look unstable.

It all seemed to make sense, except for one thing. From what I've learned about Glen, he's got a mean streak a mile long, but nobody's ever accused him of being an Einstein. I couldn't imagine him being the brains behind his own operation.

"I'm not trying to scare you, darlin', but Davis is probably tweaking, which means he hasn't slept, he's highly volatile, erratic and paranoid. A real hit could come at any time."

"What am I going to do, Nick? I feel like a sitting duck."

Nick drew me to him and wrapped me in his arms. It was the safest and most content I'd felt in weeks. "You're not going to do anything tonight except get a good night's sleep. The single malt should help."

I glanced over at the clock in the kitchen. It was one in the morning. "I have to go," I said, struggling to sit up.

Nick shook his head. "You can't go home. Not unless I go with you. Stay here for the night and we'll figure it out in the morning."

"But what about Rocky and Adrian?"

"I'll rent you the DVD."

"No, I mean my dog and kitten. I can't leave them alone. What if Glen breaks into the house? He could hurt them."

Nick untangled himself from me and picked up the phone that was sitting on his coffee table. "I have a job for you," he said to the voice that picked up on the other end. "I'm sorry. I know you need your beauty rest. I'll make sure it's worth your while." He turned to me. "What's your address?"

"But doesn't he need a key to get in?" Nick raised his eyebrows in response. There really was so much I needed to learn about the ways of the criminal world.

Thirty minutes later Rocky and Adrian were happily snuggled in Nick's spare room, courtesy of Alphonso, the B&E aficionado.

"You might want to think about an alarm system," Alphonso suggested.

Alphonso left and then it was just Nick and I and the hundreds of butterflies that suddenly took up residence in my stomach. I had stayed the night at his place once before. Nothing happened, which could have been a crushing blow to my ego, except that I chose to see it as gentlemanly restraint, given the circumstances that brought me here that night.

Nick disappeared into his bedroom, returning a few minutes later with some clean sweats and a long sleeved pullover. "Thought you might need these—unless you prefer to sleep naked." The corners of his mouth curled into a wicked grin and I felt myself go beet red.

"Uh, this is fine, thanks," I said, taking them.

He had left a new toothbrush and some fresh towels on the bathroom sink for me, with instructions to help myself to any of the toiletries. I gazed longingly at the old fashioned, cast iron bathtub. It seemed like forever since I was able to take a proper bath, with actual running water. The thought seduced me and soon I was soaking in a hot tub, filled to the brim with bubbles.

I was floating down the Mississippi River on a raft, with Rocky and Adrian. Rocky was wearing a tiny straw hat, her ears sticking out of holes on the sides. Adrian was playing the harmonica, Camp Town Races, I think. Slowly I opened my eyes as Huck Finn called to me from the dock across the way.

"Hi there."

"AHHH!" I bolted upright, forgetting for a moment that I was sitting naked in Nick's bathtub. The temperature had turned cool as the last of the bubbles floated listlessly in the water. Nick sat on the edge of the tub, smiling. Gathering the remaining bubbles I sank back under the water.

"You were in here for so long I began to get worried," he explained. "I knocked, but you didn't answer."

"Um, I must have fallen asleep."

Nick stood, and unfolded a towel for me and held it open, waiting for me to step into it. I remained rooted under water. *God, I'm such an infantile geek. If I were Alana, we'd be having mad, passionate tub-sex by now.*

"Oh," he smiled, getting it. He turned his head and I stood up at warp speed and grabbed the towel, wrapping it around myself like a cocoon.

Nick left and I brushed my hair and scrubbed my teeth and yanked on the clothes he'd left me, cursing myself all the while for being such a big, fat baby. I sat down on the edge of the tub to think things through. *Do I want Nick to "come on" to me? God, yes! Am I emotionally ready to take that step? Hell, no! Will I ever be ready for a man like Nick? Probably not.* Our relationship is so ambiguous. There'd been some sexual flirting on his part in the past, but what did it really mean? The whole thing was giving me a headache.

I found Nick in the spare room, working at the computer. He was wearing black-rimmed reading glasses, his wavy brown hair tied in a loose ponytail. He looked up when he saw me and took off his glasses. His eyes looked tired. I shoved Adrian to one side of the bed and sat down.

"I'm sorry I ruined your evening with Alana, tonight, Nick. She sounded like she had great plans for you."

"Alana is a very enterprising young lady," he agreed.

A pang of jealousy seared my insides. "Why do you keep helping me?" *Shit. I meant to say something urbane.*

He sat down next to me on the bed and brushed the hair from my eyes. "Maybe I'm just a sucker for a girl with bangs."

"No, really. I mean it. I've caused you nothing but inconvenience since the day we met. What do you get out of this?"

Nick leaned forward, the dim light from the desk lamp casting a shadow on his beautiful face. "If I were ever in trouble I'd want you on my side, because I know you'd never give up on me."

The sincerity in his voice nearly broke my heart. *Nick believed in me.* A lump formed in my throat and I swallowed hard. "Thank you," I whispered.

He turned in response and placed a hand on my cheek. My heart started beating so fast I thought it would pop right out of my chest. He gazed at me with dark, liquid eyes, and then he lowered his head and pressed his soft, full lips against mine. *Oh my God!*

I shivered in pleasure as he moved to my neck and lingered there, making small, concentric circles with his tongue. Heat spread through every erogenous zone in my body, waking up parts of me I didn't even remember I had. With agonizing slowness he worked his way back up to my earlobe, my cheek, and finally, my waiting mouth. I let out a soft moan and he pressed harder, parting his lips and pulling me to him.

Seamlessly, we rolled onto our sides and he kept on kissing me, probing my mouth with his tongue until we were completely entwined. He tasted warm and sweet and he felt so good, and I ached for him with every fiber of my being. And then he cupped my breast with the palm of his hand and I froze. *Fuck, fuck, FUCK this stupid, analytical mind. Stop thinking and just let him do it!*

Nick seemed to sense my inner struggle. He bit down gently on my lower lip and kissed me one last time. Then he wrapped his arms around me so that my head was nestled in the hollow of his neck. We laid that way until our breathing returned to normal, and then he lifted himself up on one elbow, gazing at me with those magnificent brown eyes. "You need to get some sleep, angel. You've had a busy day." He drew down the covers and I slipped between the sheets. "Sweet dreams," he said, turning out the light.

Chapter Nine

He expects me to go to sleep after *that*? It'd been four years since I'd even come close to being kissed with that kind of passion, and then I go and blow it by freaking out. What the heck was that all about? I wanted to go find him and ask if we could try it again. I'm sure I could get it right this time. Crap. He's probably called Alana by now and they're making love on his dining room table...not that he has a dining room table...maybe I should go check. I crept out of bed and listened at the door. No fevered grunting, no Bolero playing in the background. I got back in bed. Note to self: Stop being such a baby and have wild sex with Nick.

I slept straight through until eight a.m. Rocky was pawing at the door, trying to get out. Where was Adrian? I found him in the kitchen, mooching bacon off of Nick.

"Good morning," he grinned.

I decided to pretend I wasn't feeling horribly embarrassed and awkward and sat down at the counter.

Over a breakfast consisting of good strong coffee and fresh croissants, I filled Nick in on the latest developments regarding my buddy Keith. The drive had to belong to him. It was the only thing that made sense. The dog, on the other hand, clearly did not, so how did Adrian end up getting a hold of the drive? As much as I hated to admit it, I would have to track down Adrian's owner if I wanted the answer to that question.

"I think there must be something on that flash drive besides the obvious," I said. "The thing is, I don't know anything about how this computer stuff works."

"You can hide a file by erasing the file directory. It would make it harder to find, but not impossible. If you want you can leave it here and I'll take a look at it later."

I got up and cleared the dishes, wiping the table with a damp sponge. I knew I should get dressed and start the day, but I liked padding around in Nick's clothes. They were oversized and smelled like him and it made me feel sexy. Nick was already dressed in a pair of faded jeans and a black t-shirt. He wore a silver band on his left wrist. Come to think of it, I'd never seen him without it. A tiny silver cross dangled from his right ear.

My phone rang and I panicked at the sound. Nick picked it up and looked at the caller I.D. "It's okay," he said, lightly tossing the phone to me. "It's DiCarlo."

"I got a message that you called the station looking for me, last night."

"Yeah, I sorta ran into some trouble."

"Shit," he growled, when I told him. "Did you report it?"

"What was I going to say? Some phantom psycho is following me? He was driving a black Chevy Malibu, by the way."

"Where are you now?"

I hesitated. Nick is not exactly on Bobby's list of acceptable playmates and I really didn't want to get into a fight about it. "I'm at Frankie's."

"His apartment or the gym?"

"Apartment," I said. Sometimes it scares me how easily I lie.

"Put him on."

"I can't. He's in the shower." *Hah!*

"Hang on a second," Bobby said. I passed the time by eating the rest of the truffles I'd brought over the other night.

Bobby came back on the line. "You're lying. I just called your uncle and he says he hasn't seen you."

"You *what?*" My only hope was righteous indignation and I was goin' with it. "How dare you check up on me like that? Now Frankie's probably worried sick about me. See the trouble you've caused? I have to call him right now to tell him I'm okay."

"Brandy—"

I hung up before he could ask me anything else and punched in my uncle's number.

"Hey, hon, how're ya doin'?"

"Um, fine." He didn't sound all that concerned about me.

"What's up?"

"I just thought I'd call because—" Suddenly the light dawned. Have you spoken to Bobby lately?"

"No, why?" Unhhh!

Bobby called me back but I ignored him. Nick watched me, his face a picture of pure delight. "Aren't you going to answer it?"

"No."

His grin got wider.

"I'm glad this is so entertaining for you."

"You do know you're making him nuts."

"That is not my concern." I turned away but I could feel Nick's eyes on me. *"What are you lookin' at?"*

Nick offered to arrange for someone to escort me to work. He had a meeting this morning and was teaching a martial arts class in the afternoon, but Alphonso was on call if I needed him. As tempted as I was to have a personal henchman at my beck and call, I turned him down. "I can't let Glen get to me, Nick. I'll take extra precautions, but if I give in to the fear, he wins."

"Just be careful, darlin'." No lectures, no ranting about how dumb I am for wanting to handle it my way. I nodded, grateful for the vote of confidence.

I got dressed and looked out the window to check on the weather. It had snowed again in the night, which must be why I couldn't find Paul's car. It had to be buried in the snow. Okay, that was unlikely, which meant only one thing. Holy crap! Paul's car's been stolen! I am not going to have to worry about Glen killing me, because my brother is going to do it for him.

"Oh, sorry," Nick said. "I forgot to tell you, I had your car taken in to my body shop to have the dent smoothed out. You're driving the Mercedes truck out there. It comes with a tracking device. Hope you don't mind."

I almost cried with relief. But I just couldn't bring myself to accept it. While it is true that I can be very focused on my own needs, I am not, by nature, a taker.

"You've done way too much for me already," I said, shaking my head."

"I'm just thinking about Paul," Nick replied. "He's going to be heartbroken when he sees what happened to his car. I'm just trying to spare the guy a little grief." He tossed me the keys.

Well, he did have a point. I'd do anything for Paul, even if it meant driving around in a $70,000.00 truck.

I pulled up in front of the club at around noon. There was a new red T-Bird sitting out front. I went inside and found Franny, seated in one of the plush leather booths, sipping a soda. "Nice set of wheels, Fran," I said, slipping into the seat opposite her.

"Thanks," she beamed. "I was stopped at a light on

Spruce and this really hot guy pulls up besides me, rolls down his window and says, 'Beautiful car, but not as beautiful as the babe driving it.' Then he asks for my phone number."

Uh oh. The old Franny would have leaped out of the car and decked him for making such a cornball, sexist remark. But the hormonally impaired Fran was unpredictable.

"What happened then?" I asked cautiously.

"I gave him my phone number."

"Franny!"

"Relax, it was a fake number. I just wanted to remember what it felt like to be young and free."

"Have you discussed these feelings with Eddie, Fran?"

"Yeah, he says it's normal for pregnant women to feel this way. He's been reading up on the subject." Eddie is a saint.

Paul came in carrying a plate piled high with steak fries and a burger. He plunked it down in front of Franny and she scooped up the burger and began to devour it.

"Hey, kiddo," he greeted me. "I didn't know you were supposed to work today. Funny thing, I overscheduled again, so you're free to go. My mistake, so of course I'll pay you."

I looked around the room. It was packed with the usual lunchtime crowd and my brother was waiting tables.

"Paul, am I that much of a disaster? Be honest."

Paul hung his head and slowly nodded up and down. "Bran, I'm sure you were a terrific reporter, but as a waitress you basically suck. I love you, honey, but you're k- killing my business." The news was discouraging. After all, it doesn't look great on a resume to get fired by your own brother.

"Isn't there anything I'm suited for?"

Paul thought about it for a minute. Suddenly, he grinned.

"Taco and the guys are playing here tomorrow night. Their lead female vocalist is down with the flu—"

"I'll do it." I used to sing in a garage band with those guys and I filled in for them about two months ago. I had to be talked into performing after all these years, but I'd had a blast and was dying to be asked to sing with them again.

Paul left to call Taco and I settled back in the booth, happy not to be taking any more handouts from my brother. Franny finished her burger and began perusing the dessert menu. "Oh, hey, Bobby called our place this morning. He wanted to know if you'd spent the night with us."

"What did you tell him?" I tried to sound casual, but nothing gets past eagle eye Franny.

"I didn't tell him anything. Eddie talked to him and said you weren't here. So give."

She waited expectantly. The next thing I know, I'm telling Franny everything, from the fight Bobby and I had, to the kiss to end all kisses, courtesy of Nicholas Santiago. When I got to the part about Glen Davis I did an involuntary sweep of the room.

"Okay," Franny said, pushing her plate away. "I know you hate being told what to do, but I'm going to tell you anyway."

"I know, I know," I told her. "I should lay low, take Nick up on his body guard offer, go to the police and put myself in protective custody—"

She cut me off. "I was going to say you should get a gun."

"What are you, insane? Franny, You're the sensible one. I'm supposed to come up with the crazy ideas and you're supposed to talk me out of them."

"Screw that. There's a maniac on the loose and he's headed your way. You've got to learn how to protect yourself. I've been telling you this for years." Franny loves guns. She was state shooting champion three years running, back in high school.

"Look, there's a little bit of difference between knocking off clay pigeons and gunning down an actual person."

"Do you think that creep Davis knows there's a difference?" She had a good point. I told her I'd think about it and get back to her.

Franny left to go back to work and I had about six hours to kill, now that my waitressing days were officially over. Since I didn't feel safe going back to my house without Nick or a reasonable substitute, I decided to head over to Jefferson Hospital to visit my pal, Keith. Curiosity about his possible connection to the drive was eating at me. And if there turned out to be more to Keith's beating than he was willing to admit, maybe I'd uncover a juicy story to share with Barry Kaminski. I know it's not on par with a dismembered body, but I had to get my foot in the door with him somehow.

Paul walked me out to the street. "Uh, Bran, where's the car?" He tried not to show it, but there was panic in his voice.

"Oh, I'm getting it detailed. It was going to be a surprise for you," I added, "for being so nice about letting me drive it." I flashed him what I hoped was a "winning smile." Paul looked doubtful. "Don't worry, Paul. The car is absolutely perfect. I'll bring it around later on so that you can see for yourself. Okay?" Quickly I climbed into the truck and started the engine.

"Where'd you get this thing?" Paul yelled, pointing to the truck. I pantomimed that I couldn't hear him. "Roll your window down," he yelled louder. I nodded and smiled to him in response, waving as I drove away.

The woman at the information desk at Jefferson scanned the computer screen. "I'm sorry honey. It looks like Mr. Harrison has already been released."

"Oh. Do you happen to know when?" She glanced at

the screen again.

"Yesterday afternoon."

"Thanks."

Okay, now what do I do? I couldn't exactly show up at his house bearing flowers and a "Get Well" balloon. His wife seemed really nice, but I doubt she'd welcome a convalescence call from a woman her husband tried to "date".

I swung the truck around and headed off in the direction of Keith's house. Every few minutes I checked in the rear view mirror to make sure I was still flying solo. Between Marie and Glen I had developed quite the entourage.

I parked down the block and got out my phone. Keith's cell number was stuffed somewhere in the bottom of my purse. I found it and gave him a call.

After three rings a groggy, male voice said hello.

"Is this Keith?"

"Yeah?"

"This is Brandy Alexander—the woman who found the dog."

There was a moment of silence as Keith processed this news. I'd caught him off guard. Good. His tone became more alert, conciliatory, even.

"Oh, hey, hi. I'm glad you called. Sorry our lunch didn't work out. I guess the police told you I was mugged in the parking lot."

"That was some beating you took," I said. "Did they get anything valuable?"

"My wallet, a watch, you know, the usual."

What a big fat liar! The cops said nothing was taken.

"Oh, I'm so sorry. It must have been terrifying."

"You have no idea. Listen, how's the dog?"

"Fine, although it's no wonder the poor thing had stomach problems. Turns out he'd eaten a thumb drive, of all things. Can you believe it?"

"Do you still have it?"

"What?" I asked, all innocence.

"The drive, do you still have it?" His voice was tinged with desperation.

"Oh, sure. And I have to admit I was curious, so I took a peek."

"You did?" He didn't sound too happy about that.

"As porn films go, it wasn't very interesting, so I didn't sit through the grand finale. Say, Keith," I asked, as if I'd just thought of it, "the drive doesn't by any chance belong to you, does it? I know the dog isn't really yours. I've met your wife and she straightened me out about a few things. She seems very nice, by the way."

"Listen," Keith interrupted. His breathing was labored and it was obviously painful for him to speak. "I may have misled you on a few things. And I'm sorry. If I could just have a few minutes of your time to clear it up for you—"

"I'm all ears."

"Do you think you could come over here? I'd feel better talking to you face to face."

"Don't you think that might be a bit awkward, with your wife and all?"

"She's out of town for a few days."

"She left you." It wasn't a question. Keith hesitated and I could hear the lies rattling around in his brain. He settled for a gross understatement.

"We've had some problems. Listen, if you'd just come over—"

"I'm already here. I'm parked outside."

"Good." Keith sighed heavily into the phone. "Did you bring the thumb drive?"

I ignored that, asking instead if anyone was there to let me in.

"I've hired a nurse."

I took the necessary precautions by calling Nick to tell him where I was. If he didn't hear from me within the hour, send the Marines or at least Alphonso. Then I locked the car and walked up the block to the Harrisons' door.

A very attractive Indonesian woman opened it and let me in. She must have been expecting me, because she took me right into the bedroom. Keith was propped up on some pillows, his face pale against the dark sheets. She adjusted the blinds, letting in a thin filter of afternoon winter sunlight and then asked if she could get him anything else. Harrison gave her a wan smile and shook his head no. "Thank you, Amaya." I had to admit, even with his cheeks a mottled rainbow of yellow, purple and green, he still exuded a certain charm, which did not go unnoticed by the nurse. She blushed as she walked out of the room.

Now Keith turned his full attention on me. He leaned forward, making eye contact.

"Thanks for coming, Brandy. Affecting a thick Cuban accent he chuckled, "I have a lot of 'splaining to do."

Oh, I get it—Ricky Ricardo. I decided to keep the upper hand by not laughing at his attempt to be cute. Instead, I settled back in the floral print chair next to the bed and cast a steely look his way. "Okay, Ricky, start 'splaining."

According to Keith, most of what he'd told me was true. The dog was his. He'd found it at a shelter and had intended to bring it home to surprise his wife. They've been having some marital difficulties and he thought a dog would bring them closer together. But when he stopped at a client's on the way home, things went awry.

"I had the drive tucked away in the inside pocket of my jacket, which I'd left on the couch. The drive is evidence in a very sensitive custody battle—I'm not at liberty to discuss the details, but as you can see by the content, it could be very damaging to my client. This is an extremely explosive case. Anyway, long story short—and I know it sounds crazy—the dog must've thought it was a cookie—it was wrapped in an old Oreos' wrapper—and, well, he ate it. When I realized what had happened, I tried to grab him, but he bolted out the front door." Actually, it didn't sound so crazy. The dog eats everything.

"But why didn't you just tell me the truth instead of lying about it?"

"I'm truly sorry, Brandy," he said, bestowing one of his "I've-been-caught-with-my-hand-in-the-cookie-jar-but-forgive-me-because-I'm-adorable" smiles on me. "The downside to being a lawyer is sometimes you work with less than reputable people. I couldn't risk hurting my client. I didn't know if I could trust you with the truth."

"So that's it?"

"That's it."

It was time for his pain meds. I poured Keith a glass of water and helped him open the pill container.

"One last thing—why'd you ask me out to lunch?"

Keith had the grace to blush. "You sounded nice and, like I said, my wife and I have been having problems." *Gee, I can't imagine why.*

"Well, you're not getting the dog back. I named him and everything. And his name's not Fluffy"

"I guess it's a moot point, seeing as Connie's left me. But I really do need that drive. I'm happy to pay you—for your time and trouble—whatever the amount."

"The thing is I don't have it with me."

"Where is it?" His tone was sharp, and a thought that had been playing around in the back of my mind suddenly leaped to the forefront.

"It's back at my house," I lied. "I didn't know I was going to stop here this afternoon."

"Oh," he said, relaxing. "I'll send someone by to pick it up."

"No." I stood and gathered my bag. "I'm coming back this way, tomorrow. I'll drop it off on the way." I could tell by the look of frustration on his face that was not the solution he wanted, but he was in no position to argue.

"Tomorrow, then."

I needed a quiet place to think, so I drove over to the Central Library on Vine Street. Somehow Glen didn't strike me as a real literary kind of guy. I couldn't imagine him lurking in these hallowed halls, stalking me among the Twains and the Steinbecks.

I chose a quiet corner and sat with my back against a wall. Then I took out a pad of paper from my pocketbook and headlined it:

Keith—You Big Fat Liar

I began listing all of the lies he'd told me—at least the ones I knew about, ending with the most recent. Keith said he'd gotten the dog from a shelter and was going to take it home to his wife, as a sort of peace offering to her. Some peace offering. Connie Harrison is allergic to dogs. She'd told me so herself the day I visited her. Keith had no intention of giving that dog to Connie, but he wanted me to believe the dog was a stray so that I couldn't trace its owner. Where did Adrian really come from? I don't know why I was putting so much effort into this business with Keith. Maybe it's because I don't have anything of my own to occupy my time, or maybe I hate being lied to. All I know is, Keith isn't getting the thumb drive back—not until I learn the truth behind it.

It was dark when I left the library and a feeling of unease settled over me. The tracking device on the truck provided a bit of comfort—knowing that if some maniac popped up out of the back seat to kill me, they'd at least be able to figure out where he took the body—but I longed for the day I could come and go as I pleased, without looking over my shoulder every second. It was starting to feel like that day would never come.

I pulled up in front of Nick's studio on Spring Garden

Street, just as his class was letting out. Judging by the size of the huskers pouring out of there, this was definitely not Self Defense 101. These guys were some serious warriors, dressed in fatigues and black t-shirts, all with muscles to spare. A few were limping. There was one woman among the ranks. I recognized her as Tanya, one of Nick's instructors. Tanya is quite lovely and Nick seems very fond of her. Personally, I hate her, although she's done absolutely nothing to warrant my loathing. Oh well, another unsolved mystery.

Paul's car was parked half way down the block, I noted with some disappointment. Guess I'd gotten more attached to the truck than I'd realized. Nick slung an arm around me and we walked back into the studio. Tanya was picking up some mats off the floor.

"Good class, today, Tanya. Thanks for your help."

"Any time, Nick."

Nick picked up the last of the mats and helped Tanya stack them in the corner. Suddenly, they lunged for each other, doing a quick little karate dance, and then sprang apart, laughing. Note to self: Take secret lessons in martial arts. Become Martial-Arts-Expert-of-the-Universe and knock crap out of Tanya.

"Goodnight," Tanya called to me as she was leaving. "Nice to see you again."

"Yeah, you too."

Nick motioned for me to follow him into his office, and now I was sitting in my favorite spot, a plush, red velvet chair, breathing in the smell of the exotic tobacco he keeps in a drawer in his desk. Nick gave up smoking a while back, but he still enjoys the rituals.

I waited while he checked his voicemail and returned a few calls; two in rapid-fire Spanish to a country whose area code I'd never even heard of, and a local call to Ben Somebody or other. When he hung up, he said, "I gave the drive to a friend of mine today. He's real handy with computers. If there's something else on that thumb drive, Ben will find it. Oh, by the way, your brother's car is back and it looks good as new."

"How much do I owe you?" I asked, rooting around in my bag for my checkbook.

Nick put a hand out to stop me. "It's on the house, darlin'."

"No," I said. "I can't let you keep doing things for me. I'm starting to feel like a 'kept woman'—only without the 'ya know'—" I added, turning colors.

Nick laughed. "Consider it a loan, then. When you get back on your feet financially, we'll settle up."

Seeing as I was already overdrawn about forty bucks, I decided to take him up on his generous offer.

As we walked back to Paul's car, I filled Nick in on my visit with Keith. "It's like I'm just seeing the tip of the iceberg here. He's definitely hiding something and I have a gut feeling it's big."

"And he's expecting you to give back the drive tomorrow?"

"Well, it's not like he can come after me if I don't."

"Never underestimate the power of a snake, angel. He may not be able to walk, but he can slither."

Nick followed me home in the truck. While I was driving, my cell phone rang. I took a quick peek—it was Bobby, so I didn't answer. Whatever he wanted to yell at me about could wait until later.

I pulled up in front of the house and hopped out of the car. Mrs. Gentile's manger was all aglow, with my side of the porch a sad contrast. The lights Toodie had strung up had fallen down into the bushes and I couldn't help but think he'd be bummed if he saw them lying there. The thought made me want to cry.

Nick came up on the porch and reached for his gun—nothing Rambo-esque, I noted—just a small revolver tucked into the waistband at the small of his back.

"Is that really necessary?" I asked, starting to panic.

He shrugged. "Probably not, I'm just doing it to impress the old lady peering out the window next door."

"Great," I groaned. "My mother will be on the first plane back here when she hears about this, and I guarantee you, she *will* hear about it." I stuck the key in the lock and opened the door.

"Holy shit!" My house was in shambles. Every drawer was emptied, every piece of furniture overturned. The couch looked like it had been mauled to death by Bengal tigers; the cushions sliced to shreds, stuffing strewn all over the living room rug. Nick shoved me roughly behind him, his gun drawn. Cautiously, he made his way around the house, checking every crevice until he was satisfied that we were alone.

"Don't touch anything," he warned, as I instinctively reached out to set things right.

I pulled out my phone to call the police, when there was a knock on the front door and Bobby walked in. "Brandy, I—Jesus Christ. What happened?"

Nick slipped his gun back into his waistband as Bobby scanned the carnage.

"How long have you two been here?" he asked, anger lacing his words.

Nick's voice was a calm contrast. "We just got here. We walked in and everything was as you see it. Took a quick check to see if anyone was still here, but they seem to be long gone. Brandy was just about to call the police."

I nodded dumbly, taking in the sight of my mother's couch—the couch I'd grown up with—ripped to pieces. It felt like someone had steamrolled over my heart. Tears welled up in my eyes and I fought to contain them by concentrating hard on the bastard who'd done this. If I stayed pissed enough maybe I'd forget how scared I was.

Bobby called the station and minutes later, two squad cars showed up. I sat out on the back steps while they went through the house, but when they began asking me questions I lost it. Bobby pulled one of the guys aside and after a few minutes, they got back in their squad cars and left. I remained on the step, unable to face the desecration of my past.

Bobby sat down beside me. His voice was low and gentle. "Do you have any gut feelings about who did this?" For some reason, probably borderline hysteria, his question made me laugh. There was no obvious choice. Lately I've developed a real fan following that included Glen, Bulldog and Marie. Who knew how many more nuts lurked out there, waiting to get a crack at me.

Nick came out of the house and Bobby stood up. Bobby has a few inches on Nick and the skill of a professional boxer. But he's no match for the lightening quick moves of a highly trained martial arts expert. I didn't really think it would come to blows, but Bobby's been so on the edge lately, it was hard to predict. Nick defused the situation with an easy grace. "I think you two kids have some catching up to do."

Bobby gave him a begrudging nod as I walked Nick to the front door.

"Nick, I—"

"Shh," he soothed. "We'll have time to talk later. You're moving in with me."

Yikes!

Chapter Ten

Bobby came back inside and pulled up a chair at the kitchen table. All I could think of at that moment is how much I wanted, no, *needed* a chocolate cupcake. I took out a fresh pack of Tastykakes and broke open the wrapper. "Want one?" I asked. The offer was half-hearted. I really wanted both the cupcakes. Bobby hesitated, trying to gauge my sincerity. Then he shook his head, his face breaking out in a tired grin.

"Thanks, but I wouldn't want to deprive you."

"If you're sure," I said, stuffing them, whole, into my mouth.

After I ate the cupcakes I felt much better. There is nothing like a sugar high to offset bad news. Bobby waited until I cleaned off the crumbs from the table, before he broached the subject of Nick.

"I didn't know you and Santiago were such good pals. Is that where you spent the night?" It was a direct question and it deserved a direct answer.

"That is none of your fucking business."

"The guy is bad news, Brandy. He travels in circles you don't want to know from."

I was too tired to argue. Besides, he was right.

"Can we talk about something else, please? Like, how

many more times this God damn Bulldog creep is going to try to burglarize my house before the cops catch him?"

Bobby leaned forward in his chair, elbows resting on the table. He spread his hands wide and began massaging his temples. He was on the brink of exhaustion. "This was no ordinary burglary and you know it."

I did know it. I just didn't want to admit it. Because that meant it *was* personal. Whoever did this was after something besides flatware and the good china. They were after *me*.

The slicing of the couch had Glen's signature all over it. It was just his style. Dramatic. Slash and burn. It fit right in with Nick's theory that he was "playing" with me.

But then again, what if they *weren't* after me? What if whoever did this was looking for something specific—something they thought I had and maybe had hidden somewhere in the house? The thumb drive! Keith was really upset when I told him he'd have to wait until tomorrow. Could he have somehow arranged to have someone break in and steal it back from me? I wanted to go back into the living room and look it over with a fresh eye, but Bobby reached out and closed his hand around my wrist, stopping me. I shot him a puzzled look.

"Can we just talk for a minute?" he asked, letting go of my arm.

"Sure." I didn't know where this was headed, but his voice went all soft and sympathetic, like he was about to tell me my favorite aunt died or something. I sat down opposite him and said, "Shoot."

"We've located the missing head."

"Oh." My insides knotted into a hard ball. "Were you able to identify the woman?"

Bobby nodded. "Brandy, it was Ilene Werner. Toodie's ex-girlfriend."

"No!" I had to scream it really loud because the waves

157

that crashed all around my head made it hard for me to hear. Bobby caught me before I hit the floor.

"Breathe," he commanded. His hand was on the back of my neck, forcing my head between my knees. I filled my lungs with air and slowly let it out. "Again," he said, more gently.

"I'm okay. Let me up."

He released his hand from the back of my neck and I sat up. My head felt like it was filled with feathers and would be floating away any minute now.

"I'm sorry, Bran. I didn't want to have to tell you this. Preliminary report says she died of a severe blow to the left side of her head."

"How—how did the cops find it?"

"Are you sure you're up for this now?"

"I'm fine. I just need to know everything."

Bobby knew I wasn't fine. But he had the grace to let me fake it.

"We got a phone call from someone identifying himself as a neighbor. He said he'd heard some noises coming out of the Ventura's backyard and he knew the grandmother was away, so he checked it out and he saw Toodie sneaking around back there. According to this guy Toodie was carrying a shovel."

"Who was this guy?" I demanded. "If he's such a solid citizen, why didn't he identify himself?" I don't know why I was treating Bobby like this. I guess it's the old "kill the messenger" thing.

"It's not a requirement, Brandy. A lot of people phone in anonymous tips so that they don't end up involved in a long police investigation. We found the head buried in the garden. As far as circumstantial evidence goes, this is as good as it gets."

"Shit." A solitary, traitorous tear rolled down my face, and I wiped it quickly away. I stood up and got a glass out of the cabinet and tried to pour myself some water, only my hand was shaking so hard I dumped it all over the kitchen table.

Bobby took the glass from my hand and set it down. He was so close I could smell the worn leather of his jacket. He reached out and pulled me to him, enfolding me in his arms. Instinctively, I wrapped my arms around his waist, allowing myself the comfort of his warm, familiar body. "It's so hard, Bobby," I whispered into his chest. "I believed in Toodie."

"I know," he murmured stroking my hair. After a moment, I slowly let go of him.

"Listen," he said, leading me back to my seat, "would you consider going away for a few weeks, maybe visit your parents in Florida?"

"Why?"

Bobby waved his hand vaguely around the room. "You're a target, Brandy. I don't know for sure who's after you or why, but it's not safe for you to be here."

"You think Toodie did this, don't you?"

"I'm not ruling out the possibility. Look, I know you have—had a lot of affection for the guy, but he's nuts. Maybe he developed some sort of crush on you and got mad when he thought you weren't going to help him anymore. And then there's this business with Davis. Could be he and Glen had a deal going and something went wrong, and now they're trying to set each other up to take the fall. I don't know. All I know is that two women are dead, and I don't want you to be next."

That's funny, me either.

As long as we were on a roll here about all the people who wanted me dead, I thought I'd mention a few more possibilities, starting with Marie.

"Jesus Christ, my wife has been following you around for weeks and this is the first I've heard about it?" Bobby began a slow pace around the kitchen, a sure sign he was about to explode. I did my best to defuse him.

"Look, at first I wasn't even sure it was Marie. I mean I can't keep track of every Tom, Dick and Mary who's been following me. I've had a busy couple of weeks here—and I'm the one who should be mad, so calm down."

Bobby stopped his pacing, closed his eyes and sighed deeply. When he opened them again, there was a small, bemused smile playing about his lips. "How do you manage to do it?" he asked.

"What?" He shook his head, lost in private thoughts. Oh well, at least he wasn't mad anymore.

I decided to hold off on mentioning Keith Harrison. If I told Bobby about the incident with the thumb drive, he'd insist I turn it over to the police. It seemed unlikely that Keith would climb out of a deathbed to tear my house apart, when I'd already told him I'd bring the disk to him tomorrow. Plus, Nick had already given it to his friend to check out. It's not that I didn't trust Bobby or the police; I just didn't want to get caught up in all the red tape. It seemed easier going through Nick. Only I was willing to bet Bobby wouldn't see it in quite the same way.

DiCarlo offered to help me clean up the house, but I decided to let it go for now. He secured the window that whoever it was climbed in through and then I walked him to the door.

"Will you at least think about going to your parents?"

"I'll think about it," I said, only we both knew it wasn't going to happen.

"I'm not trying to tell you what to do, but I don't think you should stay here. Maybe you can move in with Frankie or Paul for awhile."

I shook my head. "I don't want to put them in any danger."

He looked at me for a long moment before he spoke again. "Brandy, about Santiago—"

"He'll keep me safe, Bobby."

"I know." He gave me a brief, hard hug and walked out the door.

"So, Alphonso. You got a last name?"

Alphonso, looking badass chic in a Terrell Owens Eagles' jersey and shades cut me a sideways glance. "Just Alphonso."

"O-kaaay." Alphonso, I was fast learning, isn't much of a conversationalist. He was driving the Mercedes truck, which he used to pick me up from my house. I'd had just enough time to throw a few essentials in a bag—toothbrush, deodorant, jeans, underwear, a nightlight—when Nick called to tell me he'd be sending an "escort" over to get me.

I tried to keep the disappointment out of my voice. "Will you be there when I get to your place?"

"Sorry, angel, I've got an appointment. But Alphonso has agreed to keep you company. Make yourself at home and I'll see you in the morning." *He'll see me in the morning? What the hell was he going to be doing all night?* Nick had offered me his protection. I don't think that included a vow of chastity. Maybe he had a date. Maybe Alana was collecting on her rain check. I guess I didn't really want to know.

Alphonso pulled into the loading zone and cut the engine. Then he turned to the back seat and swung my overnight bag over his shoulder and slid out of the truck. I followed him into the building, noting the distinctive bulge in the back of his coat where a nine- millimeter Glock rested securely in the waistband of his baggy jeans. He looked very handsome, in a homeboy gangbanger sort of way.

Alphonso held the elevator door open for me and we rode in silence up to the fourth floor. When we got to Nick's apartment, he set my bag down and fished around in his pocket for the apartment key. He unlocked the door and pushed it open and then stepped aside to let me in.

It felt like an oasis of calm in there. Alphonso found the light and flicked it on, illuminating the foyer. The view from Nick's living room window was spectacular; Ritten-house Square bathed in the glow of street lamps, reflecting powdery, snow-covered trees.

"Yo, Adrian," I yelled, and the calm was broken by the sound of a twenty-pound maniac running full-throttle into the living room. He took a flying leap right at Alphonso, who stopped him cold with a snap of his fingers. Adrian sat at his feet, soulfully gazing at him and wagging his tail so hard I thought it would fly right off the back of him.

Alphonso bent down, grinning. "Hey, Bru, how's it goin'?" He reached out a hand to Adrian, who promptly col-lapsed onto his back, rolling around in ecstasy as Alphonso rubbed his tummy.

"Do you have a dog, Alphonso?"

He nodded. "Two Pits and a Rottweiller. Hey, maybe I'll bring them around some time so this guy can have some-one to play with."

"Uh, great."

Alphonso grabbed the television remote and settled back on the couch, flicking through the channels until he found a hockey game. Was he planning to stay here all night?

"Listen," I said, "I appreciate you picking me up and all, but don't feel like you have to keep me company. I'm fine here on my own."

"Nick said to stay with you," he said, eyes glued to the game.

"Oh. But—"

"Nick said to stay."

I closed the door to the spare bedroom and punched in Nick's cell phone number.

"Hey, angel, did Alphonso come and get you?"

"Yeah. Thanks. But I don't need a babysitter, Nick. I'm

perfectly capable of spending an evening on my own."

"I'm sure that you are."

"So I can tell him to go?"

Nick hesitated. "I'd rather you didn't."

"What do you think, that I'm going to rifle through all your personal belongings the second he walks out the door?"

"The thought did cross my mind." *Okay, so that was the plan, but I could show some restraint if I had to.* "I have to go, angel. Humor me, just this once. Please?" His voice was like velvet and I caved.

"I'll see you in the morning."

"Okay, here's how it goes. I name a sit-com character and you tell me what actor played the role."

Alphonso poured us each another shot of Patron and we tossed them back on the count of three, slamming our glasses on the table. I beat him by a hair. "I won, I won!" I stood and did a little victory dance.

"You're a competitive one, aren't ya?" he said. He was seated with his back against the couch, the Glock resting on the floor next to him.

"Come on, you're stalling. Who played Greg Brady on the Brady Bunch?"

"How the hell should I know? The Brady Bunch is a little white girl's show."

"Barry Williams. I win again." I started to do my victory dance but Alphonso wouldn't let me.

It was after one and Nick still wasn't home. I went into the spare room and lay down on the bed. I hate to admit it, but I was glad Alphonso was in the next room. Whenever I have too much time to think, the fear overtakes me. I tossed and turned for about half an hour, but sleep was not a happening thing.

I opened the door and snuck a peek in the living room.

Alphonso was stretched out on the couch, watching Xtreme Wrestling. Gingerly, I made my way to Nick's room and picked up a pillow from his bed. It smelled like Nick. I took it back into the spare room with me, wrapped my arms around it and promptly fell asleep.

In the morning the sound of a ringing cell phone woke me up. I glanced at the clock on the nightstand. Seven-thirty. "Hello?"

"Brandy, it's Keith. I hope I didn't wake you." I had the distinct feeling he didn't give a rat's butt if he woke me or not.

"Nah, been up for hours."

"Oh, good. So when can I expect you to come by with the drive?" *Shit.*

"Um, later. I've got some errands to run. You're not going anywhere are you?" I joked. Only I wasn't joking.

"Look," he said, unable to keep the desperation out of his voice, "could you be more specific about when you're going to drop it off? My client is coming by in the afternoon and it really wouldn't do for you to run in to each other. You understand, client confidentiality and all that." *I understand that you are a lying scumbag.*

"I'll call you back," I said, and hung up the phone. I hopped out of bed, ignoring the persistent ringing as he tried to call me back.

I had to talk to Nick, but first I wanted to make myself presentable. I tried running my fingers through my hair, but it was so tangled I ended up yanking out a huge clump of it. I needed a mirror. I peeked out the door to make sure the coast was clear and made a beeline to the bathroom. Aahhh! My hair stuck out so far from my head it defied gravity. I spent the next ten minutes beating it into submission, and then I brushed my teeth, sprayed some water on my face and was good to go.

I wandered into the living room. Alphonso was still asleep on the couch, but he woke with a start, his gun pointed directly at me.

"Man, don't be sneakin' up on me like that," he grumbled. S'good way to get yourself killed." Okay, Alphonso was not a morning person.

"Um, sorry. Is Nick here? I really need to talk to him."

Alphonso stuck his gun back in his waistband and stretched. "He called at six. Said to tell you he'd be back around ten. You know how to cook?" he asked.

I shook my head no.

"Damn, I could really go for some eggs."

"I think I can manage eggs. It's the least I can do for a guy who played 'Name That Sitcom Actor' with me."

"Don't mention it—to anybody."

After breakfast I changed my clothes and paced around the apartment, waiting for Nick to return. Keith kept up a steady stream of phone calls, which I ignored. Uncle Frankie called me too. He'd heard about the latest break-in, from Carla, who'd heard about it from Gladys down at the beauty shop, who'd heard about it from Mrs. Gentile, when she was getting her "blue rinse." I swore I was safe and that I intended to stay that way. But he made me promise to come by the gym for a refresher course on "the art of turning a guy into a soprano."

Nick rolled in at ten; the dark shadows under his eyes telling me it had been a sleepless night. I was dying to ask him where he'd been all night, but then again, I was afraid he might tell me. "Hey, angel, did you sleep well?" he asked, giving me a weary smile.

"Yeah, great. Did you have a good evening?"

"It was—productive."

As I sat on the couch, stewing about what *that* could have meant, he took off his jacket—an ultra-expensive, black leather Bruno Magli (I knew because John's been saving up for one since his eighteenth birthday) and grabbed an apple out of the fruit basket. He joined me on the couch, sitting way too close for comfort, and offered me a bite. I shook my head and bounced off the couch, suddenly remembering I'd forgotten to feed my pets.

"Didn't you just feed them?" Alphonso asked, grinning like a fool.

"Don't you have some Brady Bunch reruns to catch up on?" I shot back.

Nick took a bite of the apple. Juice squirted out and ran down his chin to the hollow of his neck. I wanted to lick it off him.

"I'm outta here," Alphonso announced. "Listen, Santiago, the next time you need a babysitter, try Raoul. He's good with kids." Unhhh!

"Is there something you want to tell me?" Nick asked, after Alphonso left.

"Oh, he's just a sore loser. But yeah, there is something I want to discuss."

Nick motioned for me to follow him into the bedroom, and I stood in the doorway while he changed out of his street clothes. He unbuttoned his dress shirt and pulled it off. That's when I saw the Kevlar vest underneath. Wow. So probably he *wasn't* making passionate love to someone all night long, but the alternative was a whole lot scarier.

"Uh, Nick?"

"Hmm?"

"Is there something *you* want to tell *me*?"

He followed my gaze and laughed. "This is a strictly 'need to know' situation, darlin', and you don't need to know." On my worried look he added, "There are some aspects of my business that are private, but I would never leave you in the dark if it had to do with you. I hope you believe that."

I did believe it. Only it didn't stop me from worrying about him.

I filled him in on my conversation with Keith while he added a hooded sweatshirt to the t-shirt he was wearing and took his running shoes out of the closet. Just then my phone rang, and by the time I tracked it down in the kitchen, Nick had already changed out of his pants and into sweats. Dammit. He was lacing up his shoes when I walked back into the room. "That was Harrison, again," I said.

"I'm going running in Fairmount Park, but when I get back we can figure out a game plan for your pal, Keith. I should be getting the thumb drive back soon. In the meantime, when he calls, just continue to ignore it."

"Okay."

"Anything else going on?" Only that my former roommate may well have sliced n'diced his ex-girlfriend and buried her head in his backyard. It was too much to think about. I shook my head, avoiding eye contact. "Nothing that can't wait."

Nick cocked an eyebrow at me and sat on the edge of the bed, pulling me down with him. "Tell me," he said.

I took a huge breath and told him.

"I didn't want to believe Toodie was capable of something so horrible. Part of me *still* doesn't believe it. But what if I'm wrong? And now Bobby thinks he may be after me."

"And what do you think?"

"I guess it's possible. Every other criminal in town seems to be."

Nick invited me to go run with him. He thought it might help me to get out. I agreed, but a five mile jog in the park was about as appealing as a poke in the eye with a sharp stick. "I've been sitting around like a victim long enough, Nick. It's time I started taking charge of my life again."

"What do you have in mind?"

"I don't know," I admitted. Since Keith is out of commission for awhile, maybe I'll go on a little fact finding tour over at his office."

"Would you like some company?" *Desperately.*

"I've met his office manager. She's not the brightest and I outweigh her by about fifteen pounds. I think I can take her."

"My money's on you." Nick moved to the front door. "Take the truck and call me if you feel the least bit threatened." He handed me the extra set of keys that Alphonso had left on the table in the foyer.

"Thanks, Nick."

"Be careful, angel." He kissed the top of my head and walked out the door.

Outside, the snow had melted, leaving piles of gray slush all along the sidewalk. It was lunchtime and Dock Street teemed with pedestrians, shopping, dining and otherwise enjoying the crisp, December air. I felt relatively safe within the confines of the crowd, although I kept a steady watch for Glen, Bulldog and now Toodie. Marie seemed to have taken the last few days off. I kinda missed her.

It wasn't until I reached Keith's building that I realized I hadn't given an ounce of thought to what I was going to say, once I gained entrance into the office. Luckily, I didn't have to stress about it.

Ali was seated at her desk, which was piled high with her personal effects. She glanced up when I came in, a vague look of recognition on her face. "May I help you?" she asked, sweeping the contents of her desktop into a shopping bag. I extended my hand to her.

"Hi Ali. We met the other day. I'm a friend of Mr. Harrison's."

Irritation clouded her pretty face. "Keith isn't here."

So it's 'Keith' now, is it? I tried again. "I know. I met

you the day he was mugged. You were very distraught the last time I saw you, and I just came by to see how you were holding up."

Without warning, Ali burst into huge, blubbery tears.

"Oh, but Keith is doing fine, Ali. You don't have to worry about him."

"Worry about him?" she snorted and abruptly stopped crying. "I hope the asshole chokes on his feeding tube." It wasn't the adoring response I'd come to expect, and she needed little prompting to tell me why.

"He told me we couldn't be together because his wife has a terminal illness. He said he couldn't leave her in her time of need. But it was all a lie." This last statement brought on a fresh wave of sobs. I waited while she blew her nose on what looked like an invoice and then she started in again, taking stacks of office supplies out of the cabinet and adding them to her personal stash.

"So you and Keith were—close?" I prompted.

She nodded, taking the water cooler cups and dumping them into her bag of goodies.

"And on top of everything else, my paycheck bounced. Again! This is the third time this month." She disappeared into a room adjacent to the office and returned with two rolls of toilet paper, which she added to her shopping bag collection.

"Your paycheck bounced? But why?"

"Keith said he was having a little 'cash flow' problem—whatever that means. All I know is I'm sick of fielding his calls from creditors and I'm through working for free." She picked up her bag of party favors and headed for the door. "Hit the lights on the way out, will ya?"

Alone in Keith's office, I felt like a kid in a candy shop. I sat down in Ali's chair to think. So Keith has a little 'cash flow' problem. I wonder who else he owes money to? Could it be that whoever worked him over was collecting on a debt?

What was it the witness overheard the guy say to Keith? *"This one's for Conley."* I had assumed he meant Connie, but maybe this had less to do with a domestic quarrel than I'd thought. I pulled my cell phone out of my bag and called Mike Mahoe.

"Did you ever check out that lead on Connie Harrison's father, in the Keith Harrison mugging?" I asked, when Mike got on the line.

"Yeah." He sounded disgruntled. "Remind me to never listen to you. It's not even my case, but I ran it by my boss, who went ahead and spoke to Tyler Benson. That went over like a lead balloon and now Benson's making noises about suing the police department for defamation of character or something. Do me a favor, if you've got any more bright ideas, tell DiCarlo. He's had a lot more practice dealing with you." *Oh, fine.*

The door to Keith's office was open so I wandered in and began poking around. His desk drawers were locked, as well as all the file cabinets. The computer was turned off and there was no confessionary note sitting atop his desk, spilling all of his deep, dark secrets. I rifled through his Rolodex but found nothing more interesting than the name of his hair salon.

I knew I probably shouldn't be there, but it's not like I broke in or anything. I was invited—sort of. I began fiddling with the bottom drawer of Keith's desk, which wasn't locked, so much as stuck. After a few minutes of yanking, the door sprung open.

It looked like my kitchen junk drawer, filled with all the crap you pick up in the course of a year and don't know what to do with but can't bring yourself to throw out. There was a photograph of Keith and Connie, in happier days, smiling into the camera. The picture was bent and crinkled and it made me sad. These people really liked each other, once upon a time. I also found a deck of cards, some gum, a car owners'manual, a Phillies' baseball cap and a casino chip.

I picked up the chip and examined it. There were no identifying marks advertising the place it came from, but something in the back of my mind told me this was important. Keith is having financial trouble. Could this be the source of his money problems?

I'd been in Keith's office for almost a half an hour. Time to leave before I pressed my luck. Taking the chip with me, I put everything else back in its place, locked the outer door and left.

Bobby called me as I walked back to the car. "It sounds like you're outside. Please tell me you're not alone."

"I'm not alone. There is an entire squadron of Philadelphians out here with me."

"Oh, good. Well my mind's at ease now."

"Look, let's not get into a fight over this. I'm fine. Is there a reason for the call?"

"Two, actually. I spoke to my wife. She denied following you, of course, but I think I've put an end to it. I'm sorry," he added.

"Don't be. You're not responsible for her behavior. What's the other thing?"

"They just picked up a suspect in those neighborhood burglaries."

"They caught Bulldog?"

"I wish it were that simple." He let out a deep breath, a prelude to more bad news. "It wasn't Sandmeyer, Brandy, which means either Bulldog's just another burglar working the neighborhood, or—"

"Or he was targeting me specifically," I finished for him. I'd reached the truck, took a quick scan around and climbed in, locking the doors behind me.

"That seems the more likely scenario. You said nothing was taken, right? Plus, he works all the way out in Jersey.

It's not likely that he'd drive all the way up here for a random burglary."

It felt good to be on the same side of a discussion as Bobby for a change, and I wished we could've talked more, but he got called away on an emergency. *I didn't even get a chance to tell him about Keith Harrison,* I thought, when suddenly I had an idea that was so vivid I could actually *see* the light bulb hanging over my head like in a cartoon bubble. Pieces of a complicated puzzle were beginning to fall into place, and I needed time to think things through. But first I had to take care of business.

I stopped home on my way back to Nick's so that I could pick up my mail. Mrs. Gentile stuck her head out her storm door as I drove up in the truck.

"Hey you," she called out. "Girly." Never mind that in over two decades she'd never managed to learn my name. Be nice. You'll be old too some day.

I put the truck in park and ran up the steps to my house. "Yes, Mrs. Gentile?" I said, opening up the storm door. There was a pile of mail stuck inside, including a rather bulky manila envelope, devoid of an address or postage. I scooped everything up and stuffed it in my bag.

Mrs. Gentile leaned over the railing, hunkering so close to me I could smell the mothballs on her breath. "You said you'd help me get rid of the you-know-what," she whispered.

"The you-know-what *what*?" I knew what she meant, but I wanted to hear her say it.

"Shh!" She leaned over so far I thought she'd take a header over the railing. "The rat," she hissed.

"Oh. *That* you-know-what." I looked at my watch. It was getting late and I still had to stop by Janine's on the way back to Nick's to borrow an outfit for tonight's performance. My wardrobe would make any ten-year-old boy green with envy, but when I sang with the band, baggy blue jeans and a Bart Simpson t-shirt weren't going to cut it. I wanted to look *hot.* On the other hand, this was my chance to win the old gal over.

"Mrs. Gentile, I'm a little busy right now, but I promise I'll come back tomorrow and set those traps for you."

She straightened up, turning her back to me. "If that's the best you can do," she muttered, closing her door in my face.

"You're welcome. See you tomorrow." *All right! Mrs. Gentile likes me!*

I sat cross-legged on the Persian rug in Nick's living room, a legal pad balanced on my knees. Late afternoon sunlight filtered in from the big bay window, casting weird shadows on the wall. I got up and turned on a lamp.

I had spent the last hour filling up the legal pad with ideas. Connections, as Bobby would say. Whenever he had a case to solve, he'd always look for common threads. And today, when I was on the phone with him, I'd found one. I'd been thinking of Keith Harrison's money troubles. Why would a man with a thriving law practice be in such dire financial straits? Where was his money going?

For the sake of argument, I ruled out blackmail. This is a guy with an addictive personality. His wife admitted, in less delicate terms, that he had an obsession with women. My Uncle Frankie told me that when a person has one obvious addiction, there are usually a few more hanging around in the closet. Uncle Frankie should know. He's had more than his share himself.

Okay, so what, if any, were Keith's other addictions? I thought back to the casino chip I'd found in the drawer. Is it possible that Keith is a compulsive gambler? Granted, one lone casino chip did not a compulsion make, but it was a start. And that's when the connection kicked in. Ivan "Bull-dog" Sandmeyer's last known employer was the Diamond Casino, in Atlantic City, New Jersey.

173

Well, big whoop. So Bulldog worked at a casino, and Keith visited one once. But what else did they have in common? As if in answer to that question, Adrian strolled into the living room and curled up on my legs. Boy, talk about clues falling right into your lap! Keith was desperate to get his hands on the *dog*—that had already been established, and now that I looked back on it, Sandmeyer was too. And it wasn't for their mutual love of canines either.

There was no evidence that Bulldog had broken into my house in order to burglarize it. He hadn't taken a thing. He wasn't after anything but the dog. Adrian was afraid of Sandmeyer. That's why he was cowering under the couch. Sandmeyer and Harrison both wanted the thumb drive. It was the only thing that made sense.

I started to wonder if maybe Bulldog had been the one to beat up Keith at the restaurant. Maybe they were partners and he thought Keith was holding out on him. I had to get some real answers. All this speculation was making me nuts.

I'd started setting out some food for dinner when Nick walked in the door. He was in workout clothes, a tight black t-shirt and gray camouflage pants. His shirt was soaked in perspiration and the scent wafting off his skin produced a bolt of desire in me so strong I nearly fell off the kitchen stool. I never dreamed I could have such animalistic urges, and, frankly, it scared the hell out of me.

"What's all this?" Nick asked, smiling with pleasure.

"Oh, I noticed you were a little low on some of the essentials, so I went food shopping for you."

"Pat's steaks. The staff of life." He picked up a sandwich and took a bite. "Cheez-whiz. Good choice."

While he ate I filled him in on what I'd learned at Keith's office and my theory that tied in Harrison with Bulldog. "I think they're both linked to the Diamond Casino and they're both desperate to get their hands on that drive. Maybe your friend will be able to figure out what's so special about it. But in the mean time, Bobby's been wanting me to leave town for a while. Maybe I'll take Franny on a day trip to A.C. I can check out the casino, ask around about Harrison and Sandmeyer. Franny can play the slots and feel like she's having an adventure. What do you think?"

Nick eyed me with amusement tinged with exasperation. "What I think is you're going to do whatever you want to do, so just be smart and stay safe."

That was my plan.

I didn't get back from the club until after two. Nick had offered to take me there, but I ended up hitching a ride with Janine.

"That man is so hot! Why didn't you want him to come tonight?"

We were sitting in a booth in the back of the club; at least I was *trying* to sit. Janine had picked out a skirt for me that was so short it looked like a sweatband wrapped around my ass. She said I looked great. I told her the guys sitting in front were looking up my crotch.

"Oh, I get it," she said. "You're embarrassed for Nick to see your wild, sexy side."

"Pfft. That is ridiculous, Janine."

"Uh huh."

"Don't 'uh huh' me. I am not afraid to show off my 'wild, sexy' side…" *I'm freakin' petrified! This outfit is a promise of good times to come. What if I can't deliver the goods? I need a LOT more practice before I can live up to this skirt's reputation.*

"Bran—Bobby."

"And don't start in on me with Bobby."

Janine jerked her head sideways. "Will ya shut up? Bobby just walked in the door."

"Get out!" I turned slowly, as if by making minimal

movement it would turn out not to be true. It didn't work. "What is he doing here?"

He was with a bunch of other cops—Boys' Night Out, I guess. Paul headed him off at the pass, while Vince Giancola made his way to our table.

"What's the occasion, Vince?" I asked, nodding towards Philly's Finest.

"You are. We heard you were singing tonight." He leaned over and gave me a big brotherly kiss on the cheek.

"I'm surprised DiCarlo's here," Janine piped in. She was on her third Mai Tai and didn't know the meaning of discretion when she was sober. I helped her along by kicking her under the table. "What? What'd I say?"

Vince laughed. "Don't worry about it, Neenie. He's here because he got fed up with the guys calling him 'whipped'. That bitch has his balls in such a knot he doesn't know whether he's coming or going."

It was time for the second set, only knowing Bobby was in the audience changed everything. I was singing the songs I used to sing for him. And everybody knew it.

"Hey Taco, how about we drop 'Total Eclipse of the Heart'? I'm in the mood for something more upbeat."

"You kiddin'me? The crowd loves this sappy shit. Plus it's the only slow one we've got."

I was going to argue the point, but Chris and Kenny had already started playing the damn thing. *"And I need you now tonight, and I need you more than ever."* Okay, I can do this. It's just a song. *"And if you only hold me tight we'll be holding on forever."* No, I can't. I'm losin' it.

Bobby stood alone in the back of the room, arms folded across his chest, his face so full of longing it tore me apart. Oh shit. I can take my own pain but I can't take his too. Tears welled up in me as I choked out the last few notes. I closed my eyes, hoping it would stem the flow. When I opened them again, he was gone.

Chapter Eleven

When I got back to the table Vince and Janine were head to head. They straightened up when they saw me, pretending that that didn't notice my red eyes or that they weren't just talking about me and Bobby. Bobby and Marie. The whole stinking mess.

"It's okay, you guys. I'm going to be the talk of the town tomorrow, you might as well get a head start on it."

Vince scooted over in the booth, making room for me. He put his arm around me and I laid my head on his substantial shoulder. "It's not like I even want him back," I sniffed. "It's the not being able to be his friend part that's so hard."

"It's been murder on him, too, Bran," Janine told me. "The guy's always been intense—even as a kid, but you knew how to bring out the best in him. You grounded him like nobody else could."

"He's pissed off all the time now," Vince added. He's so afraid Marie will take off with his daughter he's putting up with shit I never dreamed possible. But ya know it's only a matter of time before he blows." I did know. And there wasn't a damn thing I could do about it.

Janine dropped me off in front of Nick's building and waited until I got safely through the doors. I entered the apartment as quietly as I could. He'd left the living room light on and one in the spare bedroom. His pillow was there where I'd left it. *Oh no. Now he knows I stole his pillow. How embarrassing is that?*

I pulled on a t-shirt and some Hello Kitty pajama bottoms and crawled into bed, but I was so keyed up from the evening I couldn't fall asleep. I got up, remembering the stack of mail I'd retrieved from inside my screen door.

The manila envelope fell out of my bag as I dragged it onto the bed. Must be another one of Carla's care packages. Last month she'd left me a bag of sample hair products, in the hopes that I'd discover the joys of "moussing." I tore open the envelope and spilled the contents onto the bed. It wasn't hair products. And I'd bet money it wasn't from Carla either.

I sat cross-legged on the bed, staring at a plastic doll, its arms and legs torn from its torso, the head detached and sprouting a mass of long, brown hair and crudely cut bangs. She was naked, with deep knife wounds sliced across her throat and breasts, and streaked with red paint, simulating the flow of blood.

On her stomach someone had scrawled in permanent marker, "This is you." *Hmm. No name. Maybe this was really meant for Mrs. Gentile. She's made a lot of enemies in the neighborhood over the years.* I knew the possibility of that being the case was slim, but it never hurts to be optimistic.

A strange detachment settled over me, as if I were watching the scene unfold on television. Rocky poked her chin out from under the bed and jumped up next to me. She sniffed at the head and then with a low, guttural growl, she pounced on it. Grabbing it by the hair, she raced about the room carting the damn thing around in her mouth like a prize mouse. *So much for detachment.*

I flew off the bed and began chasing after her, a sick, tight feeling forming in my belly until I was sure I was going to heave. I stopped chasing the cat and sat back down on the bed, wondering what kind of a sick bastard would do such a thing. The saddest part was candidates were lined up around the block.

When she was through having her fun, Rocky dropped the head on the rug and curled up on the pillow. I pulled a tissue out of the box and gingerly picked up the missing body part, dropping it back into the envelope. Then I gathered up the rest in the same manner and put them back as well.

"I need to talk to Nick," I thought. "But it's two-thirty in the morning. What if he's asleep? Or worse, what if he has company in there?" I picked up my cell phone and dialed.

He answered in two rings. "Yeah?"

"Hi. Are you up?" There was a brief pause, followed by a yawn.

"I am now." He didn't sound mad. Just tired.

"Are you alone?"

"Last time I checked. Where are you?"

"In the next room."

"You're calling me from the next room."

"Yeah, well, I didn't want to bother you if you were—ya know—busy."

"What time is it?"

"Late."

"Are you okay?"

"Not really." My voice faltered and a light went on under his door.

"Come on in," he said. "And bring the pillow."

When I walked into his room, Nick was sitting up in bed. He wasn't wearing a shirt and from the way the covers hung low on his exposed belly, that's not all he wasn't wearing. I dragged my eyes away from his body and tossed the envelope onto the bed.

"Somebody left me a present today."

Nick picked up the package and tipped the contents onto

the sheets. He stared at it for a few minutes. "Some present," he said, finally. "Did you touch it?"

I shook my head no. "Do you mind putting it away?" Rationally, I knew it was just a doll, but it was such a violent, vulgar, representation of me I was ashamed for Nick to see it.

With the edge of his bed sheet, he scooped everything back into the envelope and threw it onto his dresser. "How was this delivered to you?"

I told him it was left inside my screen door. "You think it could be some kid playing a prank?" I asked, although I was pretty sure of the answer.

"Afraid not, angel. I have a friend who can check it for prints. It may be faster than giving it to the cops."

I nodded glad to have a plan. "Thanks. Listen, I'm sorry I woke you," I said and began backing out the door. "Well, goodnight."

"Come here." His voice was a soft command.

As much as I wanted to go to him, I couldn't bring myself to admit how vulnerable I felt. "Nick, I'm fine."

"You're not fine. You're a mess and you have every right to be. Come here," he said again, more tenderly this time. He reached out a hand to me and I took it, allowing him to guide me to his bed. He turned out the light and pulled the sheets back so that I could climb in. Nick pulled me to him, spooning me, his warm, naked skin pressed against my back. I felt him grow hard, but he didn't make a move to touch me, other than to enfold me in his arms. I lay there, protected from the world, breathing in the smell of him, memorizing the smoothness of his skin, the hardness of his body, falling asleep to the rhythm of his every breath.

Standing in Doris Gentile's basement, armed with a flashlight, rattraps and a box of Cheez-its, which doubled as rodent bait *and* my breakfast, I couldn't stop thinking about

Nick. There must be something wrong with me. I mean I've got at least one hardcore psychopath sending me mutilated Barbies and trying to kill me, and yet the burning question in my mind is when is Nick going to kiss me again?

I'd awoken to the sound of running water and the realization that he was no longer in bed with me. A few minutes later, the shower stopped and I heard him re-enter the bedroom. I'd been faking sleep, just to see what he'd do. When nothing happened, I made a big show of stretching and opening my eyes. I was met with a grin as a semi-naked Nick pulled some jeans out of his closet.

"Good morning," he said. "Feeling better?"

I nodded, my eyes glued to the towel at his waist, the towel that he was now casually unwrapping and tossing to the floor. I looked down automatically and suddenly my eyes grew wide and my mouth flew open, and before I could stop myself I blurted out, *"What is that?"*

His eyes moved to where I was staring. "Wow, has it been that long for you?"

I felt myself go beet red. To make matters worse, the damn thing was starting to inflate.

"No, I mean—it looks—different."

Nick's grin widened as he stepped into his jeans. "I'm uncircumcised, darlin'."

"Oh." My face was so hot I'd thought I'd die of heat stroke.

"Haven't been with a lot of ethnic types, I take it."

You could say that again. I was fascinated. It was scary and beautiful at the same time, and Christ I was horny. Sadly, he put it away and zipped up his pants.

"A lot of women find sex more pleasurable with an uncircumcised partner," he told me and I believed him. "Maybe you'd like to try it some time." Was he volunteering his services? *God, I hope so.* He leaned over the bed and brushed a hand against my cheek. "You sure you're okay?

You seem warm to me." And then just when I thought things would get really interesting, the phone rang. It was Tanya. Note to self: Kill Tanya.

I'd just finished putting out two of the traps and was about to open the door to the storage area when I heard a soft, indistinct noise, something like a sneeze. *Holy Shit. I'm not just humoring an old lady. There really are rats down here.* I turned to go when I heard it again. It was coming from inside the utility closet. I shined a light under the door and saw a pair of shoes—size twelve, if I had to make a guess. Oh fuck.

Okay, don't panic. I'm panicking. Just breathe. What do I do? Part of me wanted to barge in and blast his big, goofy ass for going on the run. But another part of me said to get the hell out of the basement as fast as I could. I love Toodie, I really do, but just in case he *did* turn out to be a mass murderer, I got the hell out.

It was a little harder to convince Mrs. Gentile. "Here's the thing," I whispered when I reached the upstairs, "we need to get out of the house."

"Did you find any rats?" she asked.

"Yeah, Mrs. Gentile, a big one. We need to leave. Now."

"Why didn't you kill it? What were you doing down there?" She cut me an accusatory glare, which didn't look much different from her regular face. "Did you steal something? If you did I'll know."

"Oh my God, you old biddy, either you come with me right now, or I'm going to knock you into tomorrow."

Boy, is my mother going to be hearing about this. But she did as I told her.

The police arrived within minutes. I couldn't bear to watch Toodie being hauled away. I don't even know if I'd have called the police, except I couldn't take a chance that Toodie could hurt Mrs. Gentile. Had Toodie been hiding in her house the entire time? Ironically, the woman knows exactly what's going on in everyone else's home, but she didn't have a clue about what was happening in her own.

I felt like the worst person in the world. And it didn't help my mood, when three hours later I got a phone call from Toodie. I'd gone over to Uncle Frankie's gym to let him know what was going on. I guess I needed someone who loved me to tell me I'd done the right thing, when in my heart I felt it was all wrong.

"You didn't have a choice, sweetheart. What if he did do all the things he's been accused of?" Frankie eyed me sympathetically. "Come on, Midget Brat. You look like you could use a good meal."

"Carla's not cooking again, is she?"

"I was thinking more of Woo's Garden on Race Street."

In my family, food is the great consoler. Have a fight with your boyfriend? Eat some lasagna. Bad credit report? Cheer up with pot roast. Squeal on your roommate? Break out the chopsticks. I was just digging into the sweet and sour pork, when my cell phone went off. I ignored it and kept on eating.

"Aren't you going to answer it?"

"Nah." It was either another reporter wanting an exclusive on "the ice-box killer," or Keith Harrison, for the forty-millionth time today.

"It may be your mother." All the more reason not to answer.

I peeked at the caller I.D. City jail. I'd been calling it so often I'd decided to put it in my phone book, for easier access. I thought it would be DiCarlo, or Mike Mahoe. I wasn't prepared for the sound of my ex-roomie's voice.

"Hey, Brandy. It's me. Toodie."

I almost choked on the chow mein. "Toodie, what are you doing calling me?"

183

"I'm in jail."

"I know. I'm sorta the one who turned you in."

"It's okay. I figured you'd find me. You're really smart."

"Toodie, you should be talking to a lawyer. Why are you calling me?"

"You're my friend." *Oh jeez.* "Listen, Brandy, don't feel bad. You did what you had to do. And anyway, I don't think I could've stood another minute in that house. It smells like cat pee."

The waiter came over and started to take my plate away and I nearly stabbed him with my chopstick. "Look, Toodie, I'm glad you're not mad at me, but you need to talk to somebody who can help you."

"You still believe I'm telling the truth, don't you, Brandy?"

I hesitated a beat. "You know they found Ilene's head in your granny's winter squash garden, right?"

"I swear on my granny's life, I didn't do it." Toodie began to cry. Oh shit.

"Don't cry, Toodie. I believe you."

Uncle Frankie lectured me all the way back to the gym. Then he made me take a boxing lesson and he threw in some self-defense moves for good measure.

"Look, it's not like I baked the guy a cake with a sawed-off shot gun in it. I just told him I'd check out a few things for him, that's all."

Uncle Frankie answered me in Italian, and there were a lot of hand gestures involved. But once he calmed down, he promised not to mention anything to my mother.

The Diamond Casino on the Boardwalk, near Delaware Avenue is a mid-sized hotel-casino, with an Asian décor. According to my Internet research, it's a family owned operation, the Ellenbergs having purchased it from the Chans, back in nineteen ninety- two. In ninety-seven they were investigated for hiring illegals, but the Feds couldn't make it stick. The place looked like it had fallen on hard times. There was something really depressing about the worn carpeting, garish lighting and fake pagodas.

Fran and I played a couple of slot machines and mingled among the mostly Asian crowd. There was a group of elderly white folks at the craps table, who'd come down en masse from Philly on the Gray Panther Special, and a sprinkling of guys in polo shirts, trying their luck at Poker. I cast my eye around the room. Something was out of place, but I couldn't put my finger on it. And then it came to me. All the "worker bees"—the low level employees, were Asian, while the pit bosses and "suits" were white.

We moved to the bar and ordered a couple of cokes. Franny leaned over and whispered loud enough for the people in the next casino to hear, "This place is a dump."

The bartender snorted back a laugh. "What can I get you ladies?" He was a middle-aged Asian, Chinese, I think, with a thick accent.

I smiled and whipped out the picture of Keith that I'd taken off the Internet. "Excuse me, but I was wondering if you've seen this man in here before."

The bartender barely glanced at the photo. "No, sorry."

"If you could just take a look—"

"I told you, I don't know him," he muttered, stalking off.

"Is there some Chinese taboo against showing pictures of men around in a bar? Did I just commit the ultimate Asian faux pas?"

"I don't know," Fran said. "Let's ask this guy." She grabbed the photo from me and called to the other bartender, a stunning young man with long, jet-black hair pulled into a ponytail.

"What can I get you?" His accent was less pronounced

than the other guy, but you could tell English was not his first language either.

Franny held up the photo and flashed him a smile that could melt rocks. "I was wondering if you've seen this guy around here?"

He returned Franny's smile with one of his own, doubling the wattage. "He's not your husband, I hope." Oh jeez, he's flirting with her.

"Listen," I said, grabbing the picture back, "do you recognize him or not?"

"Yeah, I know him. Not by name, but he used to come in here, two, three times a week."

"Are you sure?" It's a real schlep from Philly to the Jersey shore.

"I remember because he used to run a weekly tab, but the last time he was in I was told to turn him down. He owed big time and they cut him off."

There was movement at the other end of the bar and then the older bartender appeared and barked at him in Chinese. The younger one shook his head. "What they gonna do? Fire me?" He laughed, but there was genuine anger behind his words. That and something else. When I tried to engage him again, he said he had things to do and went back to the other end of the bar.

The older guy refilled our glasses, on the house. "Sorry, but it's house policy not to talk about our clientele. He's new here."

"Hmm," I said, after he left.

"Hmm, what?" Franny reached over and grabbed a handful of wasabi nuts out of the bowl on the counter top.

"I was just thinking of the bartender's reaction when the other one started yelling at him. I mean he acted all cocky and everything, but underneath it, he seemed kind of scared."

"Maybe he really needs this job and was worried about

getting fired."

"Yeah, but then why would he say, 'what are they gonna do, fire me?' To me, he didn't seem all that concerned about the possibility of losing his job, but something scared him. I just don't know what."

"There you go again, reading all kinds of stuff into things that aren't really there."

"When have I ever done that, Franny? I'll bet you can't even name *one* time." *Okay, she could name about a thousand, but this wasn't necessarily one of them.*

Franny rolled her eyes and went back to eating the wasabi nuts. I decided to forgive her, since she was my ride home. And anyway, another, more pressing thought occurred to me.

"If Keith couldn't pay his bar tab, I wonder what else he wasn't paying."

"What do you mean?"

"Well, what if he ran up a tab at the tables and couldn't pay it back? It would make sense that they'd send someone after him to collect. Someone like Bulldog, maybe." But that still didn't explain what was so important about the thumb drive and why they both seemed to need it so badly.

"I have to hit the john," Franny announced. She was averaging about four times and hour, and she was only in her third month.

"Wait, I'll come with you."

"Let's go to the one at Trump Marina. I hear they've got marble toilet seats and a breath mint dispenser."

We passed the bartenders on the way out. The older one was crouched next to the dumpster, smoking a cigarette, while the younger one leaned against the side of the building, a sullen look on his handsome face. The older one was ranting in Chinese. I pulled on Franny's arm, dragging her back around the corner, out of sight.

"Wow. I wonder what they're fighting about."

"They're bartenders. They're probably arguing over whether a martini should be shaken or stirred. Come on, I have to pee!" She began to pull away, but I yanked her back again. Another man joined them. He had several bags of trash, which he tossed into the dumpster. The younger man said something in English and the guy with the trash started to shake his head, vehemently. Either he strongly disagreed with what was being said to him, or he had water in his ears.

"I think this could be important, Fran. And I'm not just playing Nancy Drew. You said you wanted an adventure. Well, here's your chance."

I pulled my cell phone out of my pocketbook and dialed Fran's cell. As soon as we connected, I handed hers to her and dropped mine back into my purse. Then I walked around the side of the building, towards the dumpsters. When the men saw me, all conversation stopped. I pulled a wad of paper out of my bag and crumpled it up, throwing it into the bin. As I went to close my purse, I "accidentally" spilled the contents onto the ground. The men paid little to no attention to me, just marking time until I left. Quickly I picked up my stuff, nudging the open cell phone under the dumpster. I walked back around the corner to Franny. She was holding her phone to her ear.

"Chinese...Chinese...Chinese..." she said, muffling the part you talk into. "Ooh, English." She shoved the phone into my hand and we stood together, listening. The voices were distant, but discernible.

"I'm sick of this. If I had known it would be so bad, I would have stayed in China."

"Well, you don't have a choice now. Unless you want to go back the way you came."

"Hah," said a voice I didn't recognize. "He'll go back in a body bag."

Fran jerked her head up, her eyes so wide I thought

they'd pop right out of her head.

There was a shuffling movement and then someone spoke. "What's this?" The words came in loud and clear. I panicked and stuck my head out from around the corner. Oh shit. The smoking bartender was bending down to pick up my phone. I disconnected Fran's, instructing her to stay put. Then I began running towards the dumpster.

Affecting a casualness I certainly didn't feel I called out to them. "Hey guys, have any of you seen my cell phone? It fell out of my pocketbook when I went to throw some trash away. Oh, you found it." I smiled, extending my hand expectantly. If suspicious looks could kill, I'd be writing this from the grave. He handed it to me and I plunked it into my bag. "Thanks."

Franny was waiting for me on the boardwalk when I reappeared around the corner. The normally unruffled Di-Angelo twin was shaking in her high-heeled booties.

"Did you hear what those guys were talking about? Body bags! I don't know what's going on, I don't *want to know* what's going on, and if you had a brain in your head, you wouldn't either."

"What happened to all that need for adventure?"

"Okay, so maybe I was wrong about needing excitement in my life. I'm going to be a mother. That's plenty exciting enough. I'm gonna go home, take up knitting and trade the T-bird in for a station wagon." We'd reached the parking lot. The T-bird was the hottest looking car there. "Maybe I'll just keep the T-bird for a little while longer."

"Yeah," I agreed. "Ya gotta work up to this motherhood business gradually."

Franny dropped me off at the martial arts studio. I'd stayed over at Frankie's last night, for various reasons, mostly having to do with my ever-growing feelings of lust for Nick. Plus, I figured he could use a break from me—too much of a good thing and all that. But the truth is, I missed him.

He was teaching a class when I walked in. I stood in the doorway and watched for a while, but all that testosterone flying around made me kind of nervous. I looked instead, for Tanya, figuring we could have some "girl talk"—you know, where do you shop for clothes, who cuts your hair, have you ever slept with Nick—but she didn't seem to be anywhere in sight. Finally, I went back into Nick's office to wait for class to be over.

While I was back there, I hit the Internet looking up articles on illegal immigration in the state of New Jersey. Bobby always told me to start with what I already knew. Okay, what did I know, or at least suspect? The casino owners had been investigated for hiring illegals. The majority of the "grunt" workers were Asian. The employees I had contact with were unhappy with their work situation, but seemed too frightened to do anything about it.

According to the articles I read, the illegals are smuggled into the country, via Mexico, and shipped to various states including New Jersey. They then pay back their passage, essentially, by becoming indentured servants. Could the bartenders have been part of an illegal alien smuggling ring? No wonder they were so grumpy.

So where did Keith fit in to all this? Was he just some hapless compulsive gambler who owed money to the Diamond Casino, which co-incidentally is a hotbed of illegal activity, or does he play a broader role in this?

I went back to looking for common threads. Bulldog and Harrison were both connected to the casino—Bulldog was the bouncer, Harrison was a patron who owed them money. Both men were after the thumb drive, ergo, the thumb drive is in some way connected to the casino. I paused for a minute. When did I start using words like ergo? But I digress.

The more I thought about it, the more I was sure Bulldog was the guy who beat up Keith. On the one hand, maybe he just did it as payback for the money Harrison owed the casino. But what if there were more to it than that? What if Harrison was supposed to bring the owners the thumb drive, only the dog ate it? The key was in finding out just what was on the damn thing. Then the pieces would start falling into place.

Carla called me, just as I was dozing off in the red velvet chair. She caught me off-guard, or else I'm sure I would have put up a better fight when she told me what she wanted. "Bran, I was talking to Mrs. Starlucci, down at the shop. Her nephew is new in town and—"

"Forget it, Carla. The last guy you set me up with was a hundred and eight."

"Will you listen? I've met this one. He's your age and he's *hot*."

"How hot?"

Okay," she conceded, "maybe not 'Nicholas-Santiago-Columbian-Underworld' hot, but a nice, respectable P.E. teacher hot. Cute, good build, never been married—"

"He's gay."

"He's not gay. He just broke up with a woman he'd been seeing for two years."

"Oh. Rebound."

"It was mutual and they're still good friends."

"Republican?" Carla paused, and I could hear her eyeballs rolling around in the back of her head.

"Independent," she said through clenched teeth. "Anything else?"

I'd run out of objections so I decided to play my Ace card. I sucked in a dramatic breath. "Now's not a good time. I've got a homicidal maniac after me."

"Well, when don't you?" She had a point.

Nick's phone rang and I automatically leaned over and checked the caller I.D. The readout said Alana. Alana of the Jimmy Choos. Was she calling for a rain check on her interrupted evening? The thought propelled me into a deep funk. I sighed.

"Okay, Carla. I'll go out with Mr. Wonderful."

"Great, honey. I'm sure you'll have fun."

Maybe Carla was right. This might actually be fun. After all, anything that could possibly go wrong on a blind date already did. The way I figured it, I was home free.

Chapter Twelve

"I saw Nick."

Janine took a sip of her diet coke and tore off a chunk of Italian bread. We were having dinner at Sargenti's, in celebration of Janine's new job as the newest member of Team Tony, Tony being Tony Tan, South Philly's premier realtor. "Aren't you staying with him?" she asked. "You must see him every day."

"No, I mean I *saw* him—ya know, in the 'biblical sense'."

"What?"

I pointed "down there."

Janine stopped eating the bread. "Shut up! I can't believe you've been holding out on me. I want details, girl."

"No. No details. He took a shower, dropped the towel, I saw him. End of discussion."

"Well, what did he look like? Oh my God, he must be incredible."

I had no choice but to tell her. "I think I insulted him."

"Did he seem insulted?"

"No, he was really cool. Said a lot of women find it more—"

"Pleasurable," Janine nodded, dreamily. "It's true. You are one lucky woman."

"Janine, he thinks I'm a sexual retard, and he's right. Now he's never going to try anything with me again. As we speak he's probably whipping it out for someone else and I'll die alone with a houseful of cats feasting on my decaying body."

"Yep," Janine agreed, tearing off another chunk of bread. "That's just what's going to happen."

Tony called, midway through our meal. Seems he had a hot prospect for a property in Bella Vista and needed Janine's special touch to seal the deal. Considering the prospect was a horny hetero twenty-nine year old, single male, I began to suspect Tony had hired Janine for more than her typing skills—which were negligible.

"Sorry to skip out on you, Bran. I hate to leave you alone. Can you call someone?"

I assured her I was a big girl and was perfectly capable of getting myself back to Nick's in one piece. Truth is, I was scared shitless, so when Bobby walked in ten minutes later, I called him over to the table and offered him a seat.

"I'm on a dinner break. Just getting some "to go" food for some of the guys." He had on his black leather bomber jacket and black jeans. He looked like he hadn't shaved in a couple of days and hadn't slept in longer than that. Crap. I hate it when he looks endearingly vulnerable. It rips my heart out.

"How's Toodie doing?" I asked. "Have you seen him?"

Bobby sat down opposite me and started tearing at the bread Janine had left. "Not great. They won't bond him out because he's a flight risk."

I still thought the cops were pinning this on the wrong guy and said as much to Bobby.

"I know your feelings about this. I mean you're not exactly shy about sharing your opinions." His eyes crinkled and his mouth curved into a grin, and for a split second there was the old Bobby. The one who used to love me. "I've been up for three days trying to track this asshole Davis down. I don't know if he was involved with Ilene Werner's death. We don't even have any proof that he knew her. There isn't much to link him to that besides Toodie's word, and let's face it, that's not worth much at the moment. But he killed Andi. I feel it in my gut. I just don't have any hard evidence to link him to her murder."

My lasagna arrived. I picked up a fork and handed Janine's to Bobby. "Help yourself. I can't finish all this."

"Since when?"

Since I realized the possibility of Nick seeing me naked.

"Do you have any clues at all in Andi's murder?" *Besides the glaring fact that if I hadn't hassled her about Glen, she'd be alive today.*

Bobby hesitated. I knew that look. He was waffling between respecting police confidentiality and telling me what all he knew. I waited and he caved.

"There were some skin samples under her nails. Looks like she put up a struggle and might've dug her nails into his scalp. But we don't have anything to compare it with. Not until we find Glen and do a DNA test."

"So if you had a sample of say, hair, you could compare that with whatever you found under her nails?"

"That's right."

"Bobby," I gulped. "I have some good news and some bad news."

The bad news was I'd forgotten (really!) that when I went through Glen's house, I'd picked up the few remaining personal items that he'd left there and stuck them in my bag. The good news is I still had the hairbrush with Glen's hair entwined in its bristles, tucked away under my bathroom sink.

Bobby stood and yanked me out of the booth by the elbow.

"Ow. What are you trying to do, break my arm?"

"You're lucky it's not your neck." He threw some bills on the table. "Let's go."

He was dragging me through the restaurant and I had to break into a trot to keep up with him.

"Where are we going?" I asked.

"Your house."

It was just as I'd left it, sliced couch and all. My eyes swept the room, taking in the devastation. I just don't understand it. Bad things never happened when my parents lived here. Although my mom did get an obscene phone call once. Turned out to be my father, trying to spice up their sex life.

I refused to go upstairs alone. It had been days since anyone had tried to break in, and I figured I was due. Bobby led the way.

"There," I said, pointing to the cabinet under the sink.

He retrieved it and opened the baggie. "Smells like Cheeze-its."

We drove back to the restaurant in silence. Once or twice I caught Bobby looking at me, but he turned away each time, careful not to make eye contact. He was mad at me. Okay, so inadvertently I'd withheld evidence—again. It's not like I did it on purpose this time, and he should be glad I'd remembered at all.

"I'm not mad at you," he said finally, breaking the ice.

"Well, you sure do a good imitation of it."

Bobby pulled over to a side street and cut the engine. "I'm worried, okay? I'm sick to my stomach that one day I'm gonna get a call to go check out some corpse and it's gonna be you."

"Well, what'd ya have to go and say that for?" I huffed. "It's not like I go around looking for trouble. It just sort of shows up at my door."

"Yeah, and then you *open* the door and invite it right in. It's just dumb luck that you haven't gotten yourself killed." Bobby started the engine while I obsessed over the image of me in a body bag.

"Okay," I said. "If I promise to butt out, will you promise to keep me totally up to date on this investigation?"

"I promise," Bobby said.

"Me too." Only we were both lying.

Bobby's cell phone rang just as we pulled into Sargenti's parking lot. It was his buddies down at the station. "Oh, Christ," he said, "I forgot all about picking up their dinner." He walked me over to Nick's truck and waited while I climbed in.

"Santiago's?"

I nodded.

"Nice," he said. "Lock the doors." He didn't have to tell me twice.

Alphonso was there when I got back to Nick's. It was after nine and Nick was headed out the door. He was wearing "date" clothes—black silk shirt, linen pants and Prada Loafers, which I recognized from John's designer wish list. His hair was freshly washed and hung in soft waves. He looked positively edible, which was, I'm sure, Alana's plan for the evening.

"Going somewhere?" I tried to appear casual, but my voice came out two octaves higher than normal. I sounded like I'd been taking hits off a kid's party balloon.

"Don't worry, Alphonso will be here. I don't like the idea of leaving you alone at night."

I glanced over at Alphonso, who was sitting on the couch, flicking the channels on the remote and looking disgruntled.

I truly hoped the overwhelming disappointment I felt at his leaving didn't show in my face, so of course, Alphonso picked up on it immediately.

"You got it bad," he called from his seat on the couch.

"I've got what bad?" I asked, only I was stuffing a TastyKake into my mouth at the same time, so it came out like, "Ah ga wha ba?"

Alphonso dropped the remote and sauntered over to the kitchen, swiping a cupcake along the way.

"It. You know—L.O.V.E. You *love* him," he singsonged. "You want to *marry* him."

"Oh grow up. I do not."

"Don't try to deny it, sweetcakes. I've seen that look on dozens of women. They get around Santiago and they're ruined for life."

"Don't you have anything better to do?"

Alphonso shrugged. "Not really."

"So, do you know where he was going tonight?" I pulled out another package of cupcakes and offered them up as an inducement to talk.

"Nick watches my back, I watch his. I don't ask questions about his personal life and he doesn't volunteer information. He pays well. It's the perfect business arrangement. All except for this baby sitting duty I keep pulling."

"You're free to go any time." It really bugged me that he thought he had me all figured out, plus he was eating my cupcakes.

"Nah, I think I'll stick around. No telling what a woman scorned will do."

"I'm not a woman scorned!" I yelled. But Alphonso was already back on the couch, flicking the remote and changing the channels.

Turk Davis walked towards MasterCarb's front office, carrying a cup of coffee from the Seven-Eleven across the street. The minute he saw me climb out of Nick's truck, he did an about face, sloshing steaming coffee down the front of his grease-stained cover-alls. He took a rag out from his pocket to wipe himself off, and it gave me time to catch up to him.

"Hi Turk," I said, real friendly. "Remember me?"

Turk heaved a big sigh. "I remember you. You were looking for my half-wit brother and I told you I've got nothing to do with him."

"Yeah, well, I was hoping things had changed since then. Ya see my friend, Toodie, just got arrested for a murder I think your brother committed, so I'm kind of anxious to find him." I didn't bother to add, "Before he finds me."

A tow truck pulled in front of us and parked. "I'm really busy," Turk whined.

"Look, I'm sorry. I don't mean to bug you. But you seem like a good guy and this is very important. Glen might've mentioned some little thing, something you wouldn't necessarily think is significant, back when you guys were still speaking."

"Like what?"

"Like, people he hung out with, anyone he might've worked for."

Turk thought about this for a minute. It was freezing outside and his breath came out his nose in little puffs of smoke. "About six months ago, he stopped by to see me. This was before he started tweaking. It seemed like he was really trying to get his life together. Anyway, he was all excited about some business type he'd hooked up with. The guy told Glen he wanted to give him a chance to work for him. The only requirement was that Glen didn't have a police record, which is hard to believe, but he didn't."

"You got a name for this guy?"

"No."

"Any idea how they met?"

"If I knew I'd tell you." Turk shook his big, woolly head. "My brother was a good kid. I don't know what the hell

199

happened." I waited an awkward moment while he swiped at his eyes with the back of his hand. "Look, I've got to get back to work."

I pulled a Hershey bar out of my pocket, which I was saving for lunch. "I really like chocolate with my coffee," I said, extending the candy to Turk.

He looked at me for a beat before taking it. "Thanks."

I waited until I pulled out of the parking lot before bursting into tears. The idea that psycho-man Glen Davis was once someone's beloved little brother had never occurred to me. After a few minutes, I wiped my nose and drove across the street to the Seven-Eleven for another Hershey Bar.

Nick called while I sat in the parking lot eating the candy. When I'd woken up this morning, I'd checked in the living room. Alphonso was gone, which meant Nick had come home last night. I felt inordinately relieved, the way I imagine my mother used to feel when she'd hear my key in the door, after I'd been out on a date with Bobby. Never mind that we'd been fucking like rabbits the entire evening. In her mind, if I didn't stay out all night, nothing happened.

"Did you have fun with Alphonso last night?" Nick asked, as if I were a five year old on a play date.

"We had a blast," I told him. "Let's see...we watched Totally Naked News until the cable went out and then Alphonso fell asleep on the couch. Ya know that guy should look into having his adenoids removed. He has some serious snoring issues."

"I'll mention it to him."

"Did *you* have fun last night?" I asked.

"Apparently not as much as you. Listen," Nick said, switching gears, "I've got the thumb drive back."

"And?"

"And you were right about there being hidden information buried on it."

"I knew it!" I yelled, practically slapping myself a high five. "So what did you find out?"

"Most of it's encrypted and my source wasn't able to crack it. But there's a list of Chinese surnames and then some dates ranging from nineteen forty-seven to nineteen eighty-six. Could be birth dates—"

"Could be anything. Crap." I finished off the candy bar and stuffed the wrapper into my pocketbook.

"Okay," Nick said, "forget for a minute that we don't know what's on the thumb drive. The important thing for now is it's not what Keith told you it was."

"True. So somehow Keith got a hold of this mysterious information—was he blackmailing the owners of the casino with it, or was he working for them when he lost it? That would be my guess, because he didn't seem to be in control. He seemed really scared and desperate."

"Either way, he must've had a coronary when the dog ate it."

And now he knows I have the damn thing and won't give it back. If Nick and I are right, I could be in a shit load of trouble here.

Nick must've been reading my mind. "Maybe it's time to turn the thumb drive over to the police and let them sort it out."

I'm sure he was right. Only something told me to hang onto it for a little while longer.

"All I know for sure is Bulldog and Keith both want the computer drive. Bulldog works for a casino that may or may not employ illegal aliens and Keith owes the casino money. Everything else is speculation. I just want to be sure I have something substantial before I go running to the cops again."

"Again?"

"Yeah, well, I may have lost a little credibility when I accidentally falsely accused Connie Harrison's father of hiring goons to beat her husband to a bloody pulp. But hey, nobody forced them to listen to me."

The sound of Nick's laughter echoed in my ears and warmed me.

"I've got to get back to work, angel. Let's talk more over dinner."

He suggested we meet at a Colombian bar and grill in Center City. The place is the new "in"spot in town, known for its exotic atmosphere, gourmet food and Latin music.

"Will there be dancing?" I squeaked. The last time Nick took me dancing, he slipped a thigh between my legs and I came in the middle of the dance floor.

"It could be arranged," he said, low and sexy, with just the barest hint of teasing in his voice. *Oh God, he knew!* I blushed from head to toe.

"Whatever," I managed to croak out.

"I'll see you at eight."

Oh boy! I'm going on an actual, sort of date with Nick. Okay, he didn't call it a date—or even imply that it was one. In actuality, all he really said was we should eat food together. But this was my chance to really make an impression.

All right...what to wear...I did a quick mental scan of my wardrobe...my blue jeans with a gray turtleneck or some black jeans with a beige one...I'm pathetic. What I need is a hotline for the fashion-impaired.

I thought about calling Janine to go shopping with me, but I'd end up looking like a South Street whore—not that there's anything *wrong* with that—I just wanted a slightly subtler look. Ditto, Carla. Okay... there's Mindy Rebowitz, but she's still wearing her maternity clothes after "delivering" six months ago. Besides, I hate her. I briefly considered Alana, but that would be inappropriate. Plus, I didn't know her phone number. Did I know *anyone* with fashion sense? Yes, in fact, I did.

"Tell me I'm dreaming. I have wanted to do a fashion makeover on you for years."

"Don't get too excited, John. It's *one* outfit, and I have veto rights."

"It's a start, Sunshine."

John schlepped me half way across town and back again, to every boutique in the city.

We finally settled on a dress. It had an off the shoulder tight black top—sexy, subtle, and sophisticated, and a short, ass-hugging skirt. It was so totally opposite who I am I could be arrested for fashion fraud. A pair of stiletto heels completed the ensemble. The only problem was, I couldn't stay upright in them.

"How am I supposed to walk in these things? I keep tipping over."

"It's the price you pay for looking gorgeous."

"John, tell me the truth. Do I look alright?"

"Brandy Renee Alexander. I don't think I've ever heard you sound insecure before."

"Then you haven't been listening. I'm a mass of self doubt."

John looked at me for so long, I thought I'd grown a third eye or something.

"What?"

"You really like this guy, don't you?"

"Well, have you *seen* him?"

"No," he said. "It's more than that. Tell me how you really feel about him."

I sighed. "It's complicated."

"How so?"

"If I knew, it wouldn't be complicated."

"Are you in love with him?"

"John, that's nuts. I barely know him."

"If I were Franny you'd tell me," John sulked. "I figured what with her being temporarily insane for the next five and a half months, you'd confide in me by default."

"I can't tell you what I don't know, John."

I was quiet the whole rest of the way home. What if John and Alphonso were right? Lust I could handle, but love? Oy.

Nick called. He was running late, so I stopped by Kenny's place on the way to the restaurant to get paid for the singing gig. It wasn't much, but it was the first honest buck I'd made in weeks.

"Be careful going up Walnut," Kenny warned, as I left. "They're doing some construction work near the St. James."

I drove carefully, looking over my shoulder about every three seconds to make sure I wasn't being followed. Traffic was light and the sidewalks deserted. A damp chill hung in the air, turning the road slick with a thin layer of ice. An SUV came up behind me, its headlights bouncing off my rearview mirror. My heart leaped into my throat but settled back down when the driver turned left at the light.

I was about two blocks from the restaurant when I heard a dull popping sound. Instantly, the truck lurched out of control. I pumped on the breaks, tightening my grasp on the steering wheel, struggling to make it to the curb. *Damn. I must've picked up a nail and popped the front tire.* The truck rolled to a stop next to a fire hydrant, and I got out to inspect the damage.

The tire was completely blown, which ruled out the possibility of driving it any further. Quickly, I hopped back into the truck and pulled open my pocketbook. If I could get a hold of Nick, he could swing by and pick me up on his way over to the restaurant—which would have been a great plan, had I remembered to charge my phone within the last five days.

I scrambled into the back of the truck and retrieved a pair of tennis shoes I'd left back there, after my training session with Uncle Frankie. Quickly, I pulled off the stiletto heels and replaced them with the sneakers. I'd change into the heels again when I got to the restaurant.

The idea of running around unprotected on the dark city streets made me a little nervous, but I couldn't just sit there in the truck, freezing to death. Besides, what were the odds of someone coming along at that precise moment to do me bodily harm?

Turns out, they were pretty good.

The SUV appeared out of nowhere and slid to a halt in front of the truck. A man flung open the door and jumped out, his shaved head gleaming in the light of the streetlamp. He wore the same drab olive green army jacket he had on when he invaded my home, and he looked about as friendly.

He began sprinting towards me and I took off running, dropping my pocketbook on the sidewalk but instinctively hanging on to the shoes. I got about five yards when he overtook me, grabbing me by the throat, pressing his meaty hands into the soft spot on my neck. "You've been a real pain in the ass," he growled. "But all that's about to change."

Rational thought went out the window as I leaped into survival mode. I lashed out with my legs, kicking him in the shins. He groaned and tightened his grip on me, forcing me backwards, towards his car. I tried to scream, but my vocal chords were stuck on mute.

Sandmeyer loosened his grip while he struggled to open his car door. I jerked and twisted beneath him and managed to free one arm. Raising the stiletto heel that was clutched firmly in my hand, I aimed straight for his face.

"Son of a bitch," he screamed, clutching at his eye.

I slammed hard against him, knocking him sideways. We both fell, but he was on his feet first, dragging me up by the hair. Pain shot through to the roots, causing my eyes to water. "This bastard is not going to make me cry," I promised myself, and with a strength born of pure fury, I took the heel of the shoe again and this time shoved it straight up his crotch. He let loose with a blood curdling scream and flew backwards. I scrambled away from him, but he quickly regained his balance and lunged for me again.

And then without warning, he was airborne. I looked up in time to see Nick grab the Bulldog by his collar and wrench him into the stratosphere, landing with a thunk on the ground. Bulldog cursed and reached into his jacket, producing a small pistol from his pocket.

"Nick," I yelled, but it was totally unnecessary.

Santiago kicked out his leg and the gun went flying. Sandmeyer took off running, but Nick tackled him, rendering him immobile. Nick tossed me his cell phone. "Do me a favor, angel, and call the police." He eyed me for a moment, a lazy grin crossing his face. "By the way, you look great."

I glanced down at my ensemble, which was, by now, torn in six places and smeared with street grime and punched in 911.

Nick hauled Bulldog to his feet and slapped a pair of cuffs on him. I stood too, my arm throbbing where I'd landed on it, and I winced in pain.

"It feels like my arm is broken," I said.

An infinitesimal frown flickered across Nick's face.

"Which one?" he asked.

"The left."

Nick reached behind Bulldog and grabbed a hold of his left arm. A split second later, Bulldog let out an agonizing yelp as his eyeballs slid towards the back of his head. Although the temperature hovered in the mid thirties, his face was drenched in sweat.

"Are you crazy, man?" he yelled. "You broke my fuckin' arm."

"Did I?" Nick asked mildly.

"Did you?" I asked, borderline hysterically.

Somewhere nearby a siren wailed. A car pulled up in

front of the truck and Bobby got out. "I was driving by when I heard the call on the radio," he told me.

"Hey," Sandmeyer called to him. "Are you a cop?"

"Yeah."

"This asshole cuffed me and broke my arm. I want to press charges."

Bobby cut his eyes to Nick.

"He fell," Nick said.

DiCarlo scanned me up and down, taking in my torn clothes and skinned knees. "He do this to you?"

I nodded mutely.

He switched his gaze back to Sandmeyer. "You fell."

"Like fuck I did."

Bobby moved in close to his face. "Why don't you just shut the hell up, unless you want to try for the other arm?"

When a six foot one inch boxer stands very close to you and gives you a direction, it's best to follow it. Unfortunately, Sandmeyer wasn't thinking too clearly. "Fuck you too."

A lightning punch to the gut and Sandmeyer was down for the count.

Mike Mahoe pulled up in a squad car and hopped out. "What happened to him?" he asked, nodding in Bulldog's direction.

Bobby shrugged. "He fell."

The "nail" that blew out my tire turned out to be a slug from a .45. Sandmeyer had doubled back in his car and waited for me to drive down the road. If Nick hadn't come along when he did—nope, I'm not even gonna go there. I already have enough to keep me up nights.

"You're awfully quiet, angel."

We were sitting in Nick's living room, sharing a bottle of Merlot and some Columbian take-out from the restaurant. The food was delicious, but somehow, after the whole attempted-kidnapping-arm-mangling-incident, I wasn't all that hungry.

I'd driven back with Nick in his jaguar, a nineteen sixty-four XKE that is rumored to have once belonged to a Beatle. My outfit was effectively ruined, so I changed into sweats and a t-shirt, feeling this suited the mood better anyway.

I thought it would have been nice to have had a chance to ask Bulldog a few questions before the police arrived, but who knew what kind of tactics Nick might've employed to extract the information. I knew Nick was dangerous. Hell, I've heard he *kills* people. Only I'd never actually witnessed that side of him—until today.

"I'm tired," I said, avoiding his gaze.

"It was the arm-breaking thing, wasn't it?"

I nodded.

"Too much?"

I pinched my thumb and forefinger together. *"A little bit."*

"He hurt you."

"Yeah," I said. "But look. It's not even broken, see?" I extended my left arm for him to inspect.

Nick held my arm, pressing his lips against the sensitive, inner part and began placing gentle kisses along the bruised area. His touch sent chills down my spine, among other places, and soon I forgot all about Bulldog and his unfortunate accident.

"I'm not a fan of violence, darlin'," Nick continued, settling back on the couch again. "Generally speaking, I only use it as a last resort." He locked eyes with mine to make sure I understood exactly what he was about to say. "But there are times when, in my opinion, it's justified. He hurt you, which is all the justification I need. You may disagree, but it won't change the way I do business."

It was hard to disagree in the middle of a mini orgasm. Okay, I was horribly ashamed of myself for being turned on in the face of such gorilla tactics, but there ya have it.

Chapter Thirteen

"Why is your shampoo lady glaring at me?"

I was sitting in the back room of Carla's hair salon, drinking coffee, while she read me the riot act over my latest choice in roommates.

Carla was the person who had first introduced me to Nick, and while she extols his virtues, (usually accompanied by a big, dreamy sigh) she is only too aware of his darker side.

She glanced over to the corner where Bonita, a nineteen year old on loan from a prison work-release program shot me death rays with frightening accuracy.

"What is *with* her?"

Carla hunched forward. She was painting her nails fuchsia to match her sweater. She had offered to paint mine too, but the polish looked radioactive so I declined.

"She's a friend of Marie DiCarlo's, honey."

I nodded sagely, but then Carla threw me for a loop.

Her voice was carefully neutral. "I overheard her talking on the phone with Marie a little while ago. It seems that Bonita saw you and Bobby leave Sargenti's the other night and drive off in his car together."

"Oh for Pete's sake, Carla," I grumbled, "it was perfectly innocent."

Bonita picked up a broom and began sweeping the already spotless floor.

"Well, you've got to admit, it looks a little suspicious, hon."

I knew Carla was saying this for Bonita's benefit. I'd explain, Bonita would report back to Marie and all would be right in the DiCarlo household once again.

I bit back my usual sarcastic response and explained. "We ran into each other at the restaurant. He was working on my case. I had some evidence. We went to pick it up. End of story."

By now Bonita wasn't even pretending not to be listening in, so I addressed my next remarks directly to her. "Sorry to disappoint you, Bonita, but Bobby and I are not having an affair. We barely even speak to each other."

At that moment my cell phone rang. I pulled it out of my coat jacket, inadvertently shifting the "speakerphone" button to the "on" position. "Hello?"

"Yo Brandy. It's Bobby." Oh crap.

Bonita's head shot up so fast it was in danger of spinning off into the stratosphere. Even Carla did a double take, her beehive swiveling from Bonita to me and back again.

"I'm sorry about before. I'm just worried about you." Of all the times for Bobby to show his sensitive side, this could win a prize for the worst possible moment.

"Tell them we're *not* having an affair," I yelled into the receiver."

"What?"

"Never mind." I hung up the phone.

Bonita resumed her death ray glare.

"Oh, bite me, Bonita."

Well, this day just keeps getting better and better. I'd woken up this morning with a world-class headache, courtesy of the half a bottle of Merlot I drank last night.

Nick thought it might help if I talked about what had

happened, but I didn't see the point in reliving my "near-death" encounter. It wasn't that much fun the *first* time around.

I did not want to go to bed. I knew from past experience that the second I closed my eyes the nightmares would start creeping into my brain. I ended up falling asleep on the couch, watching "Fresh Prince of Bel Air." Nick hung in there as long as he could, but apparently, he's not quite as enamored of old TV sit-coms as I am. Go figure.

He was gone when I woke up this morning—something to do with an appointment with rebel soldiers from Zaire.

Bobby called from the police station. "I have some good news and some bad news," he told me."

The good news was that Ivan "Bulldog" Sandmeyer was booked on assault and kidnapping charges and his bail was set so high he'd have to sell his mother, his grandmother and throw in a couple of second cousins to even come close to raising the money. The bad news is, somebody did.

"You mean he's out on the street again?" *The man tried to kill me—or at the very least, he ruined a two hundred dollar pair of high heels. Doesn't that count for anything?*

"I'm trying to get more information on who posted his bail. In the meantime, you might want to rethink visiting your parents in Florida for awhile."

I made the appropriate noises like I was really going to consider this.

"The thing I don't get is why this guy is going after you. The cops couldn't get anything out of him last night."

"Um, promise you won't get mad and I may be able to shed some light on the subject."

Bobby blew out a long air of exasperation. "I'm not going to like this, am I?"

"Probably not."

He paused while he did his mental "count to ten," only it was taking longer than usual, so I started in again.

"Look, it's not my fault. I tried to tell you a couple of times, but I got distracted—"

"Tell me," he growled, effectively cutting me off. "Now."

So I did.

"Okay, let me get this straight," he said when I was finished, and it sounded like he was laughing. "Neither of these guys actually wanted you. They were both after some magical dog who defecates computer software."

"Well, you don't have to put it that way."

"How should I put it, Brandy? Even you have to admit it sounds a little squirrelly."

"Which is half the reason I didn't mention it until now. But I got the thumb drive checked out and there's definitely something important on there. I just don't know what it all means."

"Is it worth dying over?" He said this so quietly I almost missed it. "I've got to get back to work." Bobby hung up without saying goodbye.

Okay, so at least he knew everything now. When my phone rang again, I thought he was calling back to say he was sorry for hanging up on me. It turned out to be Jason Danski, my latest blind date calling to make plans for Saturday night. *Wow. Bowling sounds great, Jason, so if nobody's managed to kill me by then, "we're on!"*

The last thing I did before heading over to Carla's was take a look through the want ads. The art museum was advertising for a curator for their Mayan exhibit and Dunkin' Doughnuts needed a counter person. I dashed off a couple of resumes and headed out the door.

My little session with Bonita left me feeling really depressed. I shouldn't have to defend my friendship with Bobby. After all, I knew him first. Plus, it's not like we have some hot romance going on. These days all our relationship consists of is me sticking my nose where he thinks it doesn't belong and him yelling at me about it—which actually reminded me that there was something I wanted to look into.

The last time I spoke to Turk Davis, he told me Glen had mentioned a business type guy who had taken Glen under his wing. Glen's old neighbor, Tom, had similarly described someone who had visited Glen on occasion. The likelihood of Glen knowing two guys who owned a suit was slim, so if I could track this man down, maybe he could shed some light on Glen's whereabouts.

Twenty minutes later I was parked in front of Glen's old building. Tom was just climbing out of his car when I pulled up.

"Hey, Tom," I called out.

Tom squinted into the sunlight. "Oh, hey. How're ya doin'? Any word on your sister?"

My sister? I quickly scanned my memory bank for the lie. Oh yeah, missing sister. I shook my head sadly. "No, not yet. But if you have a minute, I'd like to ask you about that guy you said came around every once in a while—the one you noticed because he seemed to be a cut above Glen's usual visitors."

"Oh yeah," he said. "Mr. Lexus."

"Mr. Lexus?"

"That's what I used to call him. He drove a new charcoal gray Lexus. You don't generally see a car that nice around here, unless it's stolen. In fact," Tom continued, "it was parked here not too long ago. I remember because I kept hearing some damn dog barking, so I looked outside to see what all the fuss was about, and there was that car."

"Was the guy in the car?"

"No. Sorry. Like I said, I never took any real notice of him."

I thanked Tom and got back in the Mercedes.

Okay, so the guy drives a Lexus. Where did I just see

213

something about a Lexus? And then it hit me like a hundred and sixty pound bag of lying lawyer. Keith Harrison drives a Lexus. Or if he doesn't, he at least has the owners' manual tucked into his office junk drawer.

I pulled out my cell and punched in 411for MasterCarb on Broad Street.

When Turk came on the line, I got straight to the point. "Turk, this is really important. When Glen talked to you about that guy he was going to work for, did he mention what the guy did for a living?"

"Oh man, it's you again? You're like this—this little screw that keeps twisting into my brain."

"I swear I'll never bother you again, if you could just think back for a minute."

There was a long pause, and I could hear Turk's labored breath on the other end of the line. "Yeah, come to think of it," he said finally. "He did mention something. Said the guy was a lawyer. I remember thinking that's good, because some day Glen was going to need one."

What if Keith turned out to be the guy Glen was working for? How far fetched is that? Well, I was about to find out. I got back in the car and headed on over to Keith's house.

There it was, sitting in front of the house like a clue on a silver platter. A brand new charcoal gray SC2006. I'd parked half way down the block and dragged out the binoculars, in case Keith was hanging out his bedroom window, hoping I'd show up with his thumb drive. Once I'd confirmed what I needed to know, I made a beeline out of there, looking back over my shoulder every step of the way.

"Bobby, it's Brandy."

There was a slight intake of air before he answered. "Hi. What's up?"

"Am I calling at a bad time?" I didn't want to call him

on his cell phone, in case he was in the middle of a fight with Marie, or worse, making love to her in a sudden fit of remorse over their estrangement. So I tried calling him at the station and turns out he was there.

"Nah. It's fine. I was just in talking to my captain. He says he thinks I'm a little stressed."

"And why would he think that?"

"Ah, he may have heard a rumor that I punched some scumbag suspect while he was handcuffed, but you know how it is with rumors. By tomorrow it'll all be forgotten."

I didn't want to point out that if his stress level climbed any higher it would be in the Mount Everest range. Instead, I added to it.

"I need to see Toodie."

The Plexiglas window that separated Toodie from polite society could not disguise the genuine happiness in his face when he saw me.

"Yo Brandy. I knew you'd come. I'm sorry I can't offer you anything," he added, "but there's a vending machine right down the hall. It's got fruit and candy bars. I passed it on my way in."

"I'm good, Toodie, but thanks." I turned away so that he couldn't see my eyes fill up.

I don't know what it is about the guy that makes me want to slay dragons for him. I guess it's the same feeling mama cats have when they go up against the neighborhood canines to protect their young. He's an innocent, and I couldn't help but want to take care of him.

"Are you eating all right? Getting enough rest?" He looked okay, except for the deep circles under his eyes.

"Yeah, I'm cool. It gets a little lonely in here sometimes. I'm a people person, ya know."

"Yeah," I said. "I'm sorry I didn't get by sooner."

"That's okay. I know you're busy. Bobby DiCarlo

came by. He said you're working real hard to get me out of here."

"He did?" *Wow.* "Listen, Toodie, that's one of the reasons I'm here. I've got something to show you and I want you to think real carefully before you answer."

I opened my pocketbook and extracted a folded up paper, smoothing it out on the Plexiglas barrier. It was the picture of Keith Harrison I'd printed off the Internet. "Take a good look. Have you ever seen this guy before?"

Toodie scrunched up his face in concentration. "Yeah," he said finally. "I've seen him."

"Where do you know him from?" I held my breath.

"From jail."

"What do you mean?" I'd checked Keith out. He has no record.

"I saw him once when he came to visit my cell mate, Uzi Capistrano. I think Uzi might have worked for the guy or something."

"Where's Uzi now?"

"Dead. He O.D.'ed about a month after he was released."

"Is that how you met Glen? Through Uzi?"

"Yeah. Uzi told me to look him up when I got out, but he was dead by then. He and Glen lived together for a while. Hey, I'll bet that's how Glen hooked up with Ilene."

"Yeah? How's that?"

"I'd left a bike over at Ilene's—a really sweet Harley. You should've seen it. It was gorgeous—black, with fuchsia and an engine that—"

"Uh, Toodie, stay with me now. How did Ilene meet Glen?"

"Oh yeah, well, Ilene agreed to let Uzi pick up the bike and take it back to his place. Glen must've gone with him when he went to get it."

It was a plausible explanation that would justify why

Toodie didn't know Ilene and Glen knew each other.

Toodie shrugged his big, gangly shoulders. "I don't know, Brandy. Everybody I know seems to end up dead."

I really hoped he was being nostalgic and not prophetic.

My time was up so I told him I'd come visit him again. He was in the middle of telling me how much he missed our Friday Night Scrabble tournaments, when something that had been crashing around in my brain suddenly surfaced.

"One more thing, Toodie. Did Ilene have a dog?"

I stopped in to see Bobby on the way out. He was sitting at his desk, launching paper airplanes into a wastebasket. A flow chart was tacked up on the wall in back of him with the names Ilene and Andi and dates and times and circles and arrows in different colored markers. I scanned the board, not bothering to hide my curiosity. Bobby moved in front of it, not bothering to hide his annoyance. The predictability of our actions made us both laugh. I sat down in the chair opposite him.

"Why didn't you tell me you visited Toodie?"

Bobby shrugged. "I didn't want you to get any ideas."

"What ideas?"

"That I'm a nice guy."

I smiled. "You are a nice guy. It meant a lot to him."

I filled Bobby in on our conversation, highlighting Keith's connection to Glen and the possibility that *my* Adrian could, in fact, have once belonged to Ilene.

"Toodie said she was always rescuing strays—don't say it," I added on his look. "We're talking about Ilene, here."

Bobby grinned. "I didn't say a word."

"Anyway," I continued, "the neighbor said he'd heard a dog barking the day Keith had been over there. What if it was Ilene's dog—assuming she had one. Toodie found Adrian about a half a block away from Glen's apartment.

It's possible that the dog had run off, but he didn't get very far before Toodie found him."

"You're forgetting one thing," Bobby noted. "We still only have Toodie's word that there's a connection between Glen and Ilene. We don't have any real proof that they even knew each other. And even if Glen did know her, that doesn't preclude Toodie's involvement in her murder. They could have been in it together."

"You don't really believe that."

"Yeah, alright. So I've developed a soft spot for the guy too. But that doesn't mean he's not crazy. And crazy people do crazy things."

Speaking of which, I decided I'd better clue him in about Bonita.

"Yeah, it came up around the dinner table last night. Listen, I'm really sorry about all of this." He lowered his voice and added, "I've been talking to a lawyer."

"Bobby," I stopped him. "Maybe I'm not the best person for you to be confiding in right now."

He nodded in agreement and then laughed softly. "Hey, you've been here for twenty minutes and we haven't had a fight yet. I think that's a personal record for us, these days."

"See? Miracles can happen." I stood and walked out the door.

The Barnes and Noble Café, located on the second floor of the store at Eighteenth and Walnut served as my office for the afternoon. I settled into a cushy seat next to the window, with an espresso and some dark chocolate grahams and watched a light rain tap against the glass. Sitting there I felt safe, a concept that was foreign to me these days, and I took a few minutes to enjoy the feeling.

Spread out before me was my own version of a flow chart, with names and dates, circles and arrows and little hearts and flowers edging the paper, because I'm an avowed doodler. I finished off the first chocolate graham and sat back to review my work.

"Okay," I conceded, "most of my conclusions are based on conjecture rather than hardcore facts, but it's damn good conjecture."

It was a reasonable assumption that Glen Davis and Keith Harrison knew each other. That Glen probably worked for Keith in some capacity. That Keith owed money to the Diamond Casino and that he and Ivan Sandmeyer were both after a computer thumb drive that held information that was valuable to the casino.

It had been inconceivable to me that the separate incidents that have consumed my life for the past few weeks could be related, and now it was equally inconceivable that I hadn't made the connections sooner.

What I couldn't figure out is where Ilene fit in the mix. Bobby said there isn't even any real proof that Glen and Ilene knew each other, so he was hard pressed to place Ilene at Glen's house at the time of the murder.

My coffee was gone and so were the little chocolate grahams. It was four thirty and dusk was fast approaching. I didn't want to be caught wandering the city streets after dark; it was scary enough in broad daylight, so I gathered up my pocketbook and left the cheery glow of the bookstore.

The streets were packed with holiday shoppers and people just getting off from work. I took comfort in the crowd, figuring that if anyone felt inclined to kidnap, kill or otherwise manhandle me, they'd have to do it in front of an audience. Luckily, no one seemed all that interested in me, and I got back to the car unscathed by anything except my own imagination.

I'd put my phone on mute while I was in the bookstore. When I turned it back on, there was a voicemail waiting for me from Uncle Frankie.

"Yo, Midget Brat. How about you come by for some homemade pasta tonight. And don't worry; Carla isn't going near the stove. I'm cooking. Call me."

Sounds good. I swung the car around and headed for Perini's Bakery to pick up some chocolate cannoli, Uncle Frankie's favorite.

I found a great parking spot on Christian, where a car had gotten the boot and was just being hauled away when I pulled up. I slid into the spot and got out of the car.

The bakery was crammed with customers, the line spilling out the door. I stood out on the sidewalk, tucking in behind a big guy in a Santa Claus suit. An icy wind had kicked up and set my teeth to chattering.

My cell rang again and I stuffed a frozen hand into my bag to find it. "Hello?"

The voice was friendly, cheerful even. "Hi. Did you like my little present?"

"I'm sorry?" Traffic was heavy and I could barely make out the words.

"I said, 'did you like my little present, bitch?'" *Oh shit. Here we go again.*

My heartbeat kicked into high gear as I fought down the bile rising in my throat.

"The doll is just a little preview of what I'm going to do to you when I get you alone. I'm getting hard just thinking about it."

"Shut up you fucking freak!"

Santa whipped his head around to see who the potty-mouth was. Guess I was going on the Naughty List. That is, if I survived until Christmas.

I had to stay calm, and I did, for about half a second. And then came the old sucker punch.

"You look cold."

Oh my God. He can see me. I shot a brief hard look at the people in line.

"Where are you?" I willed my voice to keep steady.

"Close by. You should've kept your Goddamn nose out of my business. You've made my life miserable and I'm gonna pay you back in spades."

I had to keep him talking. If I could keep him on the line long enough to get someone to call the cops, maybe they'd be able to catch him. I gave Santa a surreptitious poke in the back and he turned around.

"Call the police," I mouthed.

"What?"

"The Police, the police!"

He turned to the guy in front of him and stuck his index finger next to his temple, twirling it around in the universal sign for crazy.

I sighed. "Glen, could you hold on for a minute? I'm getting another call." Okay, so maybe I wasn't thinking too clearly. I just figured if I could put him on hold, I could call the cops myself. But Glen was on a roll.

"I'm used to slicing people now. I'm getting good at it. It's gonna be fun ripping into you."

"You're a real one-note guy, aren't ya Glen?" That was me being brave, but my knees had other ideas. They were buckling beneath me at an alarming rate.

"I can't wait to feel your flesh against the knife. In fact, I'm so close I could reach right out and touch you."

I didn't get to hear all the other neat plans Glen had for me, for at that precise moment I fainted.

Chapter Fourteen

Santa Claus scraped me off the sidewalk. He offered to call an ambulance, but it's embarrassing enough to pass out on a city street without being carted away on a stretcher. I was getting pretty good at recognizing the signs of a concussion, blurred vision being one of them. Only one of my eyes was blurry, and my pupils weren't *all that* dilated, so I didn't see what all the fuss was about. Still, Santa, who turned out to be Joe Morgen of the Gas Company, suggested I call someone to give me a ride home. He would have volunteered himself, to make up for the "crazy" reference, but he had to get to a Christmas party.

I picked up my cell phone off the ground and opened it, but that was as far as I got before I slammed it shut again, disgusted with myself. If I hadn't keeled over, I could've contacted the police and maybe they would've nabbed Davis. He must be half way across town by now. At least I hope he is. The thought of him watching me made my skin crawl.

Joe felt bad for me and offered to let me cut in front of him, but I was sort of out of the mood for pastry. I stood off to the side and thought about who I could call to pick me up.

Frankie, Carla, the twins, Paul, Johnny—none of them would take the news of my being threatened very well. Bobby's a professional, but his mood swings are worse than a girl's lately. That left only one person. I sighed and punched in the number.

"It's Brandy. I hate to ask, but I wonder if you could do me a favor."

Fifteen minutes later a black Bronco pulled up to the curb and Alphsonso stuck his head out the window, hollering for me.

I yanked open the door and climbed in, resting my head against the back of the seat. The strain must've shown in my face, because he studied me for a beat and then leaned across me and buckled me in.

"Thanks," I said. "I'm sorry about calling you. I just didn't know who else to ask."

I couldn't see his eyes because he was wearing shades, even though the sun had set about fifteen minutes earlier, but he was smiling so I knew he wasn't too annoyed.

"Does Nick know about this?"

I shook my head no. Alphonso raised an eyebrow but he didn't press the point.

"So what happened?"

I gave him the Readers' Digest version, skipping over the more graphic details of my conversation with Glen. When I was finished, he pulled away from the curb into the rush hour traffic.

"You're gonna have to toughen up if you plan on doing this for a living," he lectured me. "You can't be passin' out all the time. How're the bad guys gonna take you seriously?"

Alphonso was right. I have to toughen up. And I'll do just that, right after my bubble bath.

"I'll give you a hundred bucks to forget the whole thing."

I was sitting with John in the parking lot of the Kensington Rifle Club, a seedy looking building in a dicey neighborhood, overlooking a city dump. I'd found it in the yellow pages.

"Oh, come on, John. You said we need to hang out together more."

"I was thinking more along the lines of 'antiquing' and art shows."

"Think of this as a bonding experience." I pried his hands loose from the steering wheel and shoved him out the car door.

Okay, the logical choice would have been Alphonso. The man, no doubt, knew his way around a gun, but then he'd want to know why I didn't ask Nick and I wasn't ready for that conversation. Franny's pregnancy knocked her out of the running. Paul wouldn't know the port side of a gun from the starboard, Uncle Frankie isn't technically allowed to handle a firearm, after a little altercation back in '93 that the family still refers to as "the incident." Bobby would freak if he knew I was even considering carrying a weapon, and Janine and Carla—well, that's just silly. In the end, it was a toss up between John and Mrs. Gentile and I chose John.

I was hard pressed to justify in my own mind why the daughter of a '60's peace-nik would suddenly become a "gun-totin' mama," but the thing is, Glen really scared me. He'd been so close he could chart my every movement. I guess I just wanted to know I could take care of myself, should the occasion call for it.

The guy behind the counter looked like your average escapee from a chain gang. The name "Steve" was embroidered on his shirt. Steve cast an aloof eye our way and turned to the behemoth standing next to us, a two hundred and eighty pound linebacker with a penchant for large weaponry.

"Sorry, man, we're out of AK-47s. But we got some AR-15s that just came in."

John looked over at the guy, a nervous twitch developing in his right eye. He turned back to me, leaning into my ear. "Did you hear what he just asked for?" he hissed. "They're talking about semi-automatics. What would he possibly need with a semi-automatic!"

"Shhh. You're going to get us thrown out of here."

"And that would be a *bad* thing?"

Ignoring John, I stepped up to the counter. "Excuse me. We'd like to borrow some guns, please."

"Handgun or rifle?"

I looked at John. He gave me a blank stare that said, "You're on your own."

"Um, handgun. A little one."

Steve slapped a twenty-two on the counter, along with a box of ammunition. "This is good for beginners. You're new at this, I take it."

I wonder what gave it away. I handed him my driver's license and paid for the gun rental and the ammo.

Steve picked up the twenty-two and was now showing me all about gun safety and how to load the thing properly. I didn't think this was going to be necessary, seeing as I was too afraid to pick it up off the counter.

John had wandered off and was engaged in conversation with the man with the semi-automatic.

"But what if somebody all of a sudden went crazy in here and started shooting at everyone?" John asked in a voice so high it could shatter crystal. "I mean, what's to stop him?"

"Well then, we'd all just have to band together and get him," the man said, as if anticipating this very scenario.

"But how could we possibly do that?" John screeched. *"We'd all be dead!"*

In the end we were asked to leave. The counter guys said we were scaring the other patrons.

"Sorry," John told me when we were back in the car.

"That's alright. At least now I know what it's like to go to a firing range with Woody Allen."

"Shut-uh-up!"

I didn't want to be alone, so I went back to John's and stretched out on his couch, while he developed some photos in his dark room. Twenty minutes later, my cell phone rang, rousing me from an uneasy sleep. I plunged into panic mode, thinking it was Glen again. I opened the phone slowly, as if I expected him to pop right out like some psycho Jack-in-the-Box. It wasn't Glen. But I still wasn't too anxious to get on the line.

"Hey," I said.

"Are you avoiding me, angel?"

"What? No. Of course not! Don't be ridiculous. Pfft."

Okay, so I was avoiding him.

I got up from the couch and moved into the bathroom and shut the door. I didn't know where this conversation was headed, but I wanted to go there without John, the big snoop, listening in.

When Nick spoke again, there was playfulness in his voice, and I didn't know whether to feel relieved or pissed off.

"Because there's no reason to feel embarrassed by what happened—"

"I'm not!" I shouted, settling on pissed off.

"Good," he said, amicably. "Since you're not avoiding me, I'll expect to see you later on tonight at the apartment. I still owe you a dinner. And a dance," he added benignly, but he might as well have said, "and some hot Latin sex" for all the innuendo lacing his words.

"Fine," I told him. "I'll see you then." *Good girl, Bran-*

dy. *Keep it curt, business-like.*

"Oh, and see if you can salvage that outfit you wore the other night. That was very nice. I'd like to see you in it again."

There was no mistaking the message behind his request. *Oh boy.*

My original intention was not to avoid Nick, but to slowly wean myself from him. Since I'd moved into his place, I'd found myself growing more and more dependent on him, and dependence is a dangerous thing. I'd discovered that last July when my cable went out and I was forced to watch network television. I nearly went crazy until it was fixed. But there I go digressing again. The point is I was starting to form an emotional attachment to this man that went far beyond the bounds of safety for me.

Because the thing is, for all of his charm and the genuine kindness he's extended to me, Nick is a "bad boy" in the truest sense of the word. And bad boys will break your heart every time. My heart is vulnerable enough as it is, what with poor diet and little to no exercise. I don't need to add emotional turmoil to push it over the edge.

So my plan was to rein in my raging hormones, deny my growing feelings and keep Nick at bay until I was able to move out of his apartment and back into my own home again. Only you know what they say about the best-laid plans.

After Alphonso had picked me up from the bakery, he delivered me to Nick's door, did a quick, albeit unnecessary sweep of the apartment and instructed me to lock up when he left. I'd turned off my phone after Glen's call. Now, I turned it back on to check for messages. I had two.

"Brandy, honey, it's your mother. We were just wondering if you've given any more thought to visiting us over the holidays."

In the background, my dad was shouting, "Tell her I love her."

"Your father says he loves you. And he wants you to come see us."

"I didn't say that," my dad yelled.

"Lou, that's terrible. Don't you want Brandy to come for the holidays?"

"She'll come if she can. She doesn't need the pressure."

I don't recall having a direct conversation with my father in years. All of our communication is conveyed through voicemail messages, filtered and manipulated by my mom. Ya gotta love her.

Nick was call number two, letting me know he wasn't planning to be home tonight. I was equal parts relieved, disappointed and frightened. I turned on the television to keep me company and found a Seinfeld marathon.

I gave Uncle Frankie a quick call and begged off dinner, citing a colossal headache—Glen could definitely qualify as a headache, so technically, I wasn't lying. Then I fed Rocky and Adrian and played a couple of quick games of "Chase the aluminum foil ball," their favorite pastime, next to stealing food off of my plate.

At eleven thirty I turned off the television, took a quick shower, changed into a t-shirt and pajama bottoms and crawled into bed. Two minutes later I was up. The pillow wasn't right. It didn't smell like Nick. Since he wasn't planning on coming home tonight, I figured he wouldn't mind if I borrowed his pillow. I didn't want to think about where he might be. The possibilities were endless.

I padded down the hall to his room and swiped the pillow off his bed and returned to the guest room. I wrapped my arms around the pillow and closed my eyes. Then I opened them again. The pillow wasn't enough. I grabbed the pillow off the bed and marched back down the hall. "He won't even know," I thought, crawling into his bed.

Even in the dark, I knew I wasn't alone. My heart stopped and my knees quaked.

"Oh God, please don't let it be Glen...but if it is, he sure does smell good."

"You're in my bed, darlin'."

Sweet Jesus, how am I going to explain this?

"I am?" I said. I sat up and rubbed my eyes. "Oh wow. How did I end up in here?"

Nick sat down on the edge of the bed, his hand resting on my knee.

"I should probably get up," I thought, but I liked the feel of his hand on my knee way too much.

"Maybe you were sleepwalking," he said.

"Yeah, must've been," I agreed, ignoring the gently mocking tone in his voice.

A thin stream of moonlight filtered in from the window, casting a shadow on the wall. I fixated on that so I wouldn't have to think about how awkward this was.

"Um, I thought you weren't coming home tonight," I ventured.

He reached down and pulled off his shoes, tossing them in a pile next to the bed. "I finished earlier than expected." He began unbuttoning his shirt and added that to the pile as well.

I knew I shouldn't ask, but I had to. "Finished what early?"

I could hear the grin in his voice as he responded. "You don't really want to know, do you?"

I sighed. "No, I suppose not."

"Don't worry, it was nothing illegal."

Funny, that's not what I was worried about.

Nick stood up and in the next instant I heard the distinct sound of a zipper being lowered and then the rustle of material dropping softly to the floor. I held my breath as he stepped out of his pants. I had no idea where he stood on the subject of underwear and the thought made me break into a cold sweat.

"What are you doing?" I gulped.

He peeled back the covers and climbed into bed next to me, and I could feel the heat rise in my belly as he pulled me against his naked chest.

"It's been a long day, darlin'," he said. The palm of his hand rested lightly on my breast. He began slowly rubbing his thumb back and forth over the thin fabric of my t-shirt, stroking me until I squirmed against him.

"But if you give me a reason to stay awake…" He gave my nipple a light pinch, sending tiny bolts of electricity straight between my legs.

I catapulted myself off the bed, propelled by fear or common sense, I really couldn't tell which. "No, no. You need your rest." I was poised to sprint across the room, but he caught my wrist and held me there. His voice was playful but the predatory look in his eye told me he wasn't playing.

"I'm going to let you slide tonight, because Alphonso said you had a rough day. But the next time you come to my bed, you'd better be prepared to stay for the party."

I did an about face and bolted from the room.

A few minutes later there was a knock on the guest room door. When I didn't respond, he opened it and came in anyway.

"Why *did* you get into my bed tonight, angel?" His voice was soft and there wasn't a trace of teasing in his tone.

So for once I surprised even myself by opting for the truth. "Because it smells like you." I flipped onto my stomach and pulled the covers over my head. After a minute I heard the door softly close.

In the morning I waited until Nick went into the shower before I got up. I threw on some jeans and a sweatshirt, fed Rocky and Adrian, stuffed my feet into my shitkickers and snuck out of the apartment.

The only place I knew that was open this early, besides the bail bonds office and The Melrose Diner was my uncle's gym. Frankie was in the back room, lifting weights. He let out a surprised grunt when he saw me and walked over to say hello.

"Hey sweetheart. You're up early. What's the occasion?"

"I don't know," I shrugged. "I couldn't sleep, so I thought I'd get my favorite uncle to take me out for breakfast."

"Sorry, hon, I can't get away. I've got a kid coming in at seven for some private training. Did you see DiCarlo on your way in? He had an early morning sparring session."

On cue Bobby showed up, all sweaty and macho looking in faded red gym shorts and a torn, sleeveless sweatshirt. He threw his towel into the laundry bin and nodded to Frankie and me.

"Hey," I said.

"Hey. You got a minute?"

Let's see, I've got no job and no place to go. I've got all the time in the world.

"Sure."

"Wait for me, okay?"

I stood by the far wall and watched a couple of young middleweights spar for a while and then Bobby emerged from the locker room, his wavy dark hair freshly washed and slicked back from his handsome face.

We walked over to the coffee shop across the street and sat down in one of the booths. The table was coated with a thin layer of grease, and I absently began writing my name in it.

A waitress appeared and took our order. Bobby got the special—eggs over easy, toast, sausage and coffee. I hadn't eaten anything since the chocolate grahams, terror being an excellent appetite suppressant. I ordered a cup of hot chocolate and relaxed into the booth.

"Doesn't Marie feed you?" I asked, eying Bobby's plate.

"I'm not much for dining at home these days." He grabbed a forkful of eggs and began chowing down. "I tried to call you, yesterday afternoon," he said, between mouthfuls. "Your cell phone wasn't on."

"I'm having a problem with it." *A hundred and thirty-five pound problem.*

Bobby finished off his eggs and pushed his plate away. Without thinking, I began picking at the remains of his toast.

"So why are we here, Bobby?" I asked. "Unless you just wanted company for breakfast."

"The lab results came back on the hair samples found on the brush you picked up from Glen's. The DNA matches the skin found under Andi Ferguson's nails."

"Hey, that's great. Now when you find Glen you'll have positive evidence linking him to her murder."

"There's more," he said, watching me. "When the hair was tested, the lab discovered someone else's hair entwined with Glen's in the brush. I had a hunch, so I had that tested too."

"But don't you need someone to match it against?"

"I did have someone. Ilene. It was a match."

"Oh my God, Bobby. You did it. You linked Glen to Ilene. This has to be good news for Toodie."

Bobby drained his coffee cup and reached for his wallet. "It doesn't put him in the clear, but it does establish someone else as a viable suspect, and it gives more credence to his story about finding the freezer at Glen's house."

232

"Well, it's a start," I said.

Bobby nodded. "It's a start."

I couldn't get Ilene out of my mind. I mean *somebody* had to think about her. She'd been missing for over a week, and yet no one reported her absence. How sad is that?

According to Bobby, she had no known relatives in the area and fewer friends. Not a single person who thought, "Wow, haven't seen Ilene around for a while. I wonder where she is." Or at least anyone who cared enough to find out. Nobody should have to go through life so anonymously.

I left John's late in the afternoon and drove over to The Gallery at Ninth and Market. They were having a holiday shoe sale at Strawbridge's and I needed something to wear for my dinner with Nick. The night Ivan Sandmeyer tried to strangle the life out of me, I'd ruined the Jimmy Choos. Apparently, when I smashed the heel in his face, I'd broken his nose. It left a huge splotch of blood on the toe of the left shoe.

On the way back to Nick's, Center City traffic was completely gnarled up, so I took a detour down some side streets. Before I knew it, I was in a familiar looking neighborhood on the ritzy side of Society Hill. I was on Keith Harrison's block.

As long as I was here I decided to swing by his place. Maybe I'd catch some Chinese slave labor reporting for duty or Glen dropping by for a visit on his way to a Whack-o's Anonymous meeting. What I didn't expect to see was Bobby DiCarlo's Mustang parked in front of the house, right behind the Lexus.

I parked across the street and left the engine idling while I whipped out the binoculars, but the front shades were drawn and I couldn't see inside the house. I cruised down to the next block and cut the engine and dug in my bag for the cell phone.

Bobby answered on the first ring. "DiCarlo."

"What are you doing at Harrison's house?" I whispered, just in case Bobby was as cell phone impaired as I was and had left it on speakerphone.

"Where are you?" His voice was strained and he didn't sound happy.

"Down the block."

He turned back to the person in the room with him. "Sorry about this. It's the wife. You know what a pain in the ass they can be." I recognized Keith's laugh on the other end. Oh goody. The boys are bonding.

He turned back to me, his voice a hoarse whisper. "I'm working. Go home."

"Ask him if he knows Ivan Sandmeyer." There was a click on the other end of the line and it went dead. I called him right back.

"Yeah."

"We got disconnected. Ask him about Uzi Capistrano." Another click, only this time when I went to call him back it went straight to voicemail. Guess he didn't want my help. I called back one more time just to make sure he hadn't turned his phone off by mistake. It was still off. *Oh fine.*

I decided to hang out a while and wait for Bobby. While I waited I changed the channels on the radio, which had all been set to Spanish news stations. I fooled around with the dial, looking for WMMR and WIBG. I was concentrating really hard and didn't hear the car door handle turn until it was too late. The door flew open and I screamed.

"Jesus Christ, Alexander. How many times do I have to tell you to lock your God damned doors?"

Bobby nudged me out of the driver's seat and slid in next to me.

"You did that on purpose," I fumed. "You wanted to scare me half to death."

Bobby gripped the steering wheel in both hands. He

was probably envisioning my neck. "Ya know, there is something seriously wrong with you," he told me. "If I say black, you say white. If I say don't, you automatically do. You have 'Oppositional defiance disorder.'"

"Only with you. Have you ever thought about being less controlling?"

Bobby sighed deeply. "You drive me nuts."

"So what happened in there?" I knew he was going to tell me, and Bobby knew it too. This time he decided to skip the "police confidentiality" speech.

"The guy is slick. I'll hand him that. I told him I was there on a tip that he'd been seen coming in and out of Glen Davis's, a guy who's being investigated for murder.

He denied it. Said he'd never heard of Davis."

"He's lying."

"Of course he's lying. But so far we've got no one to make a positive I.D. on him and no paper trail. I asked him about Uzi Capistrano. That rang a bell. Said he'd met Uzi through some pro bono work. He'd gone to visit him a couple of times in jail, but then he'd lost touch with him. He was fairly vague."

"Did he seem nervous?"

"Hard to tell. He told me this was his first day up. He'd been on some pretty heavy painkillers and his memory is fuzzy. I told him I'd be back when he was less fuzzy."

I leaned back against the side of the door and braced myself for the inevitable.

"Maybe I should talk to him."

"No."

"Look, I have something he wants."

"Yeah, we need to talk about that too."

"I could call him. I wouldn't even have to be in the same room with him. Maybe he'll slip up and say something we can use."

"There's no "we" Brandy. You are not on this case."

Uh oh. This was DiCarlo the cop turning me down, not DiCarlo the ex-boyfriend, which made things more difficult. All DiCarlo the ex-boyfriend could do is yell at me. DiCarlo the cop could have me arrested for interfering with a police investigation. He came this close to doing it once before, and I had no doubt he'd follow through with his threat, if I called his bluff, especially if he thought it would keep me out of harm's way.

"Fine," I said. "I've got to go home." He didn't make a move to leave.

"What?"

"By 'home' do you mean Santiago's?"

"For the time being."

"How long are you planning on staying there?" Before I could work up a properly bitchy response he raised his hands in front of his chest. "Sorry. None of my business."

Bobby opened the door and climbed out. I reached over and locked it behind him. Then I watched him in the rear view mirror as he climbed back into his car. He didn't pull out right away and I realized he was waiting for me to go. He didn't trust me! I pulled out my cell phone and made a big show of calling someone. Thirty seconds later my phone rang.

"You're not really talking to anyone," he said when I answered.

"Yes, I am and I'm going to be a while, so you might as well go."

"Brandy, I'm warning you. Do not go back and try to talk to Harrison."

"It's a free country, DiCarlo." I wasn't really going to do it. I just didn't want Bobby to think he'd won.

Bobby hung up on me again and started his engine. I started mine too, because I knew I'd pushed him too far. He already had enough to worry about, without adding me to the mix. He was still sitting there as I pulled away.

Janine called. "Want to meet me for a drink?"

"I can't." It was almost seven and Nick was making dinner. "I thought you were working tonight, showing a house with Tony."

"Tony Tan is a rat," Janine said. "Hey, do you think you can get Nick to break something for me?"

"Janine!" Note to self: Don't tell Janine *anything!*

I was sitting outside Nick's apartment, in the loading zone. I'd been there for about half an hour. He'd called me at six, wanting to know if we were still "on" for dinner.

"Yeah, sure. Fine." I wasn't worried about dinner. I was worried about "dessert."

I wanted to ask Janine's advice on what to do if things turned amorous, but she was in a "men are rats" mood, so she probably wasn't the best person to consult. I told her I'd call her tomorrow and then I screwed up my courage and went inside.

Chapter Fifteen

"Truth or dare," Nick said. "Have you ever stolen anything?"

We were seated on the beige leather couch in Nick's living room, sipping some after dinner cognac and playing that childhood game in which you take turns asking each other embarrassing questions and then you either tell the truth or suffer an even more embarrassing consequence. It was Nick's idea.

The lights were dim and a candle burned low on the coffee table.

"Will you think less of me if I fess up to my life of crime?" I asked.

"Well, I don't know. I'd better hear the sordid details first."

"Okay," I told him. "When I was six I stole a box of Dots and some bright red wax lips from Pearson's Candy Store. I took them home and hid them in the washer and then I forgot about them—until my mother did the laundry and the lips melted all over an entire load of wash. My dad wore pink underwear for a month."

"Wow." Nick gave a low whistle. "You are bad to the bone."

"Yeah," I said. "To this day, I can't enjoy a box of Dots

without feeling guilty. Okay, my turn. Same question."

Nick picked up the bottle of cognac and replenished his glass. "I stole a pack of Camels from the drugstore when I was eight," he confessed. "Smoked them all that same afternoon."

"You started smoking when you were eight?"

"Where I come from, that's considered a late bloomer."

"Jeez, where did you grow up?" Riker's Island?"

Nick grinned. "Pretty close. My turn. What's your most embarrassing secret? Truth or dare," he added, slyly.

I bent my head, lowering my voice to a mere whisper. "I can't believe I'm telling you this," I said. "I've never told anyone."

Nick raised his eyebrows in anticipation.

"When I was twenty-one, I—I went to a Ricky Martin concert. There, I've said it! I even wore a t-shirt that said, 'Number One Fan.' I'm so ashamed."

Nick threw his head back and laughed. *Good. He thinks I made that up.*

I snuggled into the couch and took a sip of cognac. It burned the back of my throat and I coughed, causing the black dress, the one he'd asked me to wear, to crawl up my thigh. He cast an appreciative eye over me and smiled, and my stomach flipped, shyness overtaking me. I pulled an afghan off the back of the couch and wrapped it around my legs.

Nick was wearing loose, white linen drawstring pants and a long sleeved, white, oversized, linen shirt, open at the collar. He sported the tiny silver cross in his ear and the silver band around his wrist. He looked very handsome.

"My turn," I said.

Hmm…what did I really want to know about Nick? Considering I knew next to nothing, the field was wide open. I didn't want to waste this opportunity on something trite, so I thought really hard.

Where do you go at night? How many women are you currently involved with? Are all the rumors about you true? I rejected them all. If I really wanted to know about Nick the man, I needed to know Nick the boy.

"Tell me about your childhood," I decided.

"That's what you want to know?" he laughed.

"Why are you laughing?"

Nick leaned forward, taking both my hands in his. "Because you surprised me," he said. "I don't often get surprised."

"Was it a good surprise or a bad surprise?"

He got quiet for a minute. "A good one."

I waited expectantly for him to continue, but he didn't. "Well?" I said.

"Okay, Brandy Alexander, I'll tell you. But not tonight, okay?" There was a wistful quality to his voice I'd never heard before, and it caused a pang in my chest so deep I had to catch my breath.

"Ask me something else," he offered.

"Do you ever get scared?"

He laughed again, but this time there was an edge to it. "I've been to hell and back in this life, darlin'. Nothing much scares me anymore."

He stood up abruptly and extended his hand to me, pulling me towards him. We were face to face, his arms wrapped around my waist, his hand resting on the small of my back. I could smell the cognac, warm on his breath, intoxicating.

"My turn," he said, and I sensed his shift in mood. Cat-like. Predatory. "When was the last time you were with a man?"

I was wrong. This was my most embarrassing secret. "Um, uh…" I blushed deeply and tried to turn away, but he caught my face in his hands and held me there.

"Dare," I breathed.

"Kiss me." Before I had time to process the words, he lowered his head and brushed his lips over mine, softly at first and then harder, fuller and more insistent. He tasted sweet and hot and I kissed him back, lost in the feel of his mouth pressed against mine.

He lingered there for a moment, parting my lips with his tongue, drawing our bodies ever closer, his desire for me growing and pressing into my belly. Heat rushed through me and I let out a small, involuntary moan.

Nick pulled his head back, doing a slow scan of my body. "I want to see you," he said, slipping his tongue in my ear. "Take off your dress."

"What?"

Both hands cupped my ass, molding me to him. "You took the dare," he said, smoothly. "Take off your dress."

"I'm not playing anymore."

"Neither am I."

Oh my God!

If I had any doubt that he meant it, his ever-increasing hard-on told me he wasn't kidding. He held the hem of the dress in one hand as he slid his fingers up my leg, taking the material along with them.

I wrapped my arms around his neck, mostly so that I didn't end up on the floor. I didn't think my legs would have been able to support me.

Nick stroked the back of my knees, lingering at the thigh and then beyond.

The dress slid easily over my head, and I was left clinging to him in my Victoria's Secret silk bra and panties, bought for just such an occasion, never thinking the occasion would actually arise.

He kept kissing me the entire time, sliding his tongue around in my mouth until I was half crazed with desire. Slowly, he wedged a knee between my thighs and began to unbutton his shirt.

"Oh, please, Nick. Don't." I couldn't believe the words coming out of my mouth, but there they were, and Nick is nothing if not a good listener. He stopped and waited for me to explain.

"I, uh—" I started, in my usual articulate way.

He disengaged himself from me and sat down on the couch. Reaching for the cognac, he poured some more and drained his glass.

My mind kept drifting back to the chocolate mousse pie that was sitting on the kitchen counter, untouched. Chocolate's a real stress reliever for me, and I could've used a slab right about now, but I didn't think he'd understand if I went and cut myself a hunk. Besides, parading around practically naked is not on my top ten list of most comfortable things to do. I sat down, grabbed the afghan and wrapped it around me.

"Want to tell me what that was all about?" Nick asked, his look impassive.

Fuck if I know. I shrugged, gazing down at my lap.

He forced my chin up, demanding my full attention. "I'm attracted to you," he said. "I *think* you're attracted to me. Are you?"

"God, yes."

"Then what's the problem?"

"No problem." *Big, BIG problem.*

He waited.

"Okay, maybe there's a tiny problem."

"Do you want to tell me what it is?"

I nodded.

He waited some more.

"You scare me."

Nick choked back a laugh. "Yeah, I got that. Could you be a little more specific?"

"No."

"You *have* been with a man before, right?"

"Yes. Of course. Lots." *Two. And one doesn't count because I didn't come.*

"I don't know why this keeps happening, Nick." And then to my complete and utter humiliation, I started to cry.

Nick pulled me close, allowing me to blubber all over his white linen shirt. When I was done he wiped my tears with the palm of his hand and shifted his body so that he could look into my eyes.

"I don't scare you, angel. What scares you is losing control. But you know, it's not always a bad thing." He waited for an argument, but for once I was speechless.

"I told you once that I would never lie to you," he continued quietly. "I am not monogamous and I am not permanent. You need to understand that about me. Do you?"

I nodded.

"I want you in my bed," he said. "You need time to figure out if that's enough for you. Let me know when you're ready."

He smoothed down my hair and kissed the top of my head, an act of endearment that spoke volumes. "Good night, angel. Oh, and you can go eat that mousse pie now," he added and disappeared into his bedroom.

I was no longer interested in the chocolate mousse. I had too much to think about. Well, maybe just a bite.

I sat in the kitchen, ruminating over our conversation. Nick said he would never lie to me, which meant no promises that could later be broken. He said all he could offer me was his bed. But it *wasn't* just about sex. It was about friendship and trust and letting go. He said to tell him when I was ready. I was tired of thinking. I just wanted to "be."

I picked up my dessert plate and stuck it in the sink so that Adrian wouldn't get to it. Then I walked down the hall to Nick's bedroom. His light was still on. I hesitated a brief moment and then rapped lightly on the door.

"Come in," he said.

I opened the door and found him sitting up in bed, reading. His hair was loose and hung over the rim of his glasses. He took off his glasses and placed them on the nightstand along with the book. I glanced at the title. Sun-Tzu and The Art of War. Light bedroom reading. I don't know why, but it sounded sexy to me.

"What is it, angel?" he asked. His words were benign but the underlying electrical current could light up a city.

I walked over to his side of the bed, still wrapped in the afghan. I studied his face for any sign that he might have changed his mind about me. And when I saw none there, I dropped the blanket. "I'm ready."

"Are you sure?" He was understandably wary. After all, I'd left him "high and dry" so to speak, on three separate occasions.

Four years is a long time to go between lovers. Bobby was my first—my only—until "What's his name" in L.A. who, like I said, doesn't count.

It's not about losing control. It's about letting go.

I looked at him steadily. "I'm sure."

He reached for the lamp and turned it off, and then he threw back the covers, simultaneously pulling me onto the bed with him. *Oh boy.*

His body was hard and warm and powerful. He wrapped his legs around mine and covered my mouth with his, weaving his fingers through my hair to bring me closer. His hands were everywhere, gently tugging at my bra straps, slipping into the waistband of my panties, slowly drawing them down. His mouth was hot on my neck, my breasts, my belly. It had been so long and it felt so good. And then he moved lower and I panicked, but he stayed with me, urging me to forget everything, to give in to the feeling. I grabbed onto his powerful arms, digging my nails into his shoulders as the intensity grew, until—Oh my God—four years of pent up demand exploded in a tidal wave of sensation.

I wanted to return the favor, but he wouldn't let me.
"Tonight is for you, angel."
"But I haven't given you anything."
"Oh, you will."

He inched back up my body, laying a trail of the soft-est kisses imaginable as he went. Then he leaned over and reached into his bedstand drawer for a condom.

"I want to be inside you. Now."

I am losing control. I am letting go. I am falling without a net. Oh my God. Oh my God. Oh my God!

I woke up twice during the night, once to sneak my underwear back on, and again to finish off the mousse. Nick slept through it, or if he was awake, he didn't say anything.

He lay on his side, one arm slung over my belly, the other tucked under my rib cage, cupping my breast. I squirmed around to face him so that I could watch him sleep.

I wanted to burn every detail of this night into my brain, imprint his body on my fingertips, memorize the Spanish words he whispered in my ear as he came. I wanted to remember everything. *Because it was never going to happen again.*

When I opened my eyes in the morning, he was gone. Had a meeting, the note said. He'd be home late, if at all. *Business as usual.*

I sighed and sat up, hugging his pillow to my chest.

"I'm in big trouble." I tossed the pillow back onto the bed and hopped into the shower.

An hour later I was dressed and packed and ready to go. I couldn't stay here anymore. Not after last night. If he hadn't been so amazing, so kind, so genuinely loving, I could handle the "just buddies" treatment now. It's not like he hadn't warned me. He'd all but posted it on the Internet. But my feelings for Nick were only part of the problem.

I could deal with the unrequited "crush" thing. I'd had it bad for Scott Baio for years and I was still able to lead an independent life. It was that my life had been stolen. My freedom and sense of security had been wrenched away by a psychotic stranger, and I knew that if I didn't act now I'd descend deeper and deeper into a life of fear, until the world didn't exist for me outside of the safety of Nick's apartment—and it was bound to get crowded in there with me, Nick and his various lovers. I was grateful as hell for all that he had done for me. But it was time for me to reclaim my life.

Okay, where to begin…whenever my mom wanted to feel empowered, she would crank up Helen Reddy's "I Am Woman" on the stereo and dance around the living room. I didn't think that would do it for me. I had to find Glen and get him off the streets. And prove Toodie's innocence. And avenge Andi and Ilene's deaths. And get a job…unhhh.

I picked up the phone. "Mom, could you do me a favor…Yeah, that's right, 'I am Woman.' And could you turn it up really loud?"

Three minutes and forty-eight seconds later I was ready to tackle the world—or at least my little piece of it. So when the phone rang two seconds after that and Keith's name came up on the readout I clicked the button and said hello.

"Brandy?" He sounded shocked that I'd actually answered the phone.

"Oh, Hi Keith. I was just about to call you." I made up some lame-ass excuse for never returning the four thousand messages he'd left on my voicemail. He didn't believe me, but he pretended to, so I gave him points for playing the game.

"Look," he said, and his voice lacked the coyness I'd found so irritating the last time we spoke. "I'm going to come straight to the point here. You have something that I want, and I have something that you want. So how about we work out an exchange?"

"What exactly do you have that you think I want?"

"Information. I know your friend Toodie is in jail and I'm his ticket out."

Okay, that definitely piqued my interest. "How do you figure?" I asked.

Keith blew out a long breath. "Glen Davis," he said. "And I'm sure I don't have to point out that this is confidential information."

"I'm the soul of discretion," I assured him.

"So when can you come over?" Harrison asked.

"Actually, I was hoping we could meet somewhere. How about DiVinci's at three?"

I picked DiVinci's because it's a public place, and I didn't want to be alone with the guy. It's also kind of a dump. I wanted to get the upper hand right off the bat and I figured if Keith were worried about getting ptomaine poisoning, he'd be more likely to slip up. Plus, I'd promised Bobby I wouldn't go back to Keith's, and whether Bobby believes it or not, I don't *always* go looking for trouble.

"I'd rather you come to my place," Keith insisted. "I've only been on my feet for a few days and the pain meds make me dizzy."

Perfect. The guy's a physical wreck. If anything goes wrong, at least I'll be able to outrun him. "Sorry, Keith, maybe we'd better postpone this until you're feeling better."

"No, no. I'll be there. But this time, make sure you bring the thumb drive with you."

Okay, so employing "Illegals" isn't exactly kosher, but is it so terrible in the overall scheme of things? I mean if I turned in the Diamond Casino, wouldn't I then be obliged to blow the whistle on Mrs. Gentile for hiring that guy from Guatemala who fixed her furnace last month? And the

Costello's down the block could never have afforded their God-awful addition without the day laborers they picked up near the Pavonia rail yards in Camden. The point is everybody does it. Only the Diamond Casino does it on a slightly larger scale.

I knew I was feeding myself a load of bull, to convince myself that giving Harrison back the thumb drive was the right thing to do. But if Toodie got convicted of Ilene's murder, he could face the death penalty. When I looked at it that way, the choice was easy.

And it's not like I couldn't use this information after I got Toodie off the hook. Hey, I could do an award-winning expose and then Barry Kaminski would beg me to work for him. But I'd have to put him on hold while I entertained offers from several other networks. The more I thought about it, the more convinced I was that I was doing the right thing. But I decided to hedge my bets by stopping in at Saint Dom's for a little pre-emptive confessing, just in case it wasn't.

I ran into Marie on the way out. She was standing on the sidewalk, buying a soft pretzel off a street vendor. I tried to squeeze past her, but she turned, blocking my path.

"Hey, Bitch. Where you going? To meet your boyfriend, Bobby?"

A bunch of local boys were standing about a quarter of a block down, warming themselves by a fire they'd started in a big metal trashcan. They looked up with obvious interest at the sound of Marie's greeting.

I ignored her and kept on walking, but she reached out and grabbed my arm, spinning me around. I shook her off me and faced her head on.

"First of all, my name isn't 'Bitch'. And secondly, you should know where I'm going, you follow me around enough, which frankly is starting to get on my nerves."

Gee, I'd never noticed how tall Marie was until she was

standing directly in front of me. She glared down at me with contempt, and then she took her pretzel and smashed it on the top of my head, smearing mustard all over my hair.

"What are you, twelve?" I yelled, which brought cries of "fight, fight" from the guys down the block.

Marie tossed me a look of pure hatred. "Bobby's mine, got that? You go near him again and I'll get you way worse than this."

Oh Christ, this is just what I need. I'm supposed to meet Keith in an hour and now I have to beat the shit out of Bobby's wife. I simply don't have time for this.

I took a deep, cleansing breath the way they taught me in the one yoga class I took in L.A. and counted to ten.

"Look, Marie. I don't know what you've heard, but for the last time, Bobby's *not* cheating on you. At least not with me," I couldn't help adding.

I turned my back on her and walked away with as much dignity as one can with a head full of mustard. The next thing I knew, I felt two hands press hard into my back and I landed on my knees on the sidewalk.

The guys from down the block came closer, taking up their chant of "fight, fight" again. I threw down my bag and pushed her back. She lost her balance but remained standing. I decided to try and reason with her.

"Marie, we're adults. This is ridiculous." At least that's what I'd planned on saying, before she hurled herself at me and began yanking my hair. I fought back, tackling her to the ground. The guys from down the block were now surrounding us, taking bets on the "tall, skinny girl" and the "short, scrappy one."

A patrol car turned the corner and came cruising down the street, just as the noise from the crowd brought Father Vincenzio outside. He grabbed us each by the elbow and hauled us upright. The patrol car slowed down and idled in front of us.

Mike Mahoe rolled down a window, a big, dumb smile plastered on his face.

"Everything all right here, Father?"

Father V. nodded. "I've got it under control, officer."

My nose was bleeding and I think a chunk of my hair was missing. Marie had the beginnings of a black eye.

I watched Mike drive away and then turned my attention back to Father Vincenzio, who was wagging a bony finger in my direction.

"Brandy Renee Alexander, your mother would be so ashamed of this infantile behavior."

"She started it," I sulked, eyeing Marie, warily.

Marie scowled back, her face contorting like a pit bull on steroids.

Father V. ushered her into the church, making comforting clucking noises at her and leaving me standing alone on the sidewalk with the guys from down the block.

"You won," the biggest guy said.

"Ya think?"

"Yeah, totally."

"Thanks."

I sat in Nick's truck, fuming. It was too late to go home and change, so I took out some wetnaps and sponged off my face. The yellow mustard cast sort of a greenish glow on my hair, and it felt a little stiff, but other than that it looked okay.

I thought I deserved some TLC after my ordeal, so I stopped into the Seven-Eleven and bought a six-pack of Oreos. I was coming out of the store when Bobby rounded the corner in his Mustang and stopped in front of me, blocking my way to the truck. He leaned over and swung open the passenger door. "Get in."

He didn't look like it was up for discussion so I climbed in. *Mike, you are such a big mouth!*

Bobby cast an eye over my hair and exhaled sharply. "So it's true," he said.

"It wasn't my fault."

"It never is."

"What's that supposed to mean?" I could feel my blood pressure rising up around my ears. I opened the Oreos and popped one in.

Bobby slumped forward, holding his head in his hands. "My life isn't great, ya know? But it's tolerable. I have my kid, I have my job and Marie's been manageable. But now—shit!" he exploded, slamming his hands down on the steering wheel. "Why'd you have to come back?"

I was out of the car before he could take another breath. Bobby jumped out the driver's side door, racing to catch up with me.

"Christ, Brandy, I didn't mean it."

"Yeah, Bobby, ya did."

I made it to DiVinci's with fifteen minutes to spare. The drive over was rough going, what with me crying my heart out the entire way. Bobby's words cut deep. There was a time I was his salvation. Now I just added to his misery.

Lindsay Sargenti was waiting tables. She offered me a booth, but I told her I was meeting someone at the bar.

"I like what you did with your hair, Bran. I've never actually seen that color on anyone before." She got closer and sniffed. "How come you smell like mustard and baby wipes?"

"Long story, Linz."

I made my way to the bar and hopped up on an ancient stool. The bar top was scarred with decades-old graffiti and cigarette burns. I ordered a coke and sat with my back to the door, watching the TV that was anchored above the hanging glasses.

The news was on. I recognized the reporter. She was

my classmate at Temple University's Masters program in Journalism. She was as dumb as a rock and yet there she sat, gainfully employed, dispensing the news of the day. *Boy, this network must have some pretty low standards. I wonder if they're hiring.*

"There were protests at the U.S. Embassy in Ottawa today by Canadians, outraged by a recent decision by U.S. Immigration and Customs Services to require passports for all visitors to the United States, including Canadians, who have traditionally been exempted from this rule. This tightened security measure is intended to cut down on illegal immigration and potential terrorist attacks.

In related news, United States passports are entering the digital age. In the near future, a tiny microchip will be embedded in the cover of all U.S. passports issued. These chips will contain digitized photos, holograms and other personal data. Officials claim that the new digital technology will make counterfeiting much more difficult and will increase the security of the nation. Critics charge that the code that enables the encryption of sensitive data is far too vulnerable to theft and reproduction, making the United States an even greater target for terrorists seeking illegal entry into the country."

Theft and reproduction? Theft and reproduction! I jolted, spilling Coke all over the bar as thoughts rushed though me all at once...Diamond Casino...immigrants...charming gambling addict...dog that poops electronic devices containing names and birth dates...new passports susceptible to THEFT AND REPRODUCTION!

Suddenly I knew what was so special about the thumb drive and why people were willing to kill for it. Maybe I didn't understand how all the puzzle pieces fit exactly, but one thing I knew for sure. I had a major breach in national security sitting in the bottom of my pocketbook.

I had to get out of there. I had to get to the police and

turn this thing over to them. I had to...Keith! Shit! He was standing right behind me, watching my reaction in the beveled mirror behind the bar. I tried to remain calm, but my heart was beating a mile a minute. I swiveled around slowly, making my face as neutral as possible for someone who was about to pee her pants.

He was wearing the same black Burberry overcoat he'd worn when I'd first met him, but now it seemed to hang on him. The boyish charm was gone, replaced by the haggard look of desperation. "Oh, hey, Keith. How long have you been here?"

He studied me in tense silence. "Not long."

I could hear the gears in his bruised head turning, trying to figure out if I'd connected the dots. I gazed back at him, affecting a smile. "Have a seat," I offered.

He seemed to relax and flashed a smile of his own, showing off his newly capped teeth. "No thanks. Been doing way too much of that lately. Listen," he said, looking around, "this place isn't really conducive to conversation. How about we go somewhere else?" He pressed closer to me, crowding me on the stool.

"Uh, personal space, Keith?" He didn't seem to hear me. Or pretended not to, I couldn't tell which. My head was spinning. *How the fuck am I going to get out of here?* He looked terrible. If push came to shove I'm *sure* I could outrun him. Hey, if push really did come to shove, I was fairly confident I could handle that too.

"I've got to go to the little girl's room," I said. "I'll be right back and then we can discuss going somewhere else."

Keith turned, and for the first time I noticed his right hand had never left his coat pocket. He slung his left arm around me in a companionable embrace, squeezing me against him. "I don't think so," he said.

With surprising strength he yanked me off the stool, simultaneously whispering in my ear. "You make a scene, you're dead. I have nothing to lose. You got that?" He lifted his right hand slightly out of his pocket, enough so that I could glimpse what was wrapped inside it. At least the trip to the firing range wasn't wasted. I could now recognize a real gun when I saw one.

I nodded, my eyes wide.

"You got the thumb drive?" Keith asked, quietly.

I tried to calculate the odds of him shooting me on the spot if I said no and decided they were not in my favor. I nodded again.

"Good. Let's go."

Keith was in much better shape than he had let on. Despite his limp, we walked briskly arm in arm to the back door, the gun in his hand a constant reminder to behave myself. Frantically I searched out Lindsay, but she was on the other side of the restaurant, serving a table of frat boys.

"Wait," I shouted above the din of the crowd. "I forgot to leave a tip. Bartenders depend on it for their livelihood!"

Keith almost cracked a smile. "I guess he'll just have to go hungry tonight." He maneuvered us through the door and out into the parking lot.

A light snow had begun to fall, casting a pristine glow on the street. There should be a law against bad things happening when the world looks so peaceful. I cast my eyes around for someone to help me, or at least be a potential witness to my kidnapping, but the lot was empty. Where's Marie DiCarlo when you really need her?

We reached Nick's truck. "Get in," Keith ordered.

I looked around for the Lexus, but it was nowhere in sight. "Where are we going?"

"Look, just shut up and get in, okay?" He was nervous. I didn't think he had much practice at being a "tough guy" and I wondered what he'd do if I flat out refused to go with him.

"No," I said, taking a chance.

Keith grabbed my arm and wrenched it behind my back. The pain was excruciating and I cried out.

"I said, 'get the fuck in the car.'" He released his grip on me and waited while I fumbled with my bag looking for the keys. He grabbed them from me and pressed the pad to unlock the door. He opened the passenger side, casting furtive glances at DiVinci's back door. "Climb in," he ordered.

Oh crap. The number one rule they teach you in self-defense class is never let them get you into a car. If they do, you're a goner. I hoisted myself up onto the seat, figuring I'd spin around and surprise him with one of those nifty karate kicks I'd seen Nick do. Only I hadn't counted on what happened next. As I turned my back, there was a sudden, sharp stinging sensation behind my left ear, as Keith gave me a solid whack with the butt of the gun. Abruptly, all my fears drifted away along with conscious thought.

Chapter Sixteen

I awoke slowly, a blinding headache causing waves of nausea to ripple through my stomach. We were in some kind of warehouse. The entire contents of my bag had been dumped on the floor next to me. The thumb drive was gone, and since Keith had gotten what he so desperately wanted, I couldn't help but wonder why I was still alive.

He was on the phone. I squeezed my eyes shut, mostly to keep from vomiting all over myself and listened in on his half of the conversation.

"Yeah, I've got her… your troubles are over…well, hurry up."

I sat up carefully, leaning against the wall. The warehouse was an ancient World War II era structure, empty, except for a few odd crates and a rusting dumpster. Judging by the green slime growing on the walls, we had to be near water. My guess was we were in an old storage area for one of a handful of now defunct factories tucked between the I-95 and the river.

Harrison disconnected the call and slipped his phone back into his pocket. He appeared agitated; gone was any trace of the charming yuppie I'd first encountered. He began a slow pace back and forth in front of me.

"Ya know this whole thing could have been avoided if

you had just given me the thumb drive. I didn't want it to turn out this way."

For once we were in agreement. I didn't want it to turn out this way either.

"I don't suppose we could strike some kind of a deal," I offered.

"Afraid not. You seem to have run out of bargaining chips." He held up the thumb drive to illustrate his point.

"Who's Conley?" I asked. If I was going to die, it would not be from curiosity.

Harrison stopped abruptly and knelt beside me, his face a mottled mess in the dimming light. "Who?"

"Oh, come on, Keith. What difference does it make if you tell me now? A witness heard Ivan Sandmeyer say, 'This is for Conley' before he beat the shit out of you."

Harrison, laughed and some of the tension eased from his face, softening it.

"I guess you're right. I can tell you anything now. You're not going to tell anyone. Sandmeyer said, 'This is for *conning* me.' The people he works for thought I was holding out on them."

"The Diamond Casino owners?"

Harrison shot me a look of astonishment. "Exactly how much did you figure out?"

"Enough," I shrugged. "You've got a gambling habit. You owed money to the casino and—here it gets a little fuzzy, but I think the owners asked you to steal some government information having to do with the new passports, so that they could duplicate them. In exchange, they'd let you off the hook for the money you owed them. Am I close?"

"Close enough. I didn't have to steal it. The deal was already arranged. All I had to do was drop off the money and pick up the thumb drive."

"Jesus Christ, Keith, we're talking about national security here. How could you sell out your own country like that?"

"The price was right." Keith resumed his pacing. "If it hadn't been for that God damn dog eating the thumb drive, everything would have been fine."

"So that's really what happened?" Even in the midst of a life and death crisis, Adrian's gastric capabilities impressed me.

"You can't make that shit up." Keith emitted a rueful snort.

Slowly the puzzle was coming together. "The dog was Ilene Werner's wasn't it? She was at Glen Davis's house the night she was murdered. Why did he kill her?"

Harrison glanced at his watch, his agitation increasing tenfold with each passing minute.

"How the fuck should I know? Couple of junkies having a lovers' quarrel. According to Davis, her last boyfriend was that idiot friend of yours, Ventura," he added. "Talk about the perfect scapegoat."

"So Glen planned all along to set Toodie up for Ilene's murder?"

Keith shook his head. "You give that cretin far too much credit. He needed someone with a dolly to haul the freezer out of there and not ask questions. Ventura fit the bill."

"But Toodie said he was supposed to meet Glen at his house, only when he got there, Glen was gone. Why would he call Toodie up and then just leave?"

"Oh for God's sake," Keith barked. "The guy's hooked on ice. He has to get high about every fifteen minutes. He went out to score something and forgot all about Toodie and the freezer. If it hadn't been for me suggesting he bury the head in Ventura's back yard, Glen would be on death row by now."

I thought about this. "I don't get it, Keith. I mean I can understand you hiring Glen. He's your equivalent of Toodie. He probably did whatever you wanted and didn't ask a lot of questions. But you're really going out on a limb for him by helping him cover up his girlfriend's murder. What's in it for you?"

Suddenly the light dawned. I figured out the passport scam so now Keith wants me dead as much as Glen does. Only Keith's a white-collar kind of guy. He doesn't go in for the hardcore stuff, but he's perfectly willing to let someone else do it. I wondered if Glen knew Keith's motives weren't exactly altruistic.

"Why don't you give it a rest for awhile?" Harrison suggested, brandishing the gun at me. It didn't look entirely natural in his hand.

My head was hurting so bad he would have done me a favor by shooting me. "You don't happen to have any aspirin on you, do ya?"

"Sorry, no. But don't worry, your headache will be taken care of soon enough."

Keith resumed his pacing while I sank back along the wall again in a vain attempt at seeing only one of him. The word "concussion" was fast becoming a permanent part of my lexicon.

It was freezing in the warehouse. I stuck my hands in my coat pocket to keep warm and found an old Reese's Peanut Butter Cup in one of them. Brain fuel. I popped it in my mouth.

Okay, so Keith comes over to see Glen. Ilene is there with her dog, visiting Glen. It's hot in the apartment because of the broken thermostat. He takes off his coat, lays it on the couch. Adrian finds the thumb drive in the coat pocket and eats it, thinking it's a candy bar. Then somehow, the dog runs off and Keith goes looking for him. Is that when Glen killed Ilene? And in the scheme of things did it really matter?

I gazed around the room, trying to come up with an exit strategy that didn't include me being carted away horizontally. I decided to try my hand at bluffing. "You're not going to get away with this, Keith. You may have the information, but I left an extra copy with a friend, with a note saying that if anything happened to me to go after you."

"You made an extra copy?" His look of incredulity really ticked me off.

"Of course I made an extra copy. What do you think, I'm stupid?"

I made no extra copy. I am so stupid! I meant to make a copy. I really did. But then the whole Marie debacle happened and it just slipped my mind.

There was a sudden scuffling sound coming from outside and then someone rapped on the warehouse door. Keith inched his way toward it, keeping his gun trained on me the entire time. It really wasn't necessary. I could barely lift my head, let alone leap to my own defense.

Keith flattened himself against the wall and tugged on the sliding door. A thin shaft of light worked its way into the room, illuminating a scrawny figure standing at the entrance. A small caliber pistol jutted out from his right hand. He wore a dark, hooded sweatshirt and torn black jeans. His sunken eyes and emaciated form gave him the surreal look of a walking skeleton. Physically, he was the polar opposite of his brother, Turk. In fact, it was hard to believe he had any human relatives at all. He was unequivocally the ugliest person I'd ever seen. My phone buddy and mental tormenter, Glen Davis.

My stomach flipped at the sight of him and I automatically scooted farther back along the wall, willing myself invisible. He squeezed through the narrow entry, his entire being radiating a manic energy. Once he was all the way through, he shoved the door open wider with his hip, revealing another figure.

She was a stark contrast to Glen, with her beautiful, almost angelic face and luxurious dark hair. His arm was wrapped around her and I would have thought they were partners in crime, had it not been for the look of sheer terror on her face. There was a slight swelling under her eye, where I'd decked her. Tears stained her cheeks. Obviously, Marie DiCarlo didn't have a lot of practice being held captive by lunatics. Well, it was her own stupid fault. I didn't invite her to this shindig; she crashed it all on her own.

"Oh, Christ, who's this?" Keith grumbled.

Glen shoved Marie into the room and she tripped, landing about two feet in front of me. It was sort of nice to have the company, but I wouldn't wish this on anyone.

"I found her snooping around outside. I figured she's a friend of the bitch here."

Oh Glen, you couldn't be more wrong. And what's with everyone calling me a bitch?

Marie was openly sobbing, her entire body convulsing with fear. I completely understood how she felt, but I simply would not allow myself to give in to the urge to curl up in a fetal position and wait to die.

"Marie," I said as compassionately as possible, "shut up. This isn't helping."

"My baby," she whispered, taking in huge gulps of air. "She's in the car."

Oh fuck.

"Now what do I do?" Glen was saying to Keith.

"You have to kill them both."

This started Marie on a fresh wave of hysteria.

I braced myself against the wall and tried to stand up. It was a fruitless effort. "Let her go, you guys. She probably hates me worse than you do. In fact, you'd be doing her a favor by killing me." I glared at Marie with all the energy I could muster. Marie picked up her cue and glared back, spitting on the ground at my feet.

Glen laughed. It sounded like a cartoon hyena. "Why does she hate you?"

"I slept with her husband." I didn't add that it was before

Shelly Fredman

they'd ever met.

Marie flinched, and this time her glare was for real.

"She keeps following me around, trying to catch us in the act, I guess."

"So then why do you care if she lives or dies?" Keith asked.

I shrugged. "She's got a kid. I'm a sucker for babies."

Glen closed the gap between us. He ran the barrel of his gun along my jaw line, openly leering at me. "I'll bet you suck real good."

I turned green or whatever color revulsion is.

Harrison's voice was sharp. "Don't be an asshole, Glen." If Glen was insulted, he didn't show it. My guess was he heard that a lot.

"You sure are a funny little thing," Keith continued, directing his next comment to me. "You went to all this trouble to get a low-grade moron out of jail, and now you're trying to save a woman who despises you."

"I'm a regular Mother Teresa." It was getting harder and harder to come up with wise cracks, what with death looming over my head and all.

Glen was becoming impatient. "Hey, I don't got all day. And I'm not crazy about killing two of them. What am I supposed to do with the bodies?"

Keith limped over to the door and opened it a crack. "It'll be dark soon," he said. "Just sit tight for a little while and then we can get this thing over with. Where did the tall one park her car?" he asked as an afterthought. "Maybe we should move it before it attracts attention."

Marie paled and made the sign of the cross and began reciting a rosary in Spanish. At least I think that's what she was saying. My Spanish is limited to the holiday classic "Feliz Navidad" and old Arnold Schwarzenegger movie catch phrases.

I scooted over next to her. "Look," I whispered, "we're

262

in deep trouble here. We've got to work together if we're going to survive."

She gave a slight, begrudging nod. I guess she was still thinking about that whole 'slept with her husband' crack.

I glanced over to the door. "One of us has to create a diversion while the other one makes a break for it. Are you with me on this?"

Marie responded with a tearful hitch in her throat. "I'll do anything to keep my baby safe."

"Good. Now here's the plan—"

"Hey, you at the door." Keith whipped around and Marie stood up, arms akimbo, like Wonder Woman.

"Marie, what are you doing?" She ignored me, keeping a steady eye on Harrison.

"Look, you want her dead. I don't know why and I don't care. I just want to get out of here. I'll shoot her."

My mouth flew open and stayed that way. *So much for team building.*

"I kill her, you let me go. Everyone's a winner."

That's it. I'm gonna die. Now I'll never get to sleep with Nick again. Alright, I swore I wouldn't anyway, but now I'll really never get to. And what about Rocky and Adrian? They'll be orphans. I mean who would take in a dog who could literally eat you out of house and home?

A lump the size of Utah began to form in my throat.

"It's a trick," Glen decided.

Keith sneered at him. "Of course it's a trick."

I wasn't so sure.

"Actually, this gives me an idea," Keith continued. He grabbed Marie by the wrist. She cursed him and tried to jerk free, but he held fast, pinning her arm behind her back.

"Settle down there, honey. I'm about to make your wish come true." Keith turned to me, aiming his gun at my head. "Get up," he growled.

I struggled to get to my feet, but Keith is an "immediate needs" kind of guy and I guess I wasn't moving fast enough for him. He reached out and yanked me upwards. I stumbled against him, nearly knocking him flat.

"Take her," he called to Glen.

Glen moved in and Keith released my arm. "Put her over there."

Davis dragged me to the other side of the room. If he knew what Keith was up to, he wasn't saying.

The pain in my head worsened. Whatever Keith had in mind, I wished I could do it sitting down.

He eyeballed me for a while and then turned to Marie, who had gotten over her crying jag and had replaced it with major attitude.

"Do you know who my husband is?" Marie challenged Keith. He didn't seem to care, but she told him anyway. "He's a detective with the Philadelphia police force. He's going to hunt you down and you'll be sorry you were ever born."

"Is that true? Her husband's a cop?" he asked me.

"Yeah," I said. "A good one. He'll find you alright."

Keith shrugged. "I'm not even going to cross his mind. The poor guy is going to be overcome with grief, once he discovers that his wife shot his lover and then killed herself in a fit of remorse."

"Oh, please, who's going to believe that?" *Shit. Just about anyone who knew Marie.*

Keith began shuffling us around as if he were staging a high school production of *High Noon,* Marie on one side and me on the other. I tried to catch her eye, but she wouldn't look at me. I guess I couldn't blame her. After all, I was the one who gave him this brilliant idea by telling him she wanted me dead. I wondered if her offer to shoot me had been legitimate. Well, it was a moot point now, wasn't it?

Glen tightened his grip on my arm and rubbed up against my side. I could feel his excitement pressing into my hip, and a picture of Andi flashed through my mind. Did he have a hard-on when he slashed her throat? Bile rose up in mine and I squelched it down.

He rubbed one filthy finger against my cheek, lifting my chin so that I was eye level with him. I met his gaze, refusing to play the helpless victim.

"We need some alone time," he whispered in my ear.

"Just shoot me now," I hissed back.

Glen swung his left arm back and popped me hard in the mouth. I reeled back in pain, blood spurting from my upper lip. He let go of me and I slumped to the floor in a heap.

"What the hell are you doing?" Keith began walking toward us, his limp more pronounced now. It had been a long day for him. Marie was tucked in behind him, shackled by Keith's free hand. He released her and bent down to examine my face.

"How are we going to make this look legit if her face is all smashed in?"

Out of the corner of my eye I detected a slight movement. Marie was slowly inching her way toward the door. I decided to help her out, although it was real iffy as to whether she'd return the favor.

"He's nothing but a stinking coward," I said, nodding towards Glen. "All he knows how to do is get high and beat up on women. Is that why you killed Ilene? Because she found herself a *real* man?" I braced myself for another punch in the mouth.

"Shut up, you God damn bitch. You don't know anything about me and Ilene."

There was surprising emotion behind his words and for once it wasn't pure anger. Could it be he'd really cared for her?

Marie was almost to the door. If I could just keep their attention for a moment longer...

"Hey, maybe she was having a thing with Harrison. I

hear he's quite the ladies' man."

Confusion clouded Glen's face and he cut his eyes to Keith, who looked like he was about to strangle me with his bare hands.

"Just shut the hell up, would ya?" Keith demanded. He turned to Glen. "Can't you see what she's doing? She's trying to cause trouble between us. We've got to stick to our plan if we're going to get you out of this mess."

The warehouse door screeched open with a wrench of its rusty hinge and Marie slipped through the crack.

"Goddamit," Keith yelled, slapping Glen on the shoulder. "Go after her."

Glen shook Keith's hand off of him, a pronounced twitch pulsing above his left eye "Why don't you?" His voice was steely and left no room for argument. Harrison swore and lunged for the opening. I prayed that Marie would reach her car and drive her daughter to safety.

Glen turned back to me. "What do you know about Harrison and my girlfriend?"

The gun was trained on my temple so I chose my words carefully. "Nothing, I swear it. But haven't you ever wondered why Keith is so willing to help you cover up her murder? Let's face it, you don't exactly run in the same social circles."

"I do good work for him. He doesn't want to lose me."

"Yeah, but kidnapping is a federal crime. Not to mention accessory to murder. I'm sure you're one hell of a worker, but I'm afraid your pal Keith has an ulterior motive."

"Is that so?"

I nodded. "Keith kidnapped me because I have some information he wants to keep private. If you kill me, you'll be doing him an enormous favor."

The hand that held the gun shook and he placed the other one on top to steady it. His eyes had that glazed "overdue for a fix" look I recognized from my volunteer work at the mission in downtown Los Angeles.

"Ask him yourself."

Glen got quiet, his poor, drug-addled brain hard at work, trying to digest this new information.

"Tell me something." He didn't respond, so I plunged right in.

"Why *did* you kill Ilene? I mean I get the feeling you really liked her."

Davis seemed rooted to the spot, lost in thought. In the failing light, he didn't look quite so cadaverous, and I could see faint traces of the little brother Turk had once adored.

He lowered his head, the gun still trained on me. His entire body began to quiver, and I realized with a mixture of equal parts horror and fascination that he was crying. I held my breath, not daring to move a muscle.

"I don't know why I killed her. I loved her."

My butt was growing numb from the icy cold floor, but I didn't think now would be a good time to mention it. I shifted minimally and when Glen didn't protest, I raised myself up on my knees.

"What happened?" I asked, in what I'd hoped was a soothing, "Dr. Phil" sort of tone.

Glen rubbed at his eyes, as if trying to erase the memory. "All I know is Harrison called and was coming over to pay me for a job. Ilene had come by earlier. I was in my bedroom, getting high. The next thing I know, I'm lying on the ground next to her with a knife in my hand. Keith is standing over me, trying to wake me up, and Ilene's body is full of stab wounds." His voice broke and it was all I could do to keep from patting him on the shoulder and murmuring, "there, there."

"Keith told me what happened," Glen continued. "He'd walked in on us just as I was sticking the knife in her. He said I must've stabbed her like about twelve times before she died. He said he tried to stop me, but I was too fucked up to listen."

Something clicked in my brain. "He said he saw you stab her to death?" I repeated.

The warehouse door flung open, and Keith reappeared hauling Marie in with him. Sophia wailed in her arms as Marie desperately tried to quiet her.

"If you can't make her stop screaming, I will," Keith said, taking aim at the toddler. He was sweating like a pig, his bum leg dragging behind him.

He turned to Glen. "Let's get this thing over with."

"What do we do with the kid?" Glen asked.

"She's a witness." He didn't need to finish his thought. Even Glen got the implication. Keith pulled Sophie from his mother's arms and set her on the ground. The little girl began to wail again.

"You bastard," Marie screamed. She pounded Keith's chest with her fists, stopping only when he wrenched her arm completely out of its socket.

"Just shoot them, already," he told Glen. "We'll figure out the logistics afterwards."

There was dead silence in the room as Glen took aim at me and released the safety. Even the baby had stopped crying. Glen paused.

"Oh for Christ's sake, Davis. She knows you stabbed your girlfriend to death. If you don't kill her, you'll get 'life' or worse. Do it," he urged.

"Wait," I screamed, scrambling to my feet. My heart was in my mouth, making it difficult to speak. "Glen, you deserve to know the truth about the way Ilene died."

Keith dragged me up off the ground, his face distorted by rage. *How could I ever have found him attractive?* "Can't you *ever* just shut the fuck up?" he yelled.

"What's the matter, Keith, the truth make you nervous? Glen, Ilene was murdered all right, only you didn't do it."

"Don't mess with me, bitch."

"I'm not messing with you. You told me that Keith saw you fighting with Ilene. That he saw you stab her a bunch of times. Only that's not how she died."

Keith leveled his gun at me, but in a sudden gesture, Glen knocked it out of his hand. It landed at Keith's feet. "Keep talking," Glen said to me.

I breathed deeply, willing myself to stay calm. "The detective told me that Ilene died of severe head trauma. Not stab wounds. Keith couldn't possibly have seen you stab her while she was still alive."

"But I saw her when I woke up. There were wounds all over her body."

"Think back, Glen. Did you see any blood?"

"I can't remember." He was straining so hard he was on the verge of a mental collapse.

"You'd remember if she were lying in a pool of blood. Those wounds were inflicted *after* she was already dead. That's why there was no blood flow."

"Glen, she's lying. Kill her. Do it now."

Keith bent down to pick up his gun, but Glen kicked it across the room.

I kept a steady eye on Harrison.

"You don't know what you're talking about," Keith sneered. "Why would I concoct such an elaborate ruse?"

"Because you wanted to make sure people knew it was Glen's handiwork, not yours. If you were identified as being at the scene, no one would suspect you of doing something so heinous. Glen, on the other hand, was a natural. No offence," I added, giving a nod to Glen.

"That's crazy." Keith spun around, addressing Glen with an air of superiority. "Look, Glen, you're the one in trouble, not me. But if you choose to believe this lying cunt—"

"Excuse me?" I exploded. "Listen, you vile, disgusting, piece of—"

269

"Everybody just shut up, okay!" Glen suddenly snapped, breathing hard. He got up close to Keith, seemingly unaware of the tears that were now streaming down his ravaged face. "Why'd you do it, Keith?" he asked. Why'd you kill her?"

"I didn't. I—"

Glen backhanded him so hard I heard teeth crack.

Keith seemed to shrink before my eyes. His voice was small and thick with pain. "It wasn't my fault. Her—her dog ate something I needed. I threatened to cut him open to get it back. Ilene went crazy. She attacked me. I was just defending myself, when she fell back and hit her head on the kitchen counter. I didn't mean to do it," he ended, pathetically."

Glen stood over him, his rail thin body swaying slightly. His voice was calm, but his eyes were not. They did a manic dance over Harrison's face. "You set me up. You made me believe I'd killed her. I even killed that other girl just to cover my tracks. You said it was a good idea."

Keith took an automatic step back. "I—I was scared. I—"

Glen closed the gap between them, his finger resting on the trigger. "Are you scared now, Keith? You should be."

The sound of gunfire reverberated like a sonic boom in the empty warehouse. Keith's eyes grew wide with surprise as his brain fought to catch up with what his body already knew. He reeled back from the force of the impact, simultaneously clutching his chest as the bullet penetrated its target. A dark stain appeared and rapidly began to spread. Blood seeped through his fingers as he tried to stem the flow. It was such an ineffectual gesture, I actually felt sorry for him and I blinked back hot tears.

Glen watched with detached interest as Harrison fell backwards, landing face up on the floor. I gagged at the sight of Keith's eyes, unmoving, still wide open.

There was blood everywhere. Glen stretched out his foot

and deployed a vicious kick to Harrison's lifeless body. I shuddered with the realization that I would be next, and the thought propelled me into action.

I lunged for him, landing square on his back. He twisted violently as I latched onto his wrist and tried to wrestle the gun out of his hand. He wouldn't let go, so I grabbed him by the hair. "Marie, get Harrison's gun," I screamed. "It's over there on the floor."

Marie rushed forward, but instead of picking up the pistol, she scooped Sophia up with her good arm and bolted out the warehouse door. Boy, that woman is *so* not a team player.

By this time, Glen was spinning around like a rodeo bull, trying to buck me off him. I hung on as best I could, but I didn't have the advantage of the super-strength that comes with being a meth freak. He dug his nails into my arms, drawing blood. I let go of his hair and aimed instead for his face, clawing viciously at his eyes.

Enraged, he shoved the barrel of the gun under my breastbone. I held my breath and hurled myself sideways. Glen lost his grip and dropped the revolver. As it clattered to the floor, he reached up for me, locking his bony hands around my neck, choking the life out of me. I drew my arms up and quickly clamped down on his, breaking the hold, the way I'd seen on an old episode of Baretta. We hit the ground hard, and I landed on top of him.

A shot rang out, accompanied by a searing pain in my side. I tried to roll off him, but Glen's arms were rigid around me. When his grip suddenly loosened and unfolded from my waist I knew the struggle was over but had no idea why—and frankly, thanks to the dime-sized hole in my side, I didn't particularly care.

Chapter Seventeen

"The bullet went clean through me without hitting any vital organs," I stated with pride, as if somehow I'd had something to do with it. Glen hadn't been so lucky. When we fell, we landed on the gun, causing it to discharge. It hit both of us, lodging in his aorta. He died instantly.

I dispensed this information to Fran and Janine from my hospital bed. The doctors had insisted I stay overnight to make sure no infections set in. Franny wanted to stay with me, but the hospital staff wouldn't let her. They were afraid of her picking up an infection—ironic, isn't it? And what with her being pregnant and all...

"Per usual, I miss all the fun," she said, doing her best imitation of Eeyore.

"Don't worry, Franny, when I get home I'll make you a nice bowl of Jell-o. It'll be just like being here."

The events of the evening were hazy. After I was shot, I'd passed out from the intense pain in my gut. Upon waking, my first rational thought was, "I'm lying in the arms of a dead man. Eewww!" My next, less rational thought was, "I've got to clean up this mess. What will people think?"

I didn't have time to dwell on either one. There was a sudden explosion of light and sound as a caravan of police cars pulled up just outside the warehouse.

Nick was the first one through the door. His normally neutral expression gave way to controlled concern, until I lifted my head from Glen's prone body. Nick quickly assessed the room, noting with grim satisfaction that the two new men in my life were dead.

"You're really rough on your dates, aren't you, sport?" he said, kneeling down beside me.

I tried to laugh, but the effort it took was monumental.

Nick lifted my hand from the bullet wound and placed it in his own. Blood stained his fingers, but it he didn't seem to take notice.

Bobby appeared on the other side of me, along with two uniformed officers and a couple of paramedics. I recognized the one from that time in my basement. "Hey," I said. "Good to see you again."

"She's in shock," he explained, covering me with a blanket, "but the wound doesn't appear life-threatening."

Nick relinquished my hand and disappeared outside to speak to the hordes of reporters who had appeared like vultures, at the first whiff of human sacrifice. With any luck, some day I'd be one of them.

I looked up at Bobby. "Did Marie call you?"

"No." His tone was tense.

"Then how—"

Bobby reached over and swept my bangs out of my eyes, something he'd done a thousand times when we used to be together. "I stopped by DiVinci's about twenty minutes after you left there, this afternoon. Lindsay told me you'd been in with a guy who fit Harrison's description. The bartender said you left with him. The truck wasn't in the parking lot and I was afraid you'd taken off with Harrison, so I got in touch with Santiago and we located you through the truck's GPS."

"See, I knew you'd learn to get along with Nick. All you needed was a common project."

His smile was wan. He'd been sick with worry, and it was about to get worse.

Over in the corner, the forensics team busied themselves with Harrison's body. I tried not to think about it or the fact that it so easily could have been me. "Bobby, there's something I need to tell you about what happened here, today. I wasn't alone. Marie—"

He cut me off, barely contained anger etched on his face. "I know all about Marie. She jeopardized my daughter's life and she left you here to die." His deep blue eyes watered and he turned away. It was the last thing I remember before being lifted onto the stretcher and carried out the door.

Visitors spilled out into the hospital corridor. Predictably, the police showed up and the FBI, once they got wind of the thumb drive. When I was feeling better we'd be having a nice long chat, they assured me. For now they seemed content with restoring national security.

Barry Kaminski sent a tasteful bouquet of seasonal flowers along with a request for an exclusive. He sweetened the deal by alluding to a reporter's job that was about to open up on his network. I'm totally bribable and couldn't wait to meet with him.

Carla swung by Nick's to pick up Rocky and Adrian, and Uncle Frankie brought me a cheese steak, figuring I'd be hungry after my "ordeal." Feeding me cholesterol-packed food is his way of saying "I love you," which suited me just fine. Paul showed up wearing a Ramone's T-shirt—it was '80's night at the club, and John trailed in after him, carrying a bag from Victoria's Secret.

"Thought you might need this," he said, holding up a lacy, pink nightie. It had a plunging neckline and was, for all intents and purposes, see-through. It looked like something you'd find on the cover of a Victorian bodice-ripper. "Don't get mad at me, Sunshine," he said when I made a face. "It was your mother's idea. She thought you might run across an available doctor and you'd want to look nice."

I turned to Paul. "Mom knows already?"

"Sh-she knew b-before I did. Th-that woman is a-m-mazing."

"I'm okay, Paulie," I said quietly.

He leaned over and kissed me on my cheek. "You bet."

A nurse came in and handed me my pain meds and something to help me sleep. Then he cleared everybody out. Janine told me she'd be back later to stay the night with me. The nurse, a ruggedly handsome guy in his mid thirties said he'd look forward to seeing her again. Unbelievable.

I turned over in the darkened room and tried to go to sleep, but I couldn't stop those terrifying images from parading around in my brain. I knew from past experience that I'd be living with them for a long time.

"It's all over," I kept telling myself. "I'm fine." And then the tears that I fought to keep inside while everyone was here tumbled out of me. I cried for Ilene and Andi and Turk, and even for Glen and Keith, but most of all I cried for me.

I hadn't quite finished my little pity party, when I heard a sound at the door. Swiping a hand over my face, I sat up too quickly and groaned. Apparently, the pain meds needed a little time to kick in.

Nick was standing at the entrance. "Hey," he said.

My heart stopped beating when I saw him. Good thing I'm in a place where that sort of thing happens all the time. "Hey," I answered, shyly. Except for the brief interlude in the warehouse, I hadn't spoken to him since we shared his bed. I was off to a running start.

"I brought you something." Nick slid along the wall in the dark until he found what he was looking for. A moment later, the room was softly illuminated. He'd brought me a nightlight. It was an indescribably thoughtful gesture.

He sat down at my side while I tried, unsuccessfully, to

keep from bawling again.

"It must be the medication," I gulped. "I'm *never* like this."

"Never," he agreed. "You're a rock." He handed me some tissue and I wiped the gunk off my nose.

Nick told me the Feds had busted the Ellenbergs and closed down the casino. "Oh, and Bulldog was picked up again, this time on a weapons charge. The Ellenbergs are a little too busy to bail him out right now, so he decided to turn state's evidence in return for a shorter jail sentence."

I shook my head, amazed. "How do you know all this?"

He raised his eyebrows. "I've got friends in low places."

The sleeping pill finally kicked in and I sank back into the pillows. Nick stood up and pressed his lips lightly against mine. "Take care, angel," he said. It sounded suspiciously like the brush off and suddenly I couldn't breathe.

"Um, yeah, you too," I choked out.

He reached the door and turned to face me again. I could barely make out his features in the low light.

"Remember when you asked me if I ever got scared?" he said.

"I remember. You said nothing scares you."

The corners of his mouth twitched imperceptibly. "I was scared tonight."

Mike Mahoe stood just outside Bobby's office, his broad shoulders slumped in a show of contrition. I was still mad at him for his reaction to my fight with Marie. He'd enjoyed it entirely too much.

"I heard you were here," Mike began.

"Hm hmm." I wasn't going to make this easy for him.

He shifted uncomfortably in his heavy leather cop jacket. "Well, I just wanted to say I'm glad you're okay—and I'm sorry about—you know—the thing with Father Vincenzio," he added in a rush. I guess near-death experiences have some advantages. People go out of their way to be nice to you.

"Thanks, Mike," I said, offering him up a smile.

Bobby sat on the edge of his desk, tossing wads of paper in the wastebasket. I was in the beat up metal chair, waiting for him to miss, so that I could have my turn at "World Domination."

I had driven myself to the police station in Paul's Mercedes, having returned the truck to Nick. Now that I was safe, he was going on that business trip he'd been putting off. It was a relief to think he was in some primitive location, without access to a phone. That way, I wouldn't be hanging around mine, waiting for him to call.

After a rather lengthy interview, I was free to go. Bobby caught me on the way out and dragged me into his office. He shut the door and pulled a couple of sheets of paper out of his desk drawer, showing them to me.

"Separation agreement," he explained. "And this one gives me temporary sole custody of my little girl." A visible weight had been lifted from his shoulders. One hundred and thirty pounds, if I were to make a guess.

"So what happens to Marie now?" The woman had left me for dead, but I still couldn't bring myself to hate her.

"She knows she's sick. I'm through with our marriage, and if she wants back in Sophia's life, she's going to have to commit to some serious therapy. By the way, thanks for not pressing charges against her for stalking you."

I sank the final shot to take over Poland and stood up. I had to get home to get ready for my blind date with Jason Danski. Actually, I'd forgotten all about him until he called, that morning. It just seemed easier to meet him than to explain why I was out of the mood.

Mike walked me to the elevator. I wanted to go see

Toodie, but Mike said they'd released him a few hours ago. A uniformed officer came down the hall, towing a stocky, bald headed guy in cuffs. One of his arms was in a cast. Ivan "Bulldog" Sandmeyer. My stomach lurched when I saw him, but fear soon gave way to intense loathing as I thought about how he had destroyed my parents' couch in his quest for the thumb drive. That couch had been a part of my life for twenty-eight years. I'd logged thousands of hours watching television on that couch, was nursed through chicken pox and had gotten my first hickey, all on those familiar green velvet cushions.

Before Mike could stop me, I marched up to Sandmeyer, stopping two inches in front of his face. "You owe me a childhood memory." I reared back and delivered a solid kick to his shin.

Sandmeyer howled. "Son of a bitch!"

The officer made a move for me, but Mike shook his head, a silent warning to back off. "Come on, tiger," he grinned, throwing a meaty arm around my shoulders. "I think your work here is done."

Carla was right about Jason. He was pleasant, easy on the eye, had a respectable job and, as far as I could tell, hadn't murdered anyone recently.

Janine had called during dinner to see if I needed to invoke the "I've-got-a-sick friend-it-was-nice-meeting-you" plan.

I excused myself and went to the ladies' room. "He seems like a good one," I told her. I'm going to give him a chance."

On the way back from the restaurant we stopped at Best Buy. Jason, a self-proclaimed "electronics geek" wanted to check out the new high definition and plasma screen TV's.

We stood surrounded by dozens of televisions of various sizes, all tuned to the same channel.

"Oh, I love this show," Jason said, zeroing in on a 56 inch monster monitor.

Apparently, the rest of Northeast Philadelphia did too. A large crowd had gathered to watch the final minutes of The Nosy Neighbor. Not wanting to be a spoilsport, I chimed in with, "This show is hilarious. I mean where do they find these people?"

"And now the moment you've all been waiting for," a disembodied voice intoned. "This week's number one video, sent in by nosy neighbor Doris Gentile of South Philadelphia."

"Oh my God, Jason, she's my neighbor!"

But Jason wasn't listening. His eyes were glued to the television as a young woman filled the life-sized screen. She was standing in the front yard of a house, bent over a hose, shampooing her hair in the freezing cold. She wore only a man's trench coat, which, unbeknownst to her, had fallen open in the front, revealing her womanly wares. This being network TV, they were covered, discreetly, by two fuzzy balls of light. Sadly, her face was not.

Jason appeared even more embarrassed than I did. In the next moment, as I stood amidst snickering onlookers, he reached into his pocket, feigned a phone call, fake-answered it, and told me he hoped I didn't mind, but he had to leave immediately to visit a sick friend. Truthfully, I didn't mind so much that he was ditching me (I would have ditched me too), but he didn't even offer me a ride home.

I took a cab back to my place, made myself a large pot of hot chocolate and settled down on the patio lounge chair I'd borrowed from Fran and Eddie. (I really had to get a new couch.) Adrian sprawled at my feet while Rocky slurped the dregs of the cocoa that were cooling in the pot on the stove.

I turned on Three's Company, but the comical hi-jinks of Chrissy, Jack and Janet just weren't doing it for me. The truth is, I was lonely. I couldn't call anyone. Everybody thought I was on a date, and I didn't want to disabuse them of that notion just yet. I briefly considered knocking on Mrs. Gentile's door to tell her how much I enjoyed her home video, or inviting Bobby over, to give her something to talk about. That idea appealed to me a lot more, but in our mutually vulnerable states, I knew it wouldn't be the smartest move. The doorbell rang, saving me from a major bout of stupidity.

"Maybe it's a Jehovah's Witness," I thought hopefully, heading for the door. "They're always up for a nice, long chat." I stood on tiptoe so I could look out the peephole. "Who is it?" I called out.

A ridiculously phony British accent replied, "It's the butler."

Joyously, I ripped open the door.

"Hi Roomie…"